BRI

CONSPIR,

BRIAN FLYNN was born in 1885 in Leyton, Essex. He won a scholarship to the City Of London School, and from there went into the civil service. In World War I he served as Special Constable on the Home Front, also teaching "Accountancy, Languages, Maths and Elocution to men, women, boys and girls" in the evenings, and acting in his spare time.

It was a seaside family holiday that inspired Brian Flynn to turn his hand to writing in the mid-twenties. Finding most mystery novels of the time "mediocre in the extreme", he decided to compose his own. Edith, the author's wife, encouraged its completion, and after a protracted period finding a publisher, it was eventually released in 1927 by John Hamilton in the UK and Macrae Smith in the U.S. as *The Billiard-Room Mystery*.

The author died in 1958. In all, he wrote and published 57 mysteries, the vast majority featuring the super-sleuth Antony Bathurst.

BRIAN FLYNN

CONSPIRACY AT ANGEL

With an introduction by
Steve Barge

DEAN STREET PRESS

INTRODUCTION

> "I let my books write themselves. That is to say, having
> once constructed my own plot, I sit down to write and permit
> the puppets to do their own dancing."

DURING the war, Brian Flynn was trying some experiments with his crime writing. His earlier books are all traditional mystery novels, all with a strong whodunit element to them, but starting with *Black Edged* in 1939, Brian seemed to want to branch out in his writing style. *Black Edged* (1939) tells the tale of the pursuit of a known killer from both sides of the chase. While there is a twist in the tale, this is far from a traditional mystery, and Brian returned to the inverted format once again with *Such Bright Disguises* (1941). There was also an increasing darkness in some of his villains – the plot of *They Never Came Back* (1940), the story of disappearing boxers, has a sadistic antagonist and *The Grim Maiden* (1942) was a straight thriller with a similarly twisted adversary. However, following this, perhaps due in part to a family tragedy during the Second World War, there was a notable change in Brian's writing style. The style of the books from *The Sharp Quillet* (1947) onwards switched back to a far more traditional whodunnit format, while he also adopted a pseudonym in attempt to try something new.

The three Charles Wogan books – *The Hangman's Hands* (1947), *The Horror At Warden Hall* (1948) and *Cyanide For The Chorister* (1950) – are an interesting diversion for Brian, as while they feature a new sleuth, they aren't particularly different structurally to the Anthony Bathurst books. You could make a case that they were an attempt to go back to a sleuth who mirrored Sherlock Holmes, as Bathurst at this point seems to have moved away from the Great Detective, notably through the lack of a Watson character. The early Bathurst books mostly had the sleuth with a sidekick, a different character in most books, often narrating the books, but as the series progresses, we see Bathurst operating more and more by himself, with his thoughts being the focus of the text. The Charles Wogans, on the other hand, are all narrated by Piers Deverson, relating his adventures with Sebastian Stole who was, as per the cover of *The*

Hangman's Hands (1947), *"A Detective Who Might Have Been A King"* – he was the Crown Prince of Calorania who had to flee the palace during an uprising.

While the short Wogan series is distinct from the Bathurst mysteries, they have a lot in common. Both were published by John Long for the library market, both have a sleuth who takes on his first case because it seems like something interesting to do and both have a potentially odd speaking habit. While Bathurst is willing to pepper his speech with classical idioms and obscure quotations, Stole, being the ex-Prince of the European country of Calorania, has a habit of mangling the English language. To give an example, when a character refers to his forbears, Stole replies that *"I have heard of them, and also of Goldilocks."* I leave it to the reader to decide whether this is funny or painful, but be warned, should you decide to try and track these books down, this is only one example and some of them are even worse.

Stole has some differences from Bathurst, notably that he seems to have unlimited wealth despite fleeing Calorania in the middle of the night – he inveigles himself into his first investigation by buying the house where the murder was committed! By the third book, however, it seems as if Brian realised that there were only surface differences between Stole and Bathurst and returned to writing books exclusively about his original sleuth. This didn't however stop a literary agent, when interviewed by Bathurst in *Men For Pieces* (1949), praising the new author Charles Wogan . . .

At this stage in his investigative career, Bathurst is clearly significantly older than when he first appeared in *The Billiard Room Mystery* (1927). There, he was a Bright Young Thing, displaying his sporting prowess and diving headfirst into a murder investigation simply because he thought it would be entertaining. At the start of *The Case of Elymas the Sorcerer* (1945), we see him recovering from "muscular rheumatism", taking the sea-air at the village of St Mead (not St Mary Mead), before the local constabulary drag him into the investigation of a local murder.

The book itself is very typical of Brian's work. First, the initial mystery has a strange element about it, namely that someone has stripped the body, left it in a field and, for some reason, shaved the body's moustache off. Soon a second body is found, along with a mentally-challenged young man whispering about "gold". In common with a number of Brian's books, such as *The Mystery of The Peacock's Eye* (1928) and *The Running Nun* (1952), the reason for the title only becomes apparent very late in the day – this is not a story about magicians and wizards. One other title, which I won't name for obvious reasons, is actually a clue to what is going on in that book.

Following this, we come to *Conspiracy at Angel* (1947), a book that may well have been responsible for delaying the rediscovery of Brian's work. When Jacques Barzun and Wendell Hertig Taylor wrote *A Catalogue Of Crime* (1971), a reference book intended to cover as many crime writers as possible, they included Brian Flynn – they omitted E. & M.A. Radford, Ianthe Jerrold and Molly Thynne to name but a few great "lost" crime writers – but their opinion of Brian's work was based entirely on this one atypical novel. That opinion was *"Straight tripe and savorless. It is doubtful, on the evidence, if any of the thirty-two others by this author would be different."* This proves, at least, that Barzun and Taylor didn't look beyond the "Also By The Author" page when researching Flynn, and, more seriously, were guilty of making sweeping judgments based on little evidence. To be fair to them, they did have a lot of books to read . . .

It is likely that, post-war, Brian was looking for source material for a book and dug out a play script that he wrote for the Trevalyan Dramatic Club. *Blue Murder* was staged in East Ham Town Hall on 23rd February 1937, with Brian, his daughter and his future son-in-law all taking part. It was perhaps an odd choice, as while it is a crime story, it was also a farce. A lot of the plot of the criminal conspiracy is lifted directly into the novel, but whereas in the play, things go wrong due to the incompetence of a "silly young ass" who gets involved, it is the intervention of Anthony Bathurst in this case that puts paid to the criminal scheme. A fair amount of the farce structure is maintained, in particular in the opening section, and as such, this is a fairly unusual outing for Bathurst. There's also a fascinating snapshot of history when the criminal scheme is revealed. I won't go into details for obvious reasons, but I doubt many readers' knowledge of some specific 1940's technology will be enough to guess what the villains are up to.

Following *Conspiracy at Angel* – and possibly because of it – Brian's work comes full circle with the next few books, returning to the more traditional whodunit of the early Bathurst outings. *The Sharp Quillet* (1947) brings in a classic mystery staple, namely curare, as someone is murdered by a poisoned dart. This is no blow-pipe murder, but an actual dartboard dart – and the victim was taking part in a horse race at the time. The reader may think that the horse race, an annual event for members of the Inns of Court to take place in, is an invention of Brian's, but it did exist. Indeed, it still does, run by The Pegasus Club. This is the only one of Brian's novels to mention the Second World War overtly, with the prologue of the book, set ten years previously, involving an air-raid.

Exit Sir John (1947) – not to be confused with Clemence Dane and Helen Simpson's *Enter Sir John* (1928) – concerns the death of Sir John Wynward at Christmas. All signs point to natural causes, but it is far from the perfect murder (if indeed it is murder) due to the deaths of his chauffeur and his solicitor. For reasons that I cannot fathom, *The Sharp Quillet* and *Exit Sir John* of all of Brian's work, are the most obtainable in their original form. I have seen a number of copies for sale, complete with dustjacket, whereas for most of his other books, there have been, on average, less than one copy for sale over the past five years. I have no explanation for this, but they are both good examples of Brian's work, as is the following title *The Swinging Death* (1949).

A much more elusive title, *The Swinging Death* has a very typical Brian Flynn set-up, along with the third naked body in five books. Rather than being left in a field like the two in *The Case of Elymas the Sorcerer*, this one is hanging from a church porch. Why Dr Julian Field got off his train at the wrong stop, and how he went from there to being murdered in the church, falls to Bathurst to explain, along with why half of Field's clothes are in the church font – and the other half are in the font of a different church?

Brian's books are always full of his love for sport, but *The Swinging Death* shows where Brian's specific interests lie. While rugby has always been Bathurst's winter sport, there is a delightful scene in this book where Chief Inspector MacMorran vehemently champions football (or soccer if you really must) as being the superior sport. One can almost hear Brian's own voice finally being able to talk about a sport that Anthony Bathurst would not give much consideration to.

Brian was pleased with *The Swinging Death*, writing in *Crime Book Magazine* in 1949 that "I hope that I am not being unduly optimistic if I place *The Swinging Death* certainly among the best of my humbler contributions to mystery fiction. I hope that those who come to read it will find themselves in agreement with me in this assessment." It is certainly a sign that over halfway through his writing career, Brian was still going strong and I too hope that you agree with him on this.

Steve Barge

PART ONE
IN THE WINGS

CHAPTER I

I

As LANGLEY drove his car through the narrow streets of the town and across the bridge that spanned the river, he made a mental calculation affecting time and distance. Unless anything went radically wrong, he should be in Angel by eight o'clock. The time now was just past four and already the late Autumn day, green- and brown-tinted, was showing unmistakable signs of surrender to the enemies, Evening and Night.

But to Langley, that mattered little. The fields he had passed on his day's journey were almost entirely stubble save for the fallow strips high with weeds. The brambles had all budded and the time for ploughing had come again, in its due succession in the pageant and procession of the year. Langley, who had been driving for some hours, realized that with the approach of darkness the temperature was dropping and that there was every indication of a cold and misty night. But the moon would ride high. Few birds were in song. The trees, however, had been beautiful in their Autumn dress, and Langley, beginning to feel the increasing coldness, drew on his gloves, pulled up the collar of his greatcoat and buttoned it higher to his chin. He had driven from London and would stay in Angel for the night. Or perhaps, even, nights!

The car crossed the hump bridge at Latimer Ferris and he turned it into the Angel road with a strong feeling of pleasure, satisfaction and contented well-being. Passing the church of Fraxhill, Late Perpendicular with its tall, oak-shingled spire, he soon came to the hilltop ruins of Marnim Castle and its tall, handsome chimney-shaft. Descending to the famous park, finely wooded and stocked with deer, with its lake of 160 acres, Langley knew for certain that his earlier prognostications would be proved correct—and that before he came to the warm hospitality of Angel the mist would be at him and would curl insidiously at his eyes and throat. This prospect he found disquieting, for Langley was a most faithful disciple of Sol the Sun, and hated those twin predatory fingers of the weather, cold and wet.

But through the late afternoon the car behaved irreproachably, and soon after his watch had showed him that the time was half past seven Langley came to a signpost which he considered should afford him comfortable words of pleasing information. He stopped the car and got out. Walking to the crowned grass-centre of the road where the signpost had been erected, he flashed his torch on to it as clouds hid the moon and read the words painted on it. "Angel—two miles."

"Good," he muttered to himself; "with any luck, I shall be having dinner under the hour."

Replacing his torch in the pocket of his greatcoat, he began to make his way back to the car. And then, just as his hand fastened on to the door of the car, he saw the headlights of another car coming towards him. For a reason which he would have been unable to explain if he had been asked to do so, he lingered by the car door, with his fingers still grasping the handle. The approaching car stopped almost abreast of him and a slim figure alighted from it, with the obvious intention of crossing the road and coming over to him.

Langley saw that it was a girl. She was of middle height, and when he caught sight of her face he saw, too, that she was undeniably and most unusually attractive. Langley gave appropriate thanks in his heart that there was a moon. Her hair was dark red, her face held humour, vivacity, character and decision. There was mirth in her dark blue eyes, warm, white and covert rose of skin, and a sudden, sanguine petulance of lips. And even this hint of disdain, so Langley thought as he stood and looked at her, only enhanced her attractiveness. He placed her age at twenty-two. But she held nothing that was immature or unfinished, or even tentative. Everything about her, he thought, was eloquent of a riper womanhood. She was alive, alert and distinguished. She had race, temperament and verve.

She came to Langley and uplifted her chin a little so that she might speak to him. The approach was jaunty. Then, with a half-smile—through which there pierced, perhaps, just the faintest glimmer of secret mischief—she said, "Please forgive me—but I wonder whether you would be good enough to do something for me?"

Langley hastened to observe that any task she asked of him would be akin to an ecstatic pleasure.

She smiled again and gave her head a little pensive movement of affirmation. Had Langley known her better he would have known that this was but the beginning of her teasing mood which inevitably broke down resistance and brought success. Her eyes, still raised to Langley's, melted into yet another smile. A smile of innocence, persuasiveness, tender appeal for approbation and mocking challenge. "It's quite a little thing—but first of all—please tell me—are you making for Angel?"

Langley smiled and nodded. "Yes. Unless something goes wrong unexpectedly, I hope to be there in a few minutes."

As he spoke, he caught her, perfume. It was subtly delicate—like that of violets—and came and went in the air near her.

"Oh—good. Then you *can* do me the little service I mentioned. Please wait here for a second." She turned quickly and ran towards her own car on the other side of the road.

Langley held his breath as he watched. This was right off the beaten track and might have come straight from the pages of Dornford Yates himself. Langley squared his shoulders. "What a lovely," he murmured, "what an absolutely gorgeous . . ." But she was back in front of him and Langley, to his surprise, saw that she carried something in her arms. As he bent down to look at it, the thing moved and then wriggled up towards him.

II

Langley saw that the object at which he looked was a kitten. But by no means an ordinary kitten. It was a magnificent specimen of the Blue Persian. It possessed a wealth of smoky-blue fur and a pair of brilliant, staring, orange-coloured eyes.

"I must explain," said the girl who carried it. "This is Ahasuerus."

"By Jove," said Langley; "is it really?"

She nodded. "Yes—really! And there's quite a good reason for his name. He's a Persian and his pedigree is imposing—he was sired by 'Emperor Blue'—one of the most famous Persian sires now at the stud."

"I can quite believe it," returned Langley; "you know what most Emperors are—after all—the temptations that come their way."

The girl closured him with a toss of the head. "Please don't be absurd—or I shall be sorry I ever spoke to you."

"Heaven forbid," said Langley.

The girl flashed imperious eyes at him. "Please listen. Ahasuerus belongs to my uncle—Professor Ballantyne. He's a fellow of St. Benedict's College, Oxford. He values Ahasuerus above rubies. I found him in my car."

"Who?" inquired Langley mischievously. "Professor Ballantyne?" She tossed her head again. "No—Ahasuerus. Oh—I'm telling this all wrong, I know. I'll endeavour to explain. My uncle's staying with us at Angel. He's been ill and he's left his rooms at St. Benedict's to come to us for his convalescence. Ahasuerus must have found his way into the garage, jumped into my car, curled himself up on the seat and gone to sleep. Quite oblivious of this, I drove off and have only just discovered him. I don't know why—but he's done it twice before."

"It's pretty obvious," remarked Langley solemn-faced, "he wants to be with you. And if it interests you at all, I can jump—and I sleep remarkably well. But I'm not so sure about the curling up."

"Beast," said the girl; "and will you kindly listen to me?"

"I was," said Langley. "I was merely—"

"Being ridiculous. I know. What I want you to do for me is this. Please take Ahasuerus back to Angel for me in your car. It won't take you out of your way at all. In fact you haven't really got to leave the main road. I'll explain. Just as you run into Angel—about half a mile from the town on your right-hand side—you'll come to the Brewery. You can't miss it. It's kept by Sir George Mortimer—you've seen the name, of course. 'Mortimer's Fine Ales'. Just past the Brewery you'll come to a house—an old-fashioned white house standing well back from the road. That's ours. Daddy's. Like the Brewery—you can't miss it. Please take Ahasuerus in and just say 'Priscilla sent him back'. If you like," she concluded with a touch of roguery, "you can say 'by special messenger'."

Langley rubbed his cheek with his forefinger. "I know you'll do it for me," she said, "because you're such a dear."

Langley coughed. "Aren't you, Ahasuerus?" she continued demurely, looking down at the kitten.

Langley stifled his cough. "Ahem," he said; "all right. And in that case I'd better collect the kitten."

He bent down to receive the progeny of the Blue Emperor. The girl transferred Ahasuerus to his waiting arms.

"I ought to explain," she stated, "I shan't be back in Angel myself until very late. I'm going to Samphire, and Uncle Stephen will be most upset if Ahasuerus is missing all that time. As it is, I've no doubt that he's already very hot and bothered, and probably organizing search-parties."

"Biting the carpet perhaps?" suggested Langley.

The girl flashed him a scorching look of disdain. "It's strange," she said, "how completely one may be mistaken in a person. You *look* moderately intelligent—"

Langley grinned and interrupted her. "That's marvellous news. I read once that the finest combination one could possibly have was that of intelligence and beauty."

"You are far from beautiful," she riposted; "I can assure you on that point."

"I meant you."

"Combination?" she repeated. "I took you at your own word. I don't quite—"

Langley grinned again. "My allusion was to the state matrimonial. I should hate you to misunderstand me."

This time she tossed her head higher than ever and turned away to walk back to her car. Langley caught her by the arm.

"When do I see you again, Miss Ballantyne, and tell you of the fate of Ahasuerus?"

She pulled her arm away from him and walked across the road. "You don't," she said over her shoulder, "and my name's not Ballantyne. My uncle happens to be my mother's brother. Good-bye, and thank you."

Langley, who wore no hat, waved to her. "*Au revoir*, Priscilla."

III

Langley watched her drive off. Then he returned to his own car, made the blue-furred kitten comfortable on a rug on the back seat, and climbed back into the driving-seat. Before he set the car in motion again he turned his head and looked back at the kitten. He noted to his satisfaction that it had already settled down comfortably and was apparently asleep.

"Now for Mortimer's Fine Ales," he muttered to himself, "and just past it, an old-fashioned white house that stands well back from the road. According to my reckoning, I should make it in a few moments."

As he trod on the juice, a thought struck him. A thought which hadn't occurred to him before. "Now why in the name of thunder," he said to himself, "seeing that the house is so near, didn't she take the darned cat back herself?"

Langley drove on and pondered over the problem. "Didn't want to keep the bloke waiting, I suppose. Lucky swine—whoever he may be."

He peered through the driving-screen for a sight of the Brewery—realizing that according to Priscilla's story he must be close on it by now. Within a matter of seconds his eyes were rewarded. As Priscilla had stated, there was no mistaking it. Moreover, he recognized it down the avenue of *two* senses. He saw that the Brewery occupied commodious premises and extended for some considerable distance down the road. His next job was to pick out the old-fashioned white house which stood well back from the same road. He cut down his speed, therefore, and proceeded slowly. But he saw nothing that answered Priscilla's description for some little time. Langley began to wonder whether he had missed the house he sought.

Just as he was feeling moderately certain that he had, he saw it. Yes—it admirably fitted the description Priscilla had given of it. Langley promptly slowed down and parked the car by the side of the road, Then he went round to open the door and collect H.R.H. Ahasuerus from his corner. The gentleman in question, despite his ancient lineage and royal tradition, proved eminently tractable, so Langley gathered him up carefully and proceeded towards the white house. But when he had covered about half the distance he stopped, thought things over and decided to take Ahasuerus back to the car for the time being. He did so.

He pushed open the gate and made his way to the front door. Arrived there, he rang the bell. The ringing evoked no response. Langley promptly rang again. The second ring proved more success-ful. The door opened to him and he saw standing on the threshold a medium-sized, sallow-complexioned man in a brown tweed suit. Langley gave a quick glance at the man's face and came to an instant conclusion that he was far from being impressed by what he saw. Surely this man was neither the father nor the uncle of Priscilla!

"What's your business?" said the man at the door. Langley liked neither the tone of his voice nor his manner. But for all that he summoned his best smile to grace the occasion.

"Might I," he said pleasantly, "have a word with the Professor?" That, he considered, was the happiest opening gambit for him to employ. The man at the door frowned.

"The Professor?" he repeated interrogatively.

"Yes—if you would be so good."

"Who are you, may I ask?"

Langley smiled again. "My name's Langley. He won't know me, but the business is rather important."

The man at the door frowned again and a puzzled look came into his eyes. He ran them up and down Langley's tall, lean figure as though he were making a quick assessment of him, both physical and mental. For the space of a few seconds neither of them spoke. The man at the door seemed to be on the point of saying some-thing but hesitated. Langley waited, expectantly. The frigidity of his reception had somewhat taken him aback. Then the man spoke.

"You'd better come in, I suppose. Just wait inside, will you? I'll have a word with the Professor and find out if he'll see you. As a matter of fact he's by way of being rather busy at the moment."

The man closed the door and Langley edged further into the hall. "Funny business altogether," he thought, "but University profes-sors are proverbially eccentric—which I suppose must be regarded as the probable explanation. I'm glad now that I altered my mind and left Mister Ahasuerus in the car. He might have got restive, if he'd been in my arms all this time."

As he waited there in the hall, the murmur of voices came to him from a near room. He could hear one voice that sounded well above all the others. It was deep, harsh, guttural. He fell to surmising as to how long they intended to keep him cooling his heels in this hall. But at length his patience was rewarded. The man whom he had previously seen came out of a room farther down the hall and walked towards him.

"Mr. Langley, you said, didn't you?"

"That's right. Richard Langley—at your service."

The man nodded. "I thought you said 'Langley'. Come this way, will you, please?"

Langley followed him into the room from which, evidently, he had heard the voices coming. There were four men seated in the room. They were ranged round the table. The man in the brown tweed suit who had conducted him into the room called out his name in the manner of an introduction. "Mr. Langley."

Before Langley, however, could make any remark, the man speaking addressed himself directly to the person who was seated at the head of the table. "To have a word with you, Professor."

Langley looked at the man at the head of the table. He saw a small man with longish white hair and cold blue eyes which stared at him menacingly through horn-rimmed spectacles. When he spoke, Langley was somewhat surprised to hear that his had been the dominant voice he had heard while he had been waiting in the hall.

"What do you want with me?" asked the Professor.

"H'm," thought Langley, "charming reception, I must say." Then he cleared his throat and spoke to the Professor. He spoke as was his wont. Leaning forward towards the group of men which confronted him, he said in the pleasantest tone imaginable, "What I came to tell you, Professor, is that the cat is out of the bag." As he made this announcement, Langley smiled amiably at the circle.

IV

The effect which his words produced on the gathering was almost magical. The four men sprang to their feet and with the man in the brown tweed suit made a ring round him. As they sidled nearer and nearer to him, he was acutely conscious of the malevolence and hostility which emanated from them and which seemed to be enveloping him. Langley backed a trifle towards the wall. At least two revolvers had become visible. One was handled by a big burly man with curiously hunched shoulders and the other was in the grip of a thin rat-faced fellow who had been seated on the Professor's immediate left. Langley squinted down at them with a cool insouciance which he was far from feeling.

"I'm just a little perturbed," he said, as easily as he was able in the circumstances, "at the unusual warmth of my reception."

"Watch him, Layman," said the Professor to the big man, "don't let him play any tricks."

"Don't worry," growled Layman, "I'll see to that all right."

Langley could tell instinctively that the five men, almost, as it were, without moving, had come nearer to him. Although he realized now that he must watch his step, he was unable to avoid entirely an exhibition of indignation and resentment.

"I really don't know," he said, "what all the fuss is about! Because I happen to have brought the cat back. By special request. *Your* cat, Professor."

The man addressed came right up to him. "Cover him, Layman! And you, Webber! Now what's all this damned tomfoolery about a ruddy cat? And what's your little game? Come clean or it'll be the worse for you."

Langley heard the names mentioned and pulled at his upper lip. "I hate to contradict you," he observed, "but you've got it all wrong. The colour, for instance. It's not ruddy, by any means. It happens to be a Blue Persian. And I'm engaged in no little game. I'm merely acting as a cat-carrier. And—as I believed—on your behalf."

He smiled broadly at the ring of faces confronting him. There was no immediate reply forthcoming, so Langley seized the chance thus given to him to strengthen his position.

"If I've slipped up somehow and barged into the wrong party, let me tender my sincere apologies. Then I can get cracking out of it with no ill-will on either side."

He noticed, as he spoke, that the glances of four men went directly to the man whom they had called the "Professor". In some way, so Langley thought, they had made themselves subordinate to this undersized, white-haired man. The Professor spoke.

"Your story seems pretty thin to me. Whichever way I look at it. I don't possess a cat. I've never possessed a cat. I have no wish to possess a cat. I hate cats."

"So I gathered," said Langley, "but I wasn't to know that in the first place. Some people, though, have quite a crush on them, you know. Love to stroke them and hand them milk in saucers. Look at the ancient Egyptians, for example. They used to worship them. Don't you remember reading about the jolly old cat of Bubastes?"

Layman cut in. His lip curled as he spoke. "Cut that nonsense! Come down to brass tacks. What's your real business here—that's what we're concerned with?"

"I've told you," said Langley, "all I've done is to bring a cat back. For the Professor—I thought I was doing him a service. I imagined that I'd made that point clear to you."

"Where is it?" demanded Layman menacingly.

"In my car outside."

"In that case, then, Layman," said the Professor, "it's up to us to test Mr. Langley's rather interesting bedtime story. You and I will keep him looked after"—he gestured towards Layman's gun—"while he accompanies us to his car and produces the evidence. In the shape of this wonderful—but, I fear, mythical—cat."

"Nothing," said Langley, "that is to say, at this precise moment, would suit me better. Will you—"

"You go in front," ordered Layman curtly, "and watch your step. You see this!" He tapped his revolver.

The three other men backed away as Langley walked out of the room followed by Layman and the Professor. The former poked the gun into Langley's back.

"There's the car," announced Langley cheerfully. "Just where I left it."

"You wouldn't expect it to stray away and graze somewhere, would you?" snapped Layman savagely.

Langley grimaced to himself in the dark. "Not so good," he thought; "very definitely not so good."

The three men walked away from the house and came to the stationary car. "Here you are," declared Langley; "allow me to introduce you to Ahasuerus, who, so I have been given to understand, Professor, is one of your most prized possessions."

Langley stooped down and pointed through the car window to the back seat. Then an ice-cold shock enveloped him. One glance at the rug on which he had last placed the now notorious Persian kitten and a second at the off-side window which he had carelessly left open, were sufficient to bring the unpalatable truth home to him. In his temporary absence Ahasuerus had taken Time by the forelock and made his feline departure.

"Why," stammered Langley to his two guardians, "that's damned funny—he's gone! Well, I'm jiggered! He must have slipped out through that window as I was walking up to your house."

"Just as I suspected," said the harsh-voiced Professor, "and by God you'll pay for all this poppy-cock. Come on back to the house and keep him covered, Layman."

Langley knew he was in a jam. He knew, too, that it was up to him to get out of it as soon as possible and that anything in the shape of hesitation would be disastrous. The only way was by the exercise of quick thinking. As Layman advanced with levelled revolver to turn him towards the house again, Langley lashed out with his right foot suddenly and fiercely at Layman's wrist. The point of his shoe caught the big man a terrific crack right on the bone. The gun was sent flying in the air as Layman cried out in sheer agony. From the impetus of his kick, Langley swung round like lightning on to the Professor and planted a beautifully placed right hook to the point of the academic jaw. The Professor sagged at the knees and went down like a log, and with Layman on the ground, groping vainly for his lost weapon, Langley turned the handle of the car door, slammed the latter behind him, wriggled into the driving-seat, started the car and drove off. The last vision he had of his two acquaintances was of the Professor still lying prostrate on the ground and of Layman running hopelessly behind the car and shouting many things, all of which were entirely inaudible.

When he had covered about half a mile Langley began to feel better and grinned to himself with a certain amount of satisfaction.

"A bad start," he said to himself, "but the hell of a good finish." But suddenly his thoughts veered to Priscilla and to certain interesting problems and possibilities connected with her. "Have I slipped up anywhere?" he asked himself, "or did the lady play me for a sucker?"

A few minutes later he entered the historic town of Angel. His thoughts ran riot. What an amazing thing to have happened to him— and how strangely at times Fate works! It might well be that . . .

V

Langley drove his car straight into the courtyard of the "Bear and Ragged Staff", the inn which carried the strong recommendation and also the credentials of the R.A.C. His room had been booked in advance and he looked forward eagerly to the dinner he knew was awaiting him. As he stood in the garage after locking his car, the thought struck him that it was quite on the cards that he might have been followed from the white house near the Brewery even though the 'chase might have been a trifle tardy in getting going. All the same, he felt that he'd play for safety. So he strolled out from the courtyard unostentatiously, crossed the road and sauntered up and down the pavement opposite to the hotel to see if he were able to spot anything or anybody that he might recognize. He devoted a period of at least ten minutes to this occupation but saw nothing whatever that he regarded as in any way suspicious.

Feeling a little relieved, he returned to the "Bear and Ragged Staff" for a wash and brush-up and his long-anticipated meal. This turned out to be surprisingly good and Langley fell to with a will. But try as he would, he was unable to rid his mind completely of the events of the earlier part of the evening. These still preyed on him after he had finished his dinner and when he made his way into the smoke-room. Making his further way to a corner table, he put a tankard of beer at his elbow and proceeded to fill his pipe with the intention of more cogitation upon the surprising happenings against which he had stumbled a couple of hours previously. Langley sat there for some minutes and gradually the smoke-haze from his pipe ascended and clouded over him. He shut his eyes in a supreme effort towards intensive thought. Suddenly some reaction of mental reflection caused him to look up. After he had looked up he took a deep breath and a firm grip on himself. For there—seated in a chair exactly opposite him—Langley saw the thin rat-faced man whom the "Professor" had addressed as Webber, when Layman and he had drawn revolvers in the white house near the Brewery.

Langley steeled himself to give no sign that he had either seen or recognized this adversary. In a flash, his mind registered the decision that, come what might, he would feign complete ignorance of the fellow. That, he considered, would be by far his most politic course. He picked up his tankard imperturbably and drank from it. Before he could properly replace it on the table, the rat-faced man had sidled over and taken the chair at Langley's table, and to his immediate left. Langley puffed at his pipe complacently and continued to ignore him. He affected to sit farther back in his chair and to half-close his eyes. But at this moment Webber deliberately entered the arena.

"Good evening," he said in a singularly unpleasant voice. "So we meet again—eh?"

Langley turned to him in simulated surprise and treated him as a chance acquaintance. "Oh—er . . . good evening," he replied. He pretended to relapse again. But Webber refused to be put off and came again.

"Mr. Langley . . . I think. Not mistaken, am I?"

Langley's eyebrows went up. "That's right . . . but, honestly, old chap, you have the advantage of me."

"Is that so?" replied Webber sarcastically—"now you do surprise me! Surely I'm correct in asserting that we've met before?"

Langley smiled broadly. He flattered himself that he had become almost bucolic. "We may have done, of course," he conceded; "after all, it's a small world. I get about a bit in the course of the year—sort of here, there and everywhere—and no doubt you do likewise. You may have seen me somewhere—and I haven't noticed you—which means medals for you on the score of memory."

Having delivered himself of this masterly reply (as he thought), Langley sat back in his chair again and reached for his beer. But Webber shook his head slowly and deliberately, and a nasty expression crossed his face.

"No, Mr. Langley . . . that's all very nice and 'di-da-di-da-di-da' and all that . . . but it won't do, cock! Not on your life—it won't! And if you think you're going to get away with everything as nice and comfortable as all that—well—you've got another think coming."

He leant over the table and stuck his face unpleasantly close to Langley's. The latter, however, steadfastly repressing an intense desire to push his fist into it, stuck to his original plan. He was determined to pocket his pride and to adhere rigidly to the policy of complete denial. He smiled again—the perfect example of good temper.

"Whatever all that may mean, I don't like the sound of it. But you're wrong, I tell you—you're up against a case of mistaken identity. Still—don't worry—I shan't take offence. You aren't the first man to make a mistake. I've made 'em myself before now. And I've no doubt I shall make many more."

Webber produced a cigarette and fumbled with his matches before he lit it. "No, cock," he said at length. "It won't do, cock. I know you and you know me. And we 'aven't known each other so long neither—come to that. But listen. I don't know what your little game is—but that isn't to say that I shan't know—and before many days are past at that. You can lay to that."

Langley leant over as though the victim of a sudden impulse. "That gives me an idea," he said; "surely you aren't a relative of the late Mr. John Silver—the lengthy fellow? Because that may explain—"

Webber cut him short. "Never mind about my relations. They don't come into the picture at all. Think more of your own and of your own business. If you don't—I'll pass you the warning now—your relations'll be buying floral tributes—not because they liked you—but because it's the custom of the country." Webber buttoned his coat and rose. "And I'll wish you a very good night, *Mister* Langley. The Professor will be glad to know where you're staying."

Langley made no reply to this final effort. He watched Webber, however, walk the length of the smoke-room and make his departure. When he had disappeared from sight, Langley considered the problem from its latest aspect.

"H'm," he said to himself, "the interest grows. And they *did* take the trouble to trail me here, just as I thought they might."

He thought over the whole thing for some minutes, but the only conclusion to which he could come was that he would not be leaving Angel yet awhile, at any rate. It might have been pure chance in the first place, and, equally—it might not. All the same, his suspicions had been definitely aroused, and from at least one point of view his luck was decidedly "in"! For he had brought off the one chance in a thousand.

CHAPTER II

I

THE night passed uneventfully, and Langley, in accordance with his invariable habit, rose early and went out before breakfast for a breath of the morning air. For November it was unusually fine and clear. The bath and razor had invigorated him and the happenings of the previous evening had receded from him until they seemed to be, not only vague and nebulous, but almost as meaningless as previously they had seemed purposeful. Such is the recuperative power of young, healthy manhood. He went out from one of the back entrances of the inn and crossed the cobbled courtyard into the street.

On the point of turning towards the racecourse and the river, his mind went to his car, still standing in the garage of the "Bear and Ragged Staff". So Langley turned back towards the inn garage for the mere whim of looking at his car in the morning light of Angel. It was standing with five others, under the covering of a corrugated-roof sort of arrangement at the far end of the cobbled courtyard. When his eyes caught sight of it for the first time he gave a gasp of surprise. For there, stooping down a little and with her eyes searching the identification mark and number-plate, was none other than a girl. More than that—*the* girl! Priscilla!

"Wizard luck," though Langley, as he turned towards her. At the sound of his footsteps the girl straightened herself and stood up. Langley was unprepared for the blazing indignation with which she greeted, him. The light danced from her blue eyes and she spoke imperiously.

"And where, if you please," she said, "is Ahasuerus?"

The onslaught temporarily took the wind from Langley's sails. Paradoxically he remembered then that in the contemplation of what he considered to be the major problem he had completely forgotten the blue kitten.

"Hasn't he . . . er . . . come home . . . yet?"

"He has not," she blazed. "I shouldn't have imagined that you required to be told that, where is he? Please, I must know."

Just for a moment Langley regarded her blankly. He grinned eventually and then shrugged his shoulders. "All I know is that he handed me the dirty end. At the critical moment—too."

"How do you mean? Please explain."

"Ran out on me, left me absolutely flat. Just as I was on the point of producing him to his benevolent Professor—lo and behold—*non est Ahasuerus*. In other words—he'd 'moofed'.'"

The girl stared at Langley incredulously. "This is no laughing matter, I assure you. Please be serious—and if you can—talk intelligently."

"Lady," said Langley, "you do me more than an injustice. And when it comes to the picking of bones—I can trot out a perfectly marvellous specimen for your particular attention and edification. But on this occasion please do me a favour. We can't very well discuss things here—well—properly. Walk a little way with me on this delightful morning of mornings and you shall hear the whole story."

The girl silenced him with a look. "The sooner the better—if you please."

Langley bowed to her to show her the way and followed her from the courtyard of the "Bear and Ragged Staff".

II

"You know," he said, by the time they had reached the street, "I can guess how you're feeling, and how you'd like to tear me off a strip, but fair's fair all the world over and you really ought to let me do a spot of explaining. You owe it to me—you really do. And if you think I fell into a bed of roses in the company of your Blue Persian—well, I can tell you flatly that I didn't."

Priscilla interrupted him. "Don't you think it would be to our mutual advantage if you told me your story just plain and unvarnished and devoid of any ridiculous trimmings?"

"Oh—quite," replied Langley, "that's just what I intend to do. You must have second sight."

"That's settled, then," said Priscilla primly. "Now kindly get on with it."

Langley put his fingers momentarily on her wrist, but she angrily jerked it away from him. "You can cut the funny business," she said bitingly. "Your story—please! And in as few words as you can."

Langley's mouth set hard. "That's O.K.," he said; "put it down to sheer forgetfulness on my part. I forgot how much I was indebted to you."

Priscilla gave him a quick glance, but said no more. Langley went on. "I obeyed your instructions last night to the letter. More than that—to every comma. After I ran past the Brewery I kept my eyes glued to the window for your 'big white house, standing back from the road'. I didn't have to wait long—and I spotted it. I parked the car, left your kitten all comfy on a rug on the back seat and went to pay my respects to your dear old Uncle Steve. Such a charming old fellow."

"What on earth made you leave Ahasuerus in the car? Seems to me to have been a particularly hare-brained idea."

"My dear warm-hearted and generous critic," replied Langley, "I didn't want the animal to jump out of my arms—which was a contingency that might have happened had I carried him."

"Instead of which," replied the girl tartly, "he jumped out of the car, I suppose?"

"As a matter of fact that's precisely what did happen. Ahasuerus seized a golden opportunity. When the Professor and his pal Layman accompanied me back to the car, your little playmate had cleared out. Done a guy! He may, of course, have felt the spur of an urgent appointment—"

"Just a moment," she said, with a frown on her face; "what was that name you mentioned? In connection with my uncle."

"Layman. Evidently an old school chum of your uncle's. Captain of the Boats, probably, when Uncle Steve kept the Wall."

"Layman?" She was incredulous as she repeated the name. "I haven't the foggiest idea whom you mean—I've never heard the name in my life. My uncle knows nobody of that name."

"Well—he was there—believe me. Very much there. And quite in keeping with the general picture. In fact I should say quite disinterestedly and dispassionately that Uncle Steve was surrounded by as pretty a bunch of crooks as I've ever had the misfortune to bump alongside."

"Crooks?" said Priscilla scornfully. "What on earth are you gibbering about? My uncle's one of the most—"

This time it was Langley's turn to interrupt. "I said 'crooks' and I mean 'crooks'. Why, after I got into Angel here, one of 'em—Webber by name—came down to the pub here, sought me out deliberately and actually muttered veiled hints and threats re dirty work at some future cross-roads."

Priscilla stopped dead in her tracks and turned to face him. "But this is all completely haywire," she said, frowning at him; "these names, Webber and Layman . . . they mean nothing to me. I've never even heard of them. And as for them being friends of Uncle Steve—why, the idea's absolutely crazy."

Langley shrugged his shoulders. "Well—that's your story, of course, and you're sticking to it, but I didn't dream these things, I can assure you."

They began to walk along in step again. Priscilla's frown was still in evidence.

"Look here," she said suddenly, "I've just thought of something."

"No!" said Langley.

"Don't be a pig," she retorted, crinkling her nose at him. "Listen! And answer me this. Did you cross over the road after you had stopped and parked the car?"

"No," answered Langley, "should I have done?"

"Of course," she said; "my house is on the same side as the Brewery. When you came to it, your car should have been on the right side of the road. I mean on the left—on the proper side—oh, you know very well what I mean. You would have needed to cross over to get to it."

Langley's eyes opened wide at her statement. "Did you say, by any chance, that your house was on the same side as the Brewery?"

"Of course I did! I said as much just now. *And* last night."

"That," continued Langley with slow emphasis, "has most successfully torn it. I entered a house on the opposite side of the road to the Brewery. Good Lord!" He took out his handkerchief and mopped his brow. "I suppose I made a pills of the whole thing, but honestly, the house I picked answered your description to a T. I say, I'm frightfully sorry and all that."

"I know this other house," she said; "it belongs to a man named Gunter. He's occupied it for only a few months. I don't think any of us has ever spoken to him or even set eyes on him, and I'm pretty sure that he's made no social advances to any of us."

"Must be a mutt," said Langley. But his eyes had narrowed at the name.

"Why?" she flashed at him.

"Skip it," returned Langley.

They walked on a few yards without either of them speaking. "What's worrying me," remarked Priscilla, opening up again, "is where's Ahasuerus?"

"To my mind," replied Langley, "it looks as though Ahasuerus has 'had it'."

"Don't be absurd! According to your story, he left your car quite close to our house . . . well . . . within three hundred yards of it. . . . He shouldn't have had any difficulty in finding his way home. Should he now?"

Langley scratched his cheek. "Depends!"

"How do you mean—depends?"

"Well . . . seems to me he may have had a date. After all—can you blame him? Who are we to—"

Priscilla cut in on him. "If you don't put a sock in it and talk sensibly, I'll give you such a kick on the shin that you'll wish you'd been born legless."

"I should hate that," admitted Langley.

"I'm glad to hear it," replied the lady; "it gives me some slight degree of satisfaction even to contemplate such a contingency."

Langley thought how entirely adorable she looked when she was nettled. He was wondering how he might contrive to meet her again. He thought that he saw a way.

"Look here," he said, "it's no good you and I cussing at each other. It doesn't get us anywhere. I made a mistake—I'll admit it. But there was a certain amount of excuse for me, as I've shown you, and I've given you the gen on the whole business. Our job is to find the missing cat. Suppose I come out there later on this morning, and show you exactly where I last saw Comrade Ahasuerus? Would that help, do you think? We might be able to pick up his tracks somewhere." He cocked his eye at her appraisingly as he made the suggestion. "Well—how does the idea strike you?"

She pondered a little before she replied. "All right," she said eventually, "but you'd better come to the house, I think. The *right* house. Don't go careering about somewhere else. What time will suit you?"

Langley resisted an impulse to say "any old time" and made a pretence at calculation. "Well," he said, "supposing I come along soon after breakfast? How will that suit you?"

"It's a bit on the early side, isn't it?"

"The sooner the better—surely? Cats—especially blue-blooded specimens—are inclined to get a move on, you know. Especially when they've an attractive objective."

"All right," she said again; "there's something in what you say, I suppose. I'll expect you at . . . say . . . half past ten."

"O.K.," said Langley. "I'll be right along."

She nodded acceptance, waved a quick hand at him and darted off. Langley watched her as she went . . . walking quickly.

"Am I glad," he said to himself, "that I rose early this morning—or am I?"

III

Langley went back to the "Bear and Ragged Staff" for breakfast.

He was discomfited. Although Priscilla's explanation as to the two houses had partly cleared away one of his problems, there was still much about the entire happenings of last evening which gave him pause and much good food for thought. Into what particular nest of infamy had he unwittingly stumbled? Was there something in the long arm of coincidence after all? For that he had accomplished something of the sort he had little doubt. Priscilla had mentioned the name of Gunter.

By the time he had finished breakfast he was more determined than ever to stay in Angel itself for the next day or two. The thought came to him that by going to Priscilla's he would also be going close to the enemy's camp—which from his particular point of view was all to the good. He would keep his eyes well open while he was there. At the appropriate time he backed his car out of the garage and set off for the other "white house" that stood well back from the road and which was on the same side as the Brewery and not on the opposite side.

Langley whistled gaily to himself as he drove. The situation, as he saw it, was by no means an unpleasant one. Every cloud has a silver lining—and if the "Professor's" bunch were the cloud Priscilla, herself was certainly, from Langley's own personal angle, the silver lining. About half a mile from the Brewery, as Langley judged the distance, he spotted something interesting. Or rather—somebody. A figure approached him swinging along the road, and which he instantly recognized. It was Layman. The man whose wrist he had kicked the night before. But a Layman that was dressed differently from the Layman of the evening previous. As far as Langley could see, he was now wearing a dark-blue uniform with a blue peaked and gold-braided cap. To Langley's eye, it looked like a naval uniform of sorts. But it definitely wasn't a naval uniform that Langley knew. Or was it a uniform of the merchant service?

Langley found himself unable to place it, and as he drove on towards the house of Priscilla's father he fell to wondering at it still more. He had now run across two of the Professor's entourage since his initial encounter with them—Webber and Layman. And he had found out that the Professor's name was in all probability Gunter. Excellent! He had made *some* progress, he thought as he drove, at all events! And any progress was better than none!

IV

When Langley arrived and walked up to the front door of the house he had missed on the previous evening, he suddenly realized (and the realization brought a touch of humour to him) that he was unaware of Priscilla's surname and that also he had no idea whatever of either the name or designation of the householder—her father. Which meant that he had another minor problem to face. Whom should he ask to see? He decided to bank on the address of "Miss Priscilla" as being a fairly safe proposition. The maid's eyes popped a trifle when he put this decision into effect a moment or so later, but she nodded brightly at him and requested him to step inside.

"I'll tell Miss Priscilla she's wanted," she said hopefully, and Langley prepared himself for a period of waiting. His patience, however, was not tried too acutely, for Priscilla herself came in to him within the matter of a couple of minutes accompanied by a tall, well-built, military-looking man with a white moustache, fierce blue eyes, silvery hair and florid complexion.

"Must be a Colonel, at least," thought Langley, "and I don't even know their name. Can't possibly be 'Blimp'. Even though appropriate." Then it suddenly flashed into his mind that they were in an exactly similar predicament as far as he was concerned, and he immediately felt a little better. As Langley rose to greet his host, Priscilla came forward and said laughingly—

"This is the gentleman, Daddy, but I can't introduce him because I don't know his name. If he were to help me out—"

Langley seized the opportunity she had presented to him with eagerness. "Langley, sir. Richard Quinton Langley."

"Now I can get on," cried Priscilla. "Richard Langley—my father—Colonel Schofield."

The Colonel glared at Langley, but thrust out a powerful-looking hand. "Good morning. Glad to know you. My daughter, you know, wants a damned good larrapin'—pressing you into service like that without so much as a 'by your leave'. Dashed if I know where she gets her effrontery from. Not from me, I assure you. Must go back for generations."

Langley played up to him gallantly. "That's all right, sir. Only too pleased to help. Though I'm frightfully sorry I messed things up so. I expect Miss Schofield has told you how it occurred. If only that blessed cat—"

Priscilla burst in and silenced him. "But you didn't. And you needn't reprove yourself. Everything's all right. Ahasuerus came back for breakfast this morning none the worse for his adventures. Full of beans, apparently, and thoroughly bucked with life. Uncle Steve's in the seventh heaven of delight at his return."

"Oh—good," returned Langley; "that certainly puts a different complexion on things. I told you that he had a date, didn't I?"

"A date!" exclaimed Colonel Schofield. "My brother-in-law with a date! I can assure you, Mr. Langley, that your suggestion is thoroughly ill-founded. Anybody who knows him—"

"No, sir," Langley remonstrated, "the cat, sir, not your brother-in-law. You misunderstood me. I wouldn't dream of making such a suggestion with regard to the gentleman."

As he spoke, he could see the thoroughly delighted expression on Priscilla's face. He looked at the Colonel to see how that gentleman had taken his explanation. Evidently, from what the Colonel said next, understanding had come to him.

"The cat, eh? Yes, of course. I'm sorry. My mistake! Well—well—all's well that ends well—and Ahasuerus, or whatever his damned name is, has tidied things up a bit by putting in an appearance at the breakfast-table none the worse for wear. Priscilla, tell Taylor to bring in the sherry. You'll join us in a glass of sherry, Langley—I feel sure?"

"Thank you, Colonel Schofield—I shall be very pleased to."

A few minutes later the Colonel looked over the rim of his glass appraisingly and harked back. "Priscilla tells me you ran into a spot of bother last night when you gate-crashed into the wrong house. If you wouldn't mind, I'd like to hear all about it."

Langley told the Colonel the full facts of his interview with the "Professor", Layman, Webber and Co. Colonel Schofield punctuated the narrative with many expressive nods.

"Bunch of blackguards, I should say," he declared at length, his eyes blazing; "up to no good—not a doubt of it! People of that kind should be dealt with. Summarily. Can't think what the police are doing these days. Personally—I'd show them no quarter. The people I mean—not the police. Ought to be wiped out. Root and branch!

I'd have no mercy on 'em. Treat 'em like God Almighty used to treat some of those blasted tribes you read about in the Scriptures."

He stopped, poured himself out another glass of sherry and glared again at Langley. "Do you know your Scriptures, Langley?"

"Well, sir—it's some little time since—"

"I see. You don't. So pack up your excuses. If you knew your Old Testament, as every thinking man should—you'd be well aware that under certain circumstances Jehovah destroyed certain tribes. Mark you, sir—destroyed them! No half measures. Exterminated them. No pandering to mush and sickly sentimentality. The Amalekites, the Ammonites the . . . er . . . Jebusites and . . . er . . . many others. I commend the matter to you, Langley. You should read about it."

Colonel Schofield drank the remainder of his sherry and looked longingly at the bottle.

"No, Daddy," said Priscilla, "not a drop more—two's your allowance. You know that very well."

"H'mph," replied the Colonel—"I suppose you're right. But why I should give in to you—I'm damned if I know."

"Point that strikes me, sir," contributed Langley, and he spoke deliberately, "is what are these people afraid of? For I'll swear they *are* afraid! When I walked in on them, with the glad tidings that I'd brought the pussycat back, they all looked at me as though I were the ghost in *Hamlet*."

Colonel Schofield looked at him critically. "How do you mean—exactly?"

"Well, sir, the impression I got was that they were scared stiff. Proper breeze-up and no mistake."

"Good God! Just because you'd brought a cat back? Or thought you had. Can't understand it. Doesn't make sense to me."

"It may have been—I've considered it, you see, since—that my method of announcing myself may have caused the balloon to go up. Indeed—I think that's highly probable."

"Why? What did you say?"

Langley laughed—but the effort was far from a convincing one. "Well, sir, I blew in, thinking, of course, that I'd come to your house as Miss Schofield had directed me, and when I heard one of the people addressed as 'Professor' it seemed all—in keeping. I then remarked quite jocularly that the cat was out of the bag. Cue for general consternation."

"Dear me—extraordinary business, I must say. And do you mean to tell me, Langley, that one of this crowd is a Professor of something? Seems incredible."

"It would appear so, sir, although I can't hazard a guess as to what of. Maybe he's graduated in crime."

"Amazing coincidence," muttered the Colonel, "like one of those damned 'movies' Priscilla's always going to and chivvyin' me to go with her."

"Talkies, Daddy. March with the times, please. The industry has progressed."

"Talkies!" snorted Colonel Schofield. "That's a misnomer if ever there were one. Absolutely the last description you should give them. Whenever you lug me to one of your damned cinemas, I'm blest if I can understand a word. God knows what the language is that most of 'em 'talk', as you put it."

Langley murmured words of appropriate appreciation as Priscilla grimaced behind the Colonel's back, and then returned to the main thread of the conversation. "Well, sir, the whole thing's so stimulated my curiosity that I'm inclined to hang around for a day or two. Seems to me that I might land on something if I keep my eyes well open."

Schofield grunted disparagingly. "Don't see how you're going to do that. These people are probably pretty 'fly'—too damned 'fly' for an amateur like yourself."

Langley grinned. "Very likely, sir. Still—you never know. And if I'm lucky I might pick up something."

Colonel Schofield glanced at the clock. "In the ordinary way, my boy, I'd ask you to stop to lunch—but unfortunately today my brother-in-law's gone out and I have an appointment."

"I understand, sir—and thank you for the hospitality you have already given me."

The two men shook hands and Schofield bustled out. When he had gone, Langley shook hands with Priscilla.

"When shall I see you again?" he asked audaciously.

Priscilla crinkled her nose again and simulated consideration of the question. "I'll find a matchbox," she said, "and play 'this year, next year, sometime, never'. And I think I know where there's one with exactly a dozen matches in it."

Langley heard her out gravely before fumbling in his pocket. Eventually he produced a match, which he handed to her.

"Put this in your box for me, will you? That'll make thirteen. See how it works out then."

"I couldn't," she replied, equally seriously. "I've always been told that thirteen's frightfully unlucky."

"So it is," returned Langley, "my mistake, I should have thought of that." He pressed something into her hand. "Four more," he exclaimed with a smile, "total seventeen—see what answer that'll give you. *Au 'voir*."

"Good-bye," corrected Priscilla, decidedly coldly.

"Don't you believe it." He turned back to her from the door-way. "By the way, remember me to Ahasuerus. If cats could only talk—eh? I bet he could spill a mouthful about last night. There'd be crowds to hear him."

"Taylor," called out Priscilla, "show Mr. Langley the way out, will you, please?"

"Yes, Miss Priscilla," replied the maid primly. "This way, sir, if you please."

But Richard Quinton Langley turned round again and waved gaily as the door was opened for his departure.

CHAPTER III

I

LANGLEY drove back to Angel a prey to a conflict of mixed feelings. From some points of view he felt elated—from others he embraced depression. But Langley was not of the type which succumbs easily to the latter, and a few minutes along the road were enough to dispel the depression and to leave elation in full mastery of the general situation.

About half-way from Angel there occurred an incident which caused Langley to think a bit more. A man, standing on the near side of the road, came forward and gave him the hitch-hike sign. Deciding almost instantaneously, Langley brought the car to. a standstill and put his head out of the window.

"I'm going only' as far as Angel," he said.

The man who had accosted him smiled all over his face. "That'll suit me, Guv'nor, down to the ground, if it's all the same to you. I'm in a bit of a hurry—hence my taking the liberty."

"All right," replied Langley on the half-turn—"get in. And just shift those rugs at the back—do you mind?"

The man got into the car and moved the rugs as ordered and Langley took good stock of him as he did so. He saw a man of middle size who wore a brown suit, a brown overcoat, brown shoes and a red-brown soft hat. In age, Langley placed him as in the early forties. The pallor of his face suggested a strong degree of unhealthiness and he grew a wispy, straggling moustache that was a dirty brown-grey in colour and badly needed the hairdresser's attention. Langley was more than ordinarily interested. By this time he had become definitely curious. He knew full well that his car had probably been spotted when it had been parked outside Colonel Schofield's house and that this meeting might well be the second reaction of the gentleman known as the "Professor", and, therefore, deliberately staged. He settled back comfortably in the driving-seat, therefore, determined to be on his guard and to watch points. The man in the rear seat opened the ball almost immediately.

"Bit of luck, your bowling along. I'd been there nearly a quarter of an hour. I was whacked to the wide. Nothing on the road at all—going my way."

"Too bad," remarked Langley with a tinge of irony; "wonder you didn't accept the inevitable and pad the hoof."

Through his driving-mirror he saw his self-imposed passenger glance at him quickly and almost suspiciously. "I would have done," came a rather hesitant reply, "but my heel's been troubling me all the morning. Afraid I've blistered it. That's why I'd turned it in."

"Bad luck," returned Langley; "walked far?"

"Er . . . yes . . . all the way from Eden."

"Eden, eh? That's a good ten miles, isn't it? You must be fond of the open road. What is it? A walking tour?"

Again came the sharp, shrewd look from the passenger in the rear seat. "Not exactly," was the reply. "I'm due in Angel this afternoon on business, and things aren't so good with me these days that I can afford to pay for transport." The man laughed a trifle bitterly. "That's all there is to it," he concluded.

Langley rested his gloved hand on the wheel and took a sidelong glance at him. The man certainly didn't give the appearance of being "down and out".

"Stopping in Angel?" he asked Langley.

It was on the tip of the latter's tongue to ask abruptly what business it was of the inquirer, but a second's cool consideration gave Langley the idea that he could do better than that. "Not for long," he answered. "What's long," said the man in brown. "Bit elastic—ain't it?"

"Day or so," responded Langley laconically.

"On holiday?"

"Yes, I suppose you might call it that."

"Funny time of the year for a holiday—November."

"Funny ha-ha, or funny peculiar?"

"Oh—funny peculiar, of course."

"Why, exactly?"

"Well—weather for one thing. Fog and rain and all that muck. Should have sunshine when you're holiday-makin'. Short days too; nothing much doing in the way of entertainment."

"Depends what you want."

"Well—you look an ordinary sort of fellow—I take it you'd want the ordinary sort of pleasure."

"Tastes just as nice in November as it does in July—and there's more to go round because there aren't so many people about sharing in it." Langley grinned as he spoke.

"I didn't mean beer," retorted his passenger.

"Sorry. Thought that was what you must mean."

For the next moment or so the man was silent. The car crossed the bridge into the main street of Angel. "Tell me where to drop you," said Langley; "the best of friends must part."

"O.K.," said the man and then, "do you know—you remind me of somebody I've met before? I've been trying to place you ever since I got in, but all the time it's eluded me. I've just got it! Thought I should before I finished."

"Good man," said Langley, "and who is it—Gordon Richards? I'd love to know."

"A chap I know in the Police. K Division man. He's an Inspector now. Proper spit of him you are, and no mistake. I've just connected up with it."

"I suppose I must take that as a compliment. In what way are we so alike?"

"Oh—size,. Similar build. Physique generally. Your feet and the way you wear your clothes. You're a big fellow—you'd pass for a 'busy' anywhere."

"Really! That's interesting. And how is it you're so well acquainted with the guardians of law and order?"

"Well, the fellow I mentioned's a sort of third cousin of mine. You know—removed. That's how I happen to know him so well."

Langley became severely practical. "Afraid I shall have to drop you now. I happen to have come to the end of my journey. Hope it's not too inconvenient for you."

The man looked out of the car window. "Let me see. Where are we? I'm not altogether certain. 'Bear and Ragged Staff'?"

"Where do you want?" cut in Langley sharply.

"Er . . . Paradise Street. It's not so very far away, if my memory serves me correctly. Thanks very much, old man, for the lift—kind of you."

The man alighted, waved his hand to Langley and walked off. Langley looked out of the window and watched his retreating figure.

"H'm," he muttered, as he turned the car into the hotel court-yard. "Paradise Street, eh, and as near to Paradise, I expect, as you're ever likely to get."

II

As Langley passed down the main corridor of the "Bear and Ragged Staff", he saw a waiter hurrying in front of him, carrying a tray on which were several glasses. An idea struck him. Quickening his pace, he caught up with this waiter and at once put a question to him.

"I wonder whether you could help me," he said; "can you tell me where I can find Paradise Street? Is it very far from here—do you know?"

The man addressed answered immediately. "Couldn't say, sir. But if you were referring to the town of Angel, sir, there's no such street in this town."

Langley stared at him. "Sure of that?" he asked.

"Positive, sir. I know Angel inside out, sir. Born and bred here and have lived here all my life, so you can't tell me much I don't know about it."

"Thank you," replied Langley, "I must have misunderstood the name, I suppose."

He turned up the staircase to go to his bedroom, thinking deeply. For one thing he was anxious to see if any further approaches were to be made to him from any of the men whom he had encountered last evening. He regarded this morning's incident, although indirect, as the second of the series. When he came down to the luncheon room he gave a quick glance round the cocktail bar and the room attached to it, to see if any of the bunch had turned up at the "Bear and Ragged Staff" that morning. Both apartments were crowded. But on this occasion he drew blank. He wasn't certain as to whether he should be pleased or displeased at this. It was satisfactory, perhaps, to think that they were leaving him alone for a time, but on the other hand he realized that if they kept away indefinitely he must perforce, in the ultimate, travel to them, if he wanted to hit on a solution and satisfy himself as to their actions.

He had lunch, over which he took his time, and spent the afternoon quietly. About four o'clock he decided to take a stroll through the streets of Angel and pop into one of the shops, perhaps, for a spot of tea. He thought that he would prefer this to staying in the hotel. After wandering round for a quarter of an hour or so, and coming to the conclusion that the town was supremely crowded for the time of year, he reached what appeared to be the main street and eventually came to a rather attractive-looking tea-shop which bore the somewhat unusual sign of the "Old Spider's Web".

"This'll suit me for tea," he said to himself; "just my handwriting."

As he entered, he saw that the shop was full up with customers. Search as he might with his eyes, there wasn't a table unoccupied, or, even at a minimum, one seat at a table. Not caring to wait, he turned to make his way out again, when he felt a light touch on his arm.

"It's all right, sir," said a voice with a distinct touch of foreign accent, "we've another room downstairs. You'll find there's plenty of room down there."

The woman pointed to a descending stairway tucked away at the side of the shop. Langley cocked a quizzical eye towards the stairway and then turned to regard the woman who had directed him. He saw a woman in the early forties, probably, with a long querulous face, pointed chin and rather melancholy-looking eyes. But it was the expression that her face held which attracted the major part of his attention. It was petulant and decidedly disagreeable, and in her voice, too, was a note of thin—almost childish—peevishness.

"Thank you," said Langley, "I'll go down there, then."

"The tea's just the same down there as up here. No different at all. I'll bring one down to you in a few moments."

Langley thanked her again and half broke away from her to make for the steps that led below when he saw a second waitress approach the woman. He heard this waitress ask, evidently, for certain instructions. He noticed, too, that she addressed the woman who had spoken to him as "Madame". By this time he found himself at the head of the stairway. As he descended the stone steps, Langley was surprised to notice how the stairway itself and all the attachments thereto had been prepared and decorated so that the establishment might adequately live up to its name of the "Old Spider's Web". The steps themselves, by some artificial means, had been painted and shaded in order that this might convey the impression that they were crumbling and breaking away with the spurious evidence of grass and moss peeping between the stone steps. In the corners above his head there had been cunningly portrayed both imitation spiders' webs and cobwebs, and the mural decorations were all in the same pattern.

Langley came to an abrupt turn on the last step and entered what was evidently the "overflow" tea-room. The appointments of this tearoom were consistent with the conditions of the stairway. It gave every appearance of a disused cellar. The walls, the ceiling, the corners where wall and ceiling met and the various alcoves all suggested the dirt, the fungus,, the decay, the squalidity, the hanging festoons of dust and the dark humidity of the subterranean cellar. But the place was pleasantly warm and comfortable, and also well lighted, and as Langley took a seat at a vacant table he realized how the entire effect of squalor and begriming cellar-dirt had been cleverly and artificially created and produced. The cellar was full, too, the table to which Langley had gone being the only one not occupied. The statement of the woman upstairs that there was plenty of room below had been a convenient euphemism.

Langley counted the tables, set for the most part in cunningly-contrived corners and alcoves. There were eight of them. As in the case of the stairway to it, this cellar-room itself had cobwebs festooned in its ceiling-corners and its walls had been shaded in such a manner that their entire appearance indicated patches of coal-dust and shades of cellar-dirt. Seemingly the heritage of the years. As he considered these things, the petulant-mouthed woman came down the stairway with his tea-tray and to his elbow. With deft hands she put the tea and the tea-things in front of him. Tea, bread-and-butter, a small glass pot of jam and a plate with an assortment of fancy cakes. Langley murmured the conventional thanks.

The woman, unsmiling and plain-faced, lifted her bill-packet from her apron. "I will give you your bill so that you will not have to wait for it. We 'ave a standard charge. So I know what to charge you."

Again Langley noticed the foreign accent. The woman put the bill on the table at his side and disappeared again. The tea was good enough to disarm criticism, but when Langley had been there for a few minutes he came to the conclusion that he disliked both the place and its atmosphere and that he had no desire to have tea there again. It was the atmosphere most of all, he decided. Although the "effects" had all been merely simulated, it appeared to Langley that by some strange freak of Fate the apartment had actually taken unto itself the very atmosphere and conditions of a real cellar well below ground level.

With these thoughts uppermost in his mind, Langley didn't linger over his tea. On the contrary, he fell to with a will and made short work of it. He had finished within ten minutes and had begun to fumble in his pockets for the inevitable cigarette. As he did so, he saw the sulky-lipped woman come down the stairway again. She placed the tea-tray she carried on the table nearest Langley's. As she bent to put a spoon in a saucer, the second waitress came to the bottom of the stone steps and called to her.

"Madame—you're wanted in the shop. Will you please come at once? It's the master."

Madame nodded to show that she had heard, but a frown crossed her brows and her mouth showed its petulance more than ever. Langley formed the opinion that she was annoyed at the interruption. And, if anything, rather more than ordinarily annoyed. He watched her as she made her way up the steps, and blew a smoke-ring after her. Her face had looked like last night's soda-water at the bottom of the glass. Langley grinned to himself as he mentally toyed with one or two possible explanations of her appearance and general behaviour. He smoked his cigarette down to the stub and pressed the latter into an ash-tray. Then he collected himself and went up the stone steps. By the cash-desk, where naturally he stopped to discharge his obligation, "Madame" was standing in deep conversation with a man. The man was standing with his back to Langley. As he approached, Langley heard him say, "There'll be a show-down tonight. If the worst comes to the worst, we may have to use this place."

As Langley came alongside, the words froze on the man's lips, and "Madame" turned to take the coin which Langley put into her hand. The man with her turned too and Langley got his second surprise of that particular day. Because the man was one of the men who had been with Webber, Layman and the "Professor" when Langley had taken Ahasuerus home. Or had thought he had!

"Thank you," said "Madame" as she accepted the cash, and Langley made a slow exit from the shop. He could feel the man's eyes boring into his back as he stepped over the threshold. As he thought things over, it seemed to him much more than a coincidence that he should have run into yet another member of the "Professor's" house-party.

"Funny business altogether," he muttered to himself, "whichever way you look at it, Fate's simply throwing them at me."

Glancing up, he saw that he was abreast of a building on which were inscribed the words "Borough of Angel Municipal Library". An idea struck him, and acting upon it, he walked up the steps and made his way in. Inside, he made straight for the Reference Library section and asked a pasty-faced youth with a plenitude of pimple for a copy of the local directory. This obtained, Langley carried it to a comfortable seat and began his investigations. He had hoped to find in the directory a "Trade" index. He was successful, and under the heading "Bakers and Confectioners" he found the name "O. Newman—'The Old Spider's Web'—22, Chelt Street, Angel."

"O. Newman," he murmured to himself, "doesn't tell me much, now. Might be a man; equally—might be a woman."

He considered the various Christian names that carried the initial "O". Men first. Oswald, Oliver, Otto, Octavius, Oscar, Orlando. Six. That was all—oh—he thought of another—and Olaf. Seven! And more than one of them very definitely not English. Not so good. Now for the women's list. Olivia, Octavia, Olive, Oonagh, Odette, Ophelia and Olga. Seven. Level pegging! Nothing in it—anyhow. On the whole, he thought, and taking everything into consideration, the lists indicated that the proprietor of the establishment was a man rather than a woman. As he came to that conclusion, he remembered something. When the waitress had called down to "Madame" that she was wanted in the shop, she had used the expression, "the master".

Langley's eyes went idly to the directory again. The list of names of "Bakers and Confectioners" was still in front of him, and almost instantaneously as he looked at it he saw the name "O. Newman" occurring again in the "Trade Index" of Angel. This time the address was given as 8, Racecourse Way. Mr. (or just possibly Mrs.) Newman evidently was the proprietor of two businesses to do with baking and its attachments. Langley decided to have a look at Shop Number Two, and that as quickly as possible. He returned the directory, therefore, to the unsavoury-looking object behind the counter and set out for Racecourse Way.

He had noticed that there was a 'bus-route which served the direction he wanted, so he made tracks for the omnibus and coach station from which he knew all the Angel vehicles started. He hadn't to wait long for the right 'bus, and when the conductor arrived, asked for the Racecourse.

"Bit on the early side—ain't you, Guv'nor?" remarked the conductor, "or p'raps you've got a camp-stool tucked under your coat that I can't see."

"Don't get it," said Langley, "sorry."

"Let it ride," replied the conductor tersely, "it passed you so quick, you'd never catch up with it." He started to walk wearily to the next passenger.

"No," said Langley, "sorry I'm dumb. I'm a stranger in these parts. What was the point of your crack?"

The look on the conductor's face suggested commiseration as much as anything. "Well, chum," he said, "seeing that the meeting don't start till tomorrow, it struck me as 'ow you was on the early side—asking for the Racecourse. You'll be well in time, so to speak, going along there today. They'll list you in the overnight arrivals."

Light began to dawn on Langley. "I get you," he replied; "sorry I was so slow in the uptake. The Angel Autumn Meeting commences tomorrow—that's your point. I'm afraid that my thoughts were travelling in a totally different direction and I wasn't thinking on those lines at all."

The conductor grinned jovially. "That's all right, sir. But you see normally we only gets asked for 'Racecourse' on racecourse meeting days. That's why I chipped in." He passed along to collect the remaining fares.

Langley alighted at the terminus, which was by an hotel close to the course, and before he started looking for Racecourse Way he decided to take a glance at the course itself—the world-famous Sincil Park. From the standpoint of the picturesque he saw at once that it was ideally situated, having as it did the lapping waters of the River Seraph on the farther side. The stands, the white-painted rails and the green track of turf and the ferry-boat plying its way across the Seraph were all pleasing to the eye. Langley saw the white- and red-striped bills advertising the Angel Second Autumn Meeting, due to take place on the Wednesday and Thursday of the current week. According to the terms of the advertisement, the *pièce de résistance* was evidently the race for the "Angel Autumn Handicap", announced to be run on the second and concluding day of the meeting. It then came home to him that he had heard Angel described more than once by certain race-going friends of his as second only to Ascot in many respects.

With this in mind, he turned away from the course with the intention of locating Racecourse Way. The task presented no difficulty. Keeping on the route along which his 'bus had brought him, he quickly spotted it. It lay almost exactly parallel with the course, and therefore with the Seraph. Langley turned down it, only to discover speedily that it was a road of abnormal length. Unfortunately, too, for him and his primary object in being there, the numbers apparently started from the other end. He plodded patiently on, however, and eventually came to the baker's shop of his seeking. He saw that it lay in the shadow, as it were, of the Grand Stand itself. Over the door was the name he desired to see, "O. Newman". He also noticed with a certain tinge of interest that it combined the service of the bakery with that of a post-office. This fact, he considered, was quite an ordinary occurrence, as he had observed during the last week or so, that many country post-offices were to be found attached to bakers' shops. It seemed almost to be the rule rather than the exception.

On the spur of a momentary thought, Langley pushed open the door of the shop and went in, to the jangling accompaniment of a discordant bell. He strolled across to the post-office counter and asked for a book of postage-stamps. A pale-faced girl in a green jumper and tweed skirt put down needles and wool, served him, and then, as he took the small book from her, he spotted that the door of the shop-parlour was just a trifle ajar and that a man's face was close to it. Moreover, it was plain to see that the face was employed in watching him. Langley felt certain from the momentary glance he had been afforded that it belonged to the man whom he had seen a short time previously in the "Spider's Web". Then he began to calculate the time factor.

The man must have moved very quickly to have reached here before he himself had. Langley deduced a car. A car, starting after he had, would have passed his 'bus without the slightest difficulty. He resolved to give no sign that he had observed the watcher, so with the utmost nonchalance he strode out of the shop. On his way back to the "Bear and Ragged Staff" he again took stock of the situation as he now saw it. To the "Professor", he was able to add the names of Webber, Layman and Newman. Yes, all very satisfactory. During dinner that evening he began to think again of the man who had "hitchhiked" him on the way to Angel that morning. His statement had been that he had walked in from Eden. In that case the neighbouring village of Eden might well repay a visit. At any rate he wouldn't leave it out of his calculations. For he was as certain as he had ever been certain of anything that this man was connected with the "Professor" and his henchmen.

When Langley pushed his chair back from the table after the last course he had come to an interesting decision. It might well be that once again Truth was about to turn out stranger than fiction.

III

Langley went upstairs to his bedroom, changed his shoes for a light pair in which he knew he could move quickly and almost noiselessly, slipped an electric torch and a revolver into his overcoat pocket and went quickly down to the hotel garage. As has already been stated, this was at the end of a cobbled courtyard which ran down the side of the establishment and which gave full and easy access to the street. One of the men employed on the premises saw him as he went to his car.

"Going for a spin, sir?" he inquired. "Bit on the late side, isn't it?"

"Yes," grinned Langley, "but it's a glorious night and I've got some friends just outside the town. I shan't be coming back so frightfully late. What time do you close up?" He nodded towards the gates of the courtyard.

"Well—we aren't too particular—but about half eleven, sir. Shouldn't be later than that, if I were you."

Langley thanked him for the advice and drove off, turning the car towards the houses of the Schofields and the sinister "Professor". In other words, Langley had decided to take another look at the house into which he had intended to take Ahasuerus. As he had said to the garage hand, the night was glorious. To be true, it was raw cold, but there was a complete absence of wind and the stars hung and glittered in the dome of the sky like so many twinkling brilliants in a canopy of ebony.

Langley stepped on the juice and let the car rip "all out". Up to now, he had met nothing whatever on the road. As he approached the house of his primary interest (apart of course from that in Priscilla) he slowed down. His first objective was to find a convenient parking-place for the car. He had an idea tucked away at the back of his head somewhere that there was a lane or cart-track that ran off the main road about a couple of hundred yards from the house. If there were—and he had no reason to doubt the accuracy of his memory—he would use it for his car.

Within a few moments he knew that he was right. There was the lane—more like a cart-track than anything else—so Langley turned the car down it, ran well into the side of a hedge and switched off his lights. He felt that in doing so the risk was almost infinitesimal, as any traffic down this track at this time of the night was most unlikely. Langley gave the car a last look-over to see that it was all right and then made for the house at a quick, almost noiseless, gait. Instead of entering from the front, he worked round to the back, and soon found himself at the rear of the house. Crossing rapidly over a wide strip of grass, he found a large trellis barring his way. But Langley soon found a gap in it and came close to the windows and back wall of the house. A smallish door yielded to a handle-turn and Langley found himself in a room which smelt to him as most likely to be the kitchen scullery. He flashed a torch for a quick, stabbing second and saw that his nose hadn't let him down. Out of this room, Langley came to a wide-spaced corridor. Risking the use of the electric torch again, he saw from the various doors that at least four rooms opened on to this corridor. His ears followed the example of his nose and soon told him which of these rooms was at present occupied. The sound of voices in a buzz of conversation came from the second door on his right as he stood listening there in the corridor. And he realized that it was foolhardy of him to stand there as he was doing as the sudden opening of a door would give him no time at all for concealment but would disclose and betray him immediately. He knew that it was imperative for him to put himself into a condition of comparative safety as soon as he possibly could.

Almost opposite to the door behind which he could hear the voices, Langley spotted another door. From the size of it he thought he knew what this apartment was almost certain to be. Langley sprinted up the corridor without making the slightest sound, took a chance and turned the handle. He was right. It was an indoor toilet apartment, complete with washing-basin, mirror and towel-rack. Also, he saw—and this with unalloyed pleasure—that there was a window of ample size through which one could, if necessary, find access to the grounds at the front of the house. Also, by holding the door ajar, Langley found that he could distinguish certain words, phrases and snatches of speech as they came from the room almost opposite to him on the other side of the corridor. The one voice which Langley thought he could most certainly identify was that of the "Professor". He couldn't be certain that he could recognize either Layman's or Webber's, and having heard Newman's but once he didn't attempt to place it. But it was evident from what he could hear that a discussion of sorts was on the bill in the room opposite. A discussion which at times seemed to develop into a somewhat bitter argument. He heard a voice (which he *thought* must be that of Layman) say—

"There's only one thing to do. You all know what that is. Whether you like it or not. We must shut his mouth. The man knows far too much. Mann should never have let him in on it. It was a damned silly thing to do. I was always opposed to it."

Something was uttered in reply to this which Langley was unable to catch. Then another voice said, "When?"

And Layman (if it were he) replied, "Why be squeamish about. it? Faintheartedness never got a man anywhere. If we let him go now, there's no telling when another opportunity will come along."

For a split second Langley felt that the sinister reference might be to him, but when he considered the idea a little more carefully he knew that he was being unduly pessimistic, because the phrase "let him go" argued a condition of affairs that certainly at the moment didn't exist as far as he himself was concerned. Then the voices of the argument died down and Langley wasn't able to hear a syllable of what was being said. But occasionally he was able to detect the "Professor's" guttural tones amongst them. He determined, therefore, to take a risk. So he tip-toed across the corridor and listened outside the all-important door. Through this activity he was able to hear the "Professor" say, "Very well! Seeing that there's so much divergence of opinion, we'll put the matter to the vote. I've always held up my hand for the principles of democracy. We'll then stand or sink together. Or more realistically—shall I say—we'll stand or swing together. Ah—that makes you silent, doesn't it? But it's always the best policy to face facts. There are six of us here. Or there will be when Mann comes back. And I'm in the chair—which, if necessary, gives me the power of the casting vote. Don't be forgetting that—any one of you. And if it *is* necessary, by God, I'll use it. Don't doubt that, my brothers in crime."

There was a long silence as the "Professor" had indicated. Then Langley, craning forward anxiously, heard his voice again.

"All in favour of Layman's proposition." ("So it was Layman," thought Langley. "I was right after all.") "Come on! Show of hands! One, two, three, four. That settles it. No need to wait for Mann. There's a clear majority. And no need, either, for me to do any casting-vote stuff. Well—I think you've come to the right decision. I've always been a firm believer in decisive action."

Langley heard the noise of a chair being pushed back. He judged that he was occupying a decidedly unhealthy position where he was, so he scuttled back to the apartment from which he had previously emerged, like a shot from a gun. He was not a second too soon, and yielding to a sudden impulse as he entered the toilet-room, he quietly turned the key in the lock. If the worst came to the worst, this locked door should give him a few moments' grace that should stand him in good stead. Any doubt that he entertained on this point was soon suddenly dispelled. He heard the sound of firm steps crossing the corridor and coming directly to the door behind which he was standing. A hand turned the handle, and the door not yielding completely to the turn, the handle was shaken roughly as a result. Then it was shaken again—this second time much more violently.

Langley sized up the situation in a trice. To a certain extent, it was the one he had anticipated and for which he had partly prepared. As the door was shaken for the third time, he knew that he hadn't a moment to lose. He quietly pushed up the window at the back of the apartment and hoisted himself up to it. Luckily, it presented a good-sized aperture, and Langley was able, by a series of twists and turns, to insert his body through the space it provided and drop to the ground outside. As his feet found the path he heard an angry shout come from inside the house. Counting discretion as by far the better part of valour at this precise moment, Langley took to his heels and ran. He ran hard towards the lane in which he had left his car. He knew that he had a fair start, and that with anything like ordinary luck he should make it. As he sprinted in the lee of the wall of the house he heard and then saw a car coming towards him. He crouched down almost flat on the ground in case the headlights should pick him out for the driver's eyes, and the car swept by him safely.

Langley straightened himself and ran on again. He heard the car which had just passed him stop by the entrance to the house he had just left so unceremoniously. Langley ran on harder and faster and eventually came to the cart-track. As he turned into it his heart sank and he stopped dead in his tracks. His car had gone. The cart-track was empty!

IV

For the flash of a second Langley thought that he was badly bunkered. Directly his antagonists broke into the toilet-room, found that the key of the door had been turned on the inside and saw the opened window through which he had escaped, they would be out and after him like hounds which had put up a fox. What was the best plan, therefore, for him to adopt? In the flash of another second he found the answer, and he knew that it was a darned good answer at that. He could hear no sounds yet to indicate that the hunt was up or even in semi-cry, so Langley ran quickly across the main road in one of its darkest stretches and, still moving noiselessly, ran on in the direction of the Schofields' house. As he ran, he turned over one or two of his more pressing problems in his mind. What dark purpose was there behind the stealing of his car? What had happened to cause a man or men to do this? Had he been spotted when he had first driven up and the theft committed as a means of counter-action? Also what exactly should he tell the Schofields when he arrived there?

As he came to their house he steadied his pace a little, and a few yards further on dropped it to a respectable walk. He was fit enough, it's true—but the hot pace at which he had moved since he had made his escape had begun to tell on him, and he had no desire to be shown into the Schofields' presence panting and like a hooked fish gasping on the bank. The same maid let him in who had admitted him before.

"Yes, sir," she said brightly. "Both Colonel Schofield and Miss Priscilla are at home. If you'll kindly wait a moment, sir, I'll tell him."

Langley heard the Colonel's voice welcoming him, almost immediately, into the lounge.

"Come in, my boy! Wasn't expecting you at this time of night, but you're none the less welcome for all that."

A tall thin man, with white hair and mildly benevolent blue eyes, rose at the same time to greet him.

"My brother-in-law," said the Colonel, "Professor Ballantyne—Mr. Robert Langley."

"'Richard', sir," said Langley with a smile.

"Eh—what's that?" said the Colonel. "Richard did you say? That's what I said, my boy. I remembered it was Richard because it began with an R. Robert's the only name I can think of that fits that condition. Anyhow, my apologies. I'll have another go. Professor Langley—Mr. Stephen Ballantyne."

Langley realized the position, skipped it and shook hands with the tall, blue-eyed man. As he did so he spotted the Persian kitten on the rug, having evidently just vacated a place on Ballantyne's lap.

"Ah," he said, "he makes me feel more at home. My old china—Ahasuerus."

The kitten looked at them, hoisted his tail and strolled contemptuously away.

"He's a trifle 'high-hat'," said Ballantyne; "it's his breeding, so you mustn't consider yourself unduly snubbed."

"That's all right, sir," said Langley, "I understand. Cats have a standard of their own, I know."

"Well," said Schofield, "sit down, my dear Langley, and make yourself comfortable. And have a drink. Scotch or beer?"

"I'll have a Scotch, sir, if it's all the same to you."

The Colonel moved to the sideboard. "Say 'when'," said Schofield. Langley obliged. "Now," went on the Colonel, settling down in his chair after handing Langley his drink, "what's the latest in the way of news? Anything transpired of any consequence since I last saw you? By the way, where have you left your car?"

Langley made a quick decision. "Just up the road, sir. I motored up here from the hotel."

"Good. Now tell me the latest. Before Priscilla arrives to distract us. You know what happens once a woman barges in."

"Well, sir," replied Langley, "that's really what I came about. As it happens, I've made one or two rather important discoveries since I saw you last and there's one of them I'd like to discuss with you. Can you tell me anything about a man in Angel named Newman?" Schofield furrowed his brows. "Newman? Now let me see. I've lived here a good many years and actually I know a good many of the locals. Let me see now! Newman."

But no light of recognition showed in his eyes. Langley let him think. He made no interruption of any kind. While Schofield was pondering, the door of the lounge opened and Priscilla came in. Langley rose and bowed to her. He noticed at once her heightened colour when she saw who it was. About to speak, she seemed to sense that the silence of the room was deliberate and decided to retain the condition. Langley broke the period of tension.

"The Colonel's trying to remember something for me, Miss Schofield. That will explain the somewhat dramatic atmosphere."

"Oh," remarked Priscilla, "and why?"

"Chiefly, I think, because I asked him to."

Colonel Schofield emerged from his self-imposed trance. "I've got it, my boy," he declared. "It was damned elusive, like the Scarlet Pimpernel, but I knew if I tailed it long enough I'd run it to earth. There's a Newman keeps certain shops in Angel. Baker's and pastry-cook's—you know the kind I mean. One's not far from the Racecourse and the other's one of the more fashionable tea-shops in the town. Does a damned good trade, too. What the devil's it called now? 'The Cobweb', I fancy. Or some confoundedly silly name like that."

"The 'Old Spider's Web', Daddy," contributed Priscilla submissively.

"That's it," cried the Colonel triumphantly—"that's the name of it—the 'Old Spider's Web'. I knew I'd got the right idea."

"Thank you, sir," replied Langley, although the information told him no more than he already knew. "But do you know anything about the man himself—beyond that?"

"Afraid I don't, my boy. Not an iota. Don't move in the same circles. But what makes you so curious about the fellow? You must have something at the back of your mind to throw him up at me like this."

As he was on the point of replying, Langley noticed Ahasuerus jump on to Ballantyne's lap. For the moment he hesitated. The movement of the kitten had diverted his thoughts to another channel. But he jerked himself back to reality with an effort and framed his reply to Colonel Schofield's question.

"It's this way, sir. Unless I'm very much mistaken, Newman was one of the men in the house I told you about. I happened to spot him when I was in Angel today and recognized him."

"H'm. Interesting! Still, as I said, I can't argue about it. Know nothing about the man beyond his name. Shouldn't know him from Adam. May be an archangel in disguise—on the contrary, may be the biggest crook in the universe. Shouldn't know one way or the other." The Colonel coughed as he delivered this portentous utterance.

"My brother-in-law," put in Ballantyne, quietly, but with gentle insistence, "is nothing if not emphatic."

"Always have been, my dear fellow! Always will be! Believe in it. Never had any time at all for damned shilly-shallying."

"Well, sir," said Langley again, "many thanks and my apologies for troubling you at this time of night." He finished his Scotch and got up from his chair to place the glass on the tray. "I'll be getting back then. The people at my hotel don't like me to be too late on the return journey. Something to do with closing the garages. I understand that half-past eleven's their limit—so if you'll excuse me—"

"Certainly, my boy. I quite understand. Bit of an early bird myself. Priscilla—perhaps you'd like to see Mr. Langley out. Taylor's off duty for a few minutes."

Langley shook hands with the Colonel and Ballantyne, and Priscilla preceded him to the door.

"You're doing very well, aren't you?" she said from the side of her mouth. "Will you be along to breakfast? Or will it be—"

Langley grinned at her. "If I thought that was a spontaneous invitation—"

"It isn't," she said hastily, "it was a mere pained inquiry. If your humility weren't so frightfully overwhelming . . ." She paused as she noticed Langley staring from the porch to the highway. "What is it?" she asked. "Seeing things?"

"That," said Langley, "is almost a reversal of the situation. As a matter of fact, that's just what I'm *not* doing."

"Don't talk in riddles at this time of night, for the love of Mike!"

"I'm not. And what I intended to say was that I'm *not* seeing my car! Whereas I should be."

"Did you come in it?"

"Naturally. I thought you might possibly want me to take Ahasuerus somewhere. Cat-carrier for—"

"Pig!" she said bluntly. "Complete and utter pig! If I'd known all that I know now, I'd have run a thousand miles away from you. Why on earth I picked you out—"

Langley's voice silenced her. "And if I'd known half of what I know now, I'd have run two thousand miles towards you. And loved every inch of them. But seriously, Priscilla—"

"I am quite serious, Mr. Langley, and I much prefer you to address me as Miss Schofield, if it makes no difference to you."

"But it does, Miss Schofield. A hell of a difference. Honestly it does, Priscilla."

It was dark and Langley wasn't able to see the humorous glint in her eyes. Priscilla knew that well enough. Otherwise she wouldn't have allowed it to be there. Langley spoke again.

"Come to the kerb with me, will you? Then you can see for yourself that there's no car there."

"I don't know why I should do all these things, I'm sure. Because I'm not in the slightest degree interested."

"You don't have to know—just do as you're told—come along with me."

They came to the edge of the road and Priscilla could see that the road was clear. There was no sign of a car anywhere in the vicinity.

"What did I tell you?" declared Langley. "Somebody's won a thundering good car. And won it off me, too. Now what am I going to do?"

"My dear Mr. Langley—the reply is obvious. I'm surprised to hear you propound such a simple question. It's a well-known fact that people do far too little walking these days."

"Is such a thing possible?"

"That," said Priscilla sweetly, "is a thing that you should know, but concerning which you will probably have a much clearer idea early tomorrow morning."

"It occurs to me," said Langley severely, "that I should have a word with your good father. You shall accompany me."

Langley turned on his heel and went back to the house. Priscilla followed him, some little distance in the rear. Colonel Schofield, after he had recovered from his first surprise at Langley's return, listened to the explanation and expressed his complete sympathy.

"I've never known such a thing happen before along here. But you never can tell these days—with all these damned Communists about. Nothing's safe from them. Get their hands on anything and that's the end of that. You'd better report it to the Police at once. There you are. Don't delay a minute. Use my 'phone."

Schofield pointed to the instrument. Langley thought things over quickly and decided to take the Colonel's advice. After all—his story was true in its essentials and why worry over a matter of a couple of hundred yards, which was all there was in it? As far as he could see from the point of view of the Police, this was immaterial.

"Thank you, sir. I'll take your advice. I don't think I can do better. After all—there's nothing like striking while the iron's hot."

So Langley went across to the Colonel's telephone and rang the Angel police-station. He was lucky enough to get through to the proper quarter without undue delay. Within a couple of minutes he had supplied the Police authorities with a full description of his car and of the circumstances (slightly amended to fit the present situation) under which it had been stolen. He concluded his message by saying, "And if you want me, you'll find me at the 'Bear and Ragged Staff'; I'm staying there for a few days." Then he replaced the receiver, and had he but known it at the time he did so, he had just accomplished an extremely satisfactory piece of work. That knowledge, however, was destined to come along to him a little later. He spoke to the assembled company.

"Now, sir—I'd better be getting back. Perhaps the tramp will do me good."

"Not at all, my boy," said Schofield at once; "don't you bother about walking back. Shouldn't dream of letting you do that. Not on your life! We can arrange that. Priscilla will drive you back to the hotel in our car."

Langley looked across and saw Miss Schofield's lips tighten.

"That's awfully decent of you, sir, I'm sure—"

Priscilla's voice cut in ruthlessly. "I don't know that I'm particularly keen, Daddy. As a matter of fact, I've a bit of a head coming on, and if Mr. Langley—"

But Colonel Schofield yielded no point in ruthlessness to his daughter. "Stuff and nonsense, my dear! Do you good! Do you no end of good—especially that headache of yours. A breath of night air'll blow all the cobwebs away. Couldn't have anything better. You take Langley along and then breeze back. I'll lay a wager that by the time you return you'll be feeling as right as a trivet."

Priscilla realized that the contest was hopeless and conceded the issue. Shrugging her shoulders, she turned away and in a cold, even-toned voice, said, "Very well, I'll go and get the car now. I'll be ready for you in five minutes, Mr. Langley."

Langley said good-night again and in five minutes' time went out to the Schofields' car. Priscilla, seated in the driving-seat, received him with a stony stare. For all the recognition she afforded to his presence beside her, Langley might well have been non-existent. They drove in a well of silence for over a mile, with no word issuing from the lips of Miss Schofield. When the words did come, they were decidedly trenchant.

"This is rather a new one on me. The gag of the stolen car. Although I'm acquainted with many of the ordinary devices, I can't remember that I've heard that one before."

"Devices?" echoed Langley, secretly delighted at the turn things had taken.

"You heard! I've come across the grit put in the petrol tank to choke the feed. Usually used, I believe, in attempted seduction cases. A friend of mine had it played on her once in a lonely part of the Lake District. And then, I fancy, there's that other—"

"Miss Schofield," interrupted Langley severely, "please consider my extreme youth. There are limits, you know. And how, may I ask, is your friend now?"

"My friend?" inquired Miss Schofield coldly. "Which friend do you mean?"

"Why, the one you were telling me about. The one that was seduced in the Lake District. The sad case of the grit in the petrol tank."

"That wasn't the way it went, if you must know. You jumped at conclusions," she said more frigidly than ever. "By an exercise of extreme ingenuity my friend avoided the . . . er . . ." Miss Schofield seemed at a loss for a word. Langley, not a muscle of his face moving, attempted to supply the deficiency.

"Fate worse than death?" he suggested hopefully.

Miss Schofield averted her head and kept it firmly fixed on the road ahead. "I have no wish," she said icily, "to discuss the question any further."

"I'm sorry," returned Langley, "and I think it's a great pity, because we were getting down to something jolly interesting. Still, I suppose you're right."

Miss Schofield drove the car to the street of the "Bear and Ragged Staff". A hundred yards or so away from the entrance Langley said:

"Here we are, this will do splendidly for me. Please don't trouble to come all the way. And—er—many thanks for the service. Most charming of you."

"Don't mention it," responded Miss Schofield. "It's been an extraordinary pleasure for me."

"I say," said Langley, brightening, "I'm tremendously bucked to hear you say that."

"The actual pleasure," went on Miss Schofield, as though Langley had not spoken, "lay in the entrancingly delightful thought that I should soon be going back alone and that you would be in every way a thing of the past. Good night and good-bye, Mr. Langley! And, if it's any consequence to you to know, the knee-cap of your left trouser-leg is rather badly slit. I'm wondering where you had been before you broke in on us."

Langley looked down at his left trouser-leg. It was as Priscilla had pointed out. When he looked up again she had swung the car round and away from him.

"When shall I see you again?" he called out.

"You won't," were the words that Langley heard, but nevertheless he waved assiduously at the departing car.

V

Langley went in the main entrance of the "Bear and Ragged Staff" and straight up the staircase to his bedroom. As he opened his bedroom door, he looked at the time by his wrist-watch. It was twenty-two minutes past eleven. Not quite as late as he had anticipated. Contemplation of the torn cloth of his left trouser-leg failed to remove entirely the smile that had been on his face for some time.

"I must have done that," he said to himself, "when I climbed through that blasted lavatory window. All the same, cheers for the jolly old Colonel! Good scout that—doesn't stand any damned nonsense—what! Only daughter or no only daughter."

He was soon in bed and, despite the happenings of the evening, quickly asleep. His sleep was such that dreams came to him. He dreamt that Ahasuerus had grown into a huge blue tiger which, with Colonel Schofield astride, hunted him through a weird succession of gradually-narrowing lavatory windows. But eventually the dream receded and his sleep became comfortable and placid. When he woke up in the morning he decided that with the weather so promising he would, if nothing untoward transpired, go to the first day of the Angel race-meeting. It seemed too good an opportunity for him to miss, especially when he reviewed all his problems, and, bearing in mind that he had no car, an extremely attractive proposition as a means of spending the day.

After breakfast, which he had as late as he conveniently could, he walked round to the police-station to make inquiries as to whether any information had been received with regard to the missing vehicle. It struck him that this was a step he should take. The sergeant whom he interviewed, however, had no good news for him. No information concerning his car had so far come through to the station.

"If anything *does* come along, sir," stated the sergeant with cheerful optimism, "I'll 'phone straight through to your hotel."

"Suppose I'm not there, Sergeant?"

"Then we'll leave a message for you, sir, which you can pick up when you come back."

Langley had perforce to be content with this promise. The time was now half past ten. Study of his newspaper had elicited the fact that the first race was timed to be run at noon. Langley decided that he would have an early snack at a likely-looking pub and then meander along to the Racecourse at his comparative leisure.

The "Dog and Partridge" afforded the snack, plus two pints of the wine of the country drunk from a tankard, and soon after eleven o'clock Langley found himself *en route* for the Angel Racecourse. Several thousands had managed to arrive before he did, but with twenty minutes or so to go before the first event on the card, Langley had successfully passed through the turnstiles and was on his way to one of the higher-priced Rings. It was at this moment that he encountered his first stroke of luck for the day. As he passed along the wrong side of the Members' Enclosure he heard his name called by a familiar voice, and called in no puny tones, either! Turning quickly at the sound of it, he saw Colonel Schofield waving to him enthusiastically from inside the enclosure. Langley waved back. Schofield came nearer to him. Langley heard him calling something out across the barrier. He heard the Colonel say, "Come round to the entrance of the Members' Enclosure, my boy, and I'll pass you in. I'm allowed the privilege of introducing one guest per day, and so far today I'm on my own."

"This," said Langley to himself, "has very definitely got jam on both sides." He called to the Colonel, "O.K., sir! I'll be round there right now. It's very kind of you."

"Not at all," boomed Schofield. "I'll be there to meet you. Look slippy. I want to get on for the first race, and there isn't a lot of time."

The Colonel met him as he had indicated and seemed overjoyed at the prospect of his company. "Damned glad to see you, my boy! Always partial to good company. Didn't expect it, I can tell you. Why didn't you tell me last night that you were coming? I'd have come round for you in the car, seeing the plight you're in. By the way—any news of your car yet?"

Langley laughed. "Not a whisper, sir. I've been round to the police-station this morning. They'd heard nothing. I expect the first news that I shall get will be in about three days' time. I shall be informed that the car's been found abandoned in some remote district of Scotland or Westmoreland. That, I believe, is the usual formula."

"H'm! Not much satisfaction in that. Still, we'll hope that your pessimism is unfounded. By the way, this may interest you. Priscilla will be along before the big race. It's the fourth event on the card. The Angel Autumn Handicap. Do you follow the Turf at all, Langley?"

"Not to any extent, sir. Usually have a flutter on one or two of the big races, like most ordinary citizens. You know what I mean—the Derby, Grand National, the Guineas—perhaps the Cesarewitch and Che Hunt Cup. But I have no real or sound appreciation of current form, I'm sorry to say."

"That's all right," replied the Colonel almost ecstatically. "You must be guided by me. Put yourself unreservedly in my hands, and at the end of the day you'll be patting yourself on the back. In the first race—it's only a Selling Plate—you must be on the favourite. Sticks out a mile. It's bound to be 'Blue-eyed Susan'; she ran second in a similar event last week. By 'Vineyard' out of 'Palairet's Pride'— that's damned good breeding, I can tell you, for a small race of this character. Now come along and see what's the best price we can get. I always put my stuff on with Louis Isaacs. You can't beat him. Safe as the Bank of England! Come on, Langley."

They walked along the Members' Enclosure and into the Ring, until they discovered the bookmaker of Colonel Schofield's recommendation.

"What's the price of the favourite?" asked the Colonel of Langley. "Can you see?"

"Eleven to ten, sir. We shan't get fat on that, I'm afraid."

The Colonel shook his head at Langley's statement and wagged an admonitory finger. "Now don't talk tripe, my boy. When you talk in that strain you betray your ignorance. Little fish are sweet and an eleven-to-ten winner's a damned sight more good to a man than a twenty-to-one loser. Or a smack in the belly with a wet turbot."

He spoke to the bookmaker and handed over a tenner. "Book me eleven pounds to ten the favourite, Isaacs, will you?"

"Eleven pound to ten to you, sir," called out the bookmaker, and Colonel Schofield pocketed the ticket that was handed over to him.

"What about you, Langley? Going to have a nibble?"

"I'll be content with a modest quid's worth, sir. Just as a pipe-opener."

Langley's bet was booked at the same price and the two men strolled back together to the rails. By this time the horses were going down to the starting-post. The Colonel waited for his "Blue-eyed Susan" to thud by.

"Here's the favourite," he said at length. "Apricot jacket. Stretching out well, too. Beautiful action. Couldn't be bettered. Ought to walk it, if I'm any judge."

The race was soon over. The favourite, after making all the running, was beaten a neck by a ten-to-one chance on the rails, which challenged at the distance and won comfortably.

"H'm," muttered the Colonel. "Bad start, I must say. Still, mustn't be discouraged—a bad start often means a good finish."

"What do you fancy for the second race, sir?" inquired Langley. "Two-year-old race," grunted Schofield. "And I'm on 'Lanfranc'. Ought to get a fair price if we get in early."

Langley referred to the previous form of the horse the Colonel had mentioned. "Doesn't appear to have much form, sir," he said.

The Colonel chuckled. "Don't you worry! Only been out once. About a fortnight ago. Down the course. But it was backed by the right people—which is good enough for me. There they are. The prices are going up. What's old Isaacs laying against 'Lanfranc'?"

Langley went along to have a look. He was soon back. "Nine to two, sir. Is that rather less than you were expecting?"

"No," replied the Colonel. "It's just about what I expected. Fives was the most I thought we might get. Nine to two's all right. I'm going to take forty-five quid to ten. What about you, this time?"

"Just a quid, sir—like the previous race. No more."

"Come on, then—we'll get it on," replied Colonel Schofield. "Shouldn't be surprised if the price shortens before the off. What are they making favourite?"

"'Snake in the Grass', I fancy. Seven to four. With 'Molly Madcap' second favourite at five to two."

"H'm," grunted the Colonel. "'Lanfranc' should take good care of those, if I'm any judge of form."

Isaacs laid the bets and less than five minutes after the transaction Langley noticed that 'Lanfranc' shortened to seven to two. Schofield chuckled again.

"There you are. What did I tell you? We got on just in time and collared the best of the market. Shouldn't be surprised if it's a 'springer'. Here they come! Black jacket, lilac sleeves and cap—that's 'Lanfranc'. By 'Abbot's Trace' out of 'Caprifolia'. Good breeding, that. For a short cut like this is. You'll be drawing your money in a few minutes, Langley."

Langley, sobered by the experience of the first race, by no means shared the Colonel's confidence, but as it happened, he was wrong. The race was a procession. 'Lanfranc' took an early lead which he never at any time surrendered, and he raced past the stick an easy winner by the comfortable margin of two lengths. Colonel Schofield was jubilant. With his face shining like the morning sun and wreathed in smiles, he clapped Langley on the back.

"Do we collect, my boy? I'll say we do! Forty-five quid to a tenner! And very nice, too! Much nicer than that slap in the belly with a wet turbot that I was talking about just now. Come along down to old Isaacs and we'll draw the 'bees'. His dial'll be a picture."

The Colonel pocketed his winnings and, lusting for more worlds to conquer, turned enthusiastically to the third race on the card.

"H'm," he grunted again. "Maiden Three-year-old Handicap. Don't like 'em, Langley! Not a little bit. Trappy affairs, believe me. Usually give 'em a wide berth. Real bookmakers' benefits. Shan't chance much on this. Damned sight too dangerous."

"Why not leave it alone altogether, sir, if it's pretty certain you'll lose on it? That would seem sound policy, wouldn't it?"

The Colonel regarded him with something akin to indignation. "Must have a flutter, Langley! Good lord, what are we here for? Never attend race-meetings merely to study human nature in the raw. No, I'll pick something out that should have a fair chance of getting 'in the money'."

Schofield ran his finger down the entries on the card. "What about backing the favourite, sir?" said Langley. "Isn't it about time one turned up?"

"Eh? What's that? The favourite, did you say? What is it? Have a look, will you, Langley?"

Langley walked along the Ring. He soon saw that "Bus Conductor" was favourite, round about seven to two. He reported on these lines to the Colonel.

"'Bus Conductor'? Don't know it. What's its breeding? Let me have a glance at the card again. H'm. By 'Trade Union' out of 'That's the Ticket'. Don't care for that overmuch, my boy. No, I think I'll have a modest couple of quid on 'Fanny Bracegirdle'. Like her breeding much better—by 'Timothy Titus' out of 'Canteen'. You please yourself, my boy."

"O.K., sir. I'll risk a trifle on the favourite, as I said. Just on the law of average."

Langley got "threes", and the Colonel a hundred to eight, but neither of the fancies was concerned with the finish.

"Ah well," said the Colonel, as the winning numbers went into the frame. "That's that! Good job I played light. Never like those three-year-old handicaps, as I told you. Now we'll have a spot of lunch, Langley, before we turn our attention to the *pièce de résistance* on today's card—the Angel Autumn Handicap. Priscilla should be along in a moment or so with the luncheon-basket. By Jove, there she is! Not looking too pleased, either."

The Colonel waved to his daughter and sailed in with indescribable enthusiasm. "Halloa, my darling. Good news for you. Run into Langley, of all people. The last person on earth I expected to see here."

"I don't know about that," said Priscilla with a frosty smile.

"Mr. Langley seems to have an extraordinary knack of turning up in most places. In fact, I almost despair of ever losing him."

The Colonel ignored the allusion. "And we're not doing too badly, Priscilla. Just pulled off a nice little nine-to-two shot. Very tasty, Priscilla, very sweet."

"Hope you remembered me," murmured Priscilla, "otherwise I shall feel—"

Langley intervened. "It would be impossible to forget you, Miss Schofield."

Priscilla turned her back on him and proceeded to unpack the hamper. The Colonel eyed her activities greedily.

"Cold chicken, lobster and oyster patties and a couple of bottles of G.H. Mumm—that's the stuff, Priscilla. Ah ha—I don't mind if I do! Come along, Langley—into the Services Club canteen. We can make ourselves fairly comfortable in there."

Langley lunched with a garrulous Colonel and a silent Priscilla, and the garrulousness of the Colonel was so marked that Priscilla's silence was scarcely noticeable. Luncheon ended, the Colonel turned immediately to the task of finding the big race winner. For many years now his enthusiasm for the Turf had shown no signs of abating.

"Two and three-quarter miles, Langley! And pretty heavy going at that! Only a true stayer can do it. Don't forget that. What's the strength of the field? How many starters? The numbers are going up."

Langley counted them. "Five, sir. Five only."

"Oh, it's dried up, has it? What are they, Langley?"

"Numbers 2, 3, 9, 14 and 16," replied Langley.

"Let's sort 'em out—2, 3, 9, 14 and 16, you said. Let's see now. 'Booming Alfred', 'Doctor Fell', 'Baby Austin', 'Numskull' and 'Wilkins Micawber'. H'm. Open race—say what you like about it."

Langley waited in patience for Colonel Schofield to arrive at a definite selection. But the Colonel hummed and hawed for some time. He was examining pedigrees. Langley listened. "'Numskull', by 'Hot-Pot' out of 'Round the Corner'. H'm. Nothing much there." Langley could hear him muttering and grunting to himself, and saw how he repeatedly referred to the bundle of assorted morning papers which he had brought with him to the course.

"Moderate lot," he murmured, "moderate lot. What's favourite, Langley?" he blurted at length.

Langley went along and then came back with the desired information. " 'Doctor Fell', sir, two to one. 'Wilkins Micawber', second favourite, eleven to four. 'Baby Austin' fours."

"H'm," muttered Schofield again. "In a quandary. Don't dislike the breeding of 'Booming Alfred', by 'Executive' out of 'Summer Season'. The dam was a thunderin' good stayer in her time. Had the knack of always poppin' up when least expected. Won the Alexandra Stakes at Ascot in a common canter. Think I'll have a dabble at it. Ought to get the distance at any rate. Like the trainer, too! Always have. Ever since I started racing. Old Alec Naylor knows a good old 'stomper' when he sees one—and it's an old 'stomper' that'll do the trick this afternoon with the going as it is. What do you say, Langley? Going to chance a fiver?"

Langley looked at Priscilla and then shook his head with a laugh. "No, sir. Not more than a quid of mine, sir. Think I'll chance a quid on 'Wilkins Micawber'."

"What about you, Priscilla? Going to have a flutter? You ought to, you know—you've missed three races already."

"I'm backing the favourite," she said calmly. "'Doctor Fell'. For what reason? My dear Daddy—the reason why I cannot tell. Put me on a pound, will you, Daddy?"

The Colonel nodded. "'Doctor Fell', eh? Don't care for its breeding at all. By 'Paint Pot' out of 'Old Nannie'. Neither of 'em great shakes."

The men walked down to the bookmaker and placed the three separate bets. In a slowly-run race 'Doctor Fell' justified Priscilla's non-foundationed confidence and won by a length and a half from "Baby Austin", and it was Priscilla alone who handed a winning ticket to the bookmaker for settlement.

While he was in the act of congratulating her, Langley saw two men coming towards him along the enclosure, and something seemed to tell him that these two men were there for business with him. His premonition was sound. The taller of the two men came forward and spoke.

"Mr. Richard Langley, sir?"

"My name," said Langley, but he was puzzled for all that. "What's your business with me at this time of day?" he added.

"You reported a lost car, sir, last night. You rang up from Nirvana 2222, sir—some time after ten o'clock last night, sir. Is that correct?"

"Quite right," said Langley; "have you come to tell me that it's found?"

"Yes, sir. That is so, sir. I'm Detective-Sergeant Lawton. It was reported found about eleven o'clock this morning, sir. Soon after you spoke to the sergeant on duty. We've been trying to find you ever since that time."

"Where was it found?" demanded Langley. "Nowhere near here, I'll bet."

The man's face was set and grave as he answered, "Yes, sir. Quite near, as it happens. One might almost say at home, sir, come to that."

"How do you mean?" said Langley curiously. The phrase had startled him.

"Your car was found in the garage at the 'Bear and Ragged Staff', sir. According to the chap on the job there, sir, almost exactly in the spot where you've been keeping it."

"What?" exclaimed Langley. "You're joking, surely?"

The Detective-Sergeant shook his head. "I wish I were, sir. But I assure you I'm not. And what's more, sir, there's a bit more to it than that."

"What do you mean?" queried Langley, still puzzled.

He was fully aware that Colonel Schofield and Priscilla were listening intently to the conversation. Detective-Sergeant Lawton eyed him up and down before he replied to the question.

"There's a dead man in it," said Lawton curtly.

The news hit Langley hard. "What!" he exclaimed incredulously. "A dead man in my car? But how can that be? Do you mean somebody—er—that was taken ill or something?"

"No, sir," replied Lawton with even more gravity than before. "I don't mean that, sir. The dead man in your car was murdered."

As he finished speaking, Langley could hear the runners thudding down to the starting-post for the next race.

CHAPTER IV

I

IT IS no exaggeration to say that Langley was momentarily stunned by the information. Before he could say anything, he heard Lawton speaking again. The detective's voice seemed far away and distant.

"And I'm afraid I must ask you to come along and have a look at him, sir. It occurs to me that as he's in your car you may be able to identify him."

Langley frowned at the statement. "Now?" he inquired. "At once?"

"If you don't mind, sir?" replied Lawton.

"Well, in that case," declared Langley, "I suppose I'd better do as you suggest and come along with you. But I must first of all submit my apologies to my host and hostess here. Please pardon me for a moment." Langley turned and made a quick explanation to the Colonel. "You've heard the news, sir. A man murdered in my car. Last night. The Police want to see if I can identify him. It's a piece of execrable luck, and my sincere apologies for breaking up the party."

"That's all right. We thoroughly understand. Not your fault. Damned funny business, though, say what you like about it. Pretty fishy—it seems to me. Let's know how you get on."

"I will, sir. At the earliest opportunity."

Langley waved to the Colonel, bowed to Priscilla and made his way with Lawton and his assistant to a waiting car. A few minutes' driving time brought the party to the Angel police-station. Langley was taken through to the stone-paved yard at the rear of the building. A car was standing there. Langley saw at once that it was his.

"Your car?" asked Lawton. "You identify it?"

"My car."

"I thought so. Thought there was no mistake from the number-plate and description. Now I'll take you to see the body. The Divisional-Surgeon should be just finished by now. Come along in, sir, will you, please? This way."

In the part of the building which had been allotted for the purposes of a mortuary, a man was standing, wiping his hands on a towel.

"Good afternoon, Doctor," opened Lawton. "Mr. Richard Langley—Doctor Maidment."

The doctor acknowledged the introduction with a rather curt nod of the head.

"What's the verdict, Doctor?" asked Lawton.

"Dead from fracture of skull," replied the Divisional-Surgeon laconically—"and once again, Lawton, you can be looking for a heavy, blunt instrument as the weapon used for the attack. Sorry I can't be more original." Maidment grinned cynically as he made the statement.

"Such as?" asked Lawton.

Maidment screwed up his face in consideration of Lawton's question. "Oh—I don't know. You fellows always want such damned exactitude. Poker in all probability. I'd bank on a poker. Common or garden poker. Also, Lawton—and here's something for you to put in your note-book—the blow was delivered from behind."

"That's interesting. And important. I shall certainly remember that. How long's the fellow been dead? Approximately?"

"There you go again. More perishin' precision asked for. Want me to take temperatures, add 'em up, subtract, take away the number I first thought of and the answer's a lemon. If you take it that he was snuffed out about midnight last night you won't be far wrong, Lawton. But I'm not sending any man to the scaffold on a matter of a quarter of an hour, and that's as near as I'm giving. I'll tell you that now—straight."

"All right, Doctor," expostulated Lawton hastily and uneasily, "that's all right. Don't worry your head over that. I pride myself on being a reasonable sort of fellow."

He turned to Langley, who had been listening attentively. "Now, sir—take a good look at the dead man, will you? And remember he was found dead in your car. Ever seen him before?"

Langley advanced to the slab on which the body was lying, with a certain amount of diffidence. He was little prepared for what he was about to see. Lawton watched him intently as Langley strode up to the slab and then bent down over it to examine the body. He saw Langley give way to an immediate and undoubted start of surprise. Lawton's suspicions were at once aroused, but they were dispelled somewhat a minute afterwards.

"Yes," said Langley quietly. "I know something about this man."

"Good," exclaimed Lawton in quick acceptance. "Let me hear what it is, will you?"

II

"I don't know," said Langley, "whether the Judges' Rules apply to the present circumstances—but at any rate—"

Lawton broke into the sentence and Langley stopped. "I'm only asking you to identify, sir—if you're in a position to. Nothing more than that. Anything else, of course, you care to add . . ."

Langley gestured with his hand. "Suits me," he announced, "so rest easy."

"What's the man's name, Mr. Langley?"

"Couldn't tell you. Haven't the foggiest."

Lawton frowned. "Sorry to hear that—was hoping otherwise— don't mind admitting it. But I'm a bit mystified. Because I thought you said—or rather I understood you to say—"

Again Langley gestured with his hand. "I think it would be better for both of us if you let me tell you my story in my own way. Not that I've a great deal to tell you when it comes to the point. But I was travelling into Angel yesterday morning. Not over-early. It was getting on for lunch-time. I'd been visiting my friend Colonel Schofield, who lives a little way out, and had left his place to get back to my hotel for the midday meal. Well—the fellow over there stood by the side of the road and thumbed a ride out of me. I drove him into Angel and he told me to drop him near my hotel because he wanted an address in Paradise Street. I had no wish to be hard on the chap, so I did as he asked. That was the last time I saw him until a moment or so ago. Both the first and the last."

"H'm—I see." Lawton made notes. There was a curious expression on his face and Langley couldn't help noticing it. "Tell me," said the Detective-Sergeant suddenly, "what did he say to you during' the time he was in your car?"

"Not a great deal," replied Langley, "but one or two things, perhaps, that you might be all the better for knowing. He told me that he had walked in from Eden and had blistered his heel in doing so. According to his story he had walked nearly ten miles. He told me he had business to transact in Angel and was 'on his uppers'. Couldn't afford to pay for transport."

Lawton looked up shrewdly. "I don't altogether get that. His appearance, when I first saw him, didn't altogether tally with that statement. What did you think yourself, Mr. Langley, when you were talking to him?"

"Much the same as you. From the sartorial point of view I'd say he didn't look at all bad."

"Good. Did he spill anything else to you on the journey?"

Langley considered the question. "I wouldn't say that he did. But I'll tell you what I did think. He seemed unusually interested in *my* movements. At least—as I said—that's how it appeared to me."

Lawton's face took on a shrewder expression than ever. "Oh?" he exclaimed briskly—"that's a new angle, and an interesting one at that. Would you mind telling me what gave you that idea? It must have been pretty obvious for you to cotton on to it so quickly. What exactly did he ask you?"

"Well—general questions—I admit, but they were more or less of a personal nature and had reference either to my movements or to my future intentions."

"How do you mean?"

"Well—I'll give you certain examples—why was I on holiday at this particular time of the year? How long was I staying in Angel, etc., etc.? That was the general trend of his remarks to me. Excessive curiosity."

"H'm. Don't quite know what to make of this. Seems to me more in it than meets the eye. You say he deliberately stopped your car, eh?"

"That's so. Gave me the accepted sign. I was travelling light, and, as I told you, I stopped for him. I was only going to Angel, so that the incident didn't seem to have any particular importance. Just a few minutes' run—no more."

"That's so. I can appreciate that. Now another point, Mr. Langley, if you don't mind. You stated just now that he asked you to drop him at an address in Paradise Street. Is that correct?"

Langley shook his head. "Not quite. I dropped him at my hotel and he told me, as he alighted, that he wanted Paradise Street."

"Oh yes. I remember now." Lawton hesitated for a minute or two. But he came to his point eventually and translated it into words. "Are you familiar with the town of Angel, Mr. Langley?"

"No. I can't say that I am. Actually I haven't been here before this occasion."

"You aren't aware, then, that there's no such street as Paradise Street anywhere in the town?"

Langley thought matters over and decided to tell the truth. "Yes, as a matter of fact I am."

"Oh—you are? How's that, then, bearing in mind your previous answer?"

"The explanation is a simple one. After the fellow had left me and walked away I inquired of a waiter at the 'Bear and Ragged Staff' as to where the street was. He told me there's no street of that name in the town."

"Why did you do that? What made you do it?"

"I think that the reason was this. Directly after I had dropped this chap, I went into the hotel and barged straight into one of the waiters there. As this Paradise Street address was uppermost in my mind at the time, I asked the chap direct if he could tell me where it was. He answered me without the slightest hesitation. Said that he had been born and bred in Angel, knew the place inside out and that there wasn't such an address anywhere within the borough. That's how I came to know, my dear chap. Quite a simple business."

"H'm," said Lawton again, "there's no doubt about your waiter chap being right. There isn't a street of that name in Angel. Funny business, all of it, no matter which way you come to look at it. Smells 'phoney' all the way through. You think this chap that's 'had it' deliberately waited for your car, don't you? That, I take it, is the point you are making?"

"I formed that opinion, certainly, but, of course, I've nothing whatever to go on beyond the extraordinary way he tried to pump me when he got inside the car."

Lawton considered the answer but made no immediate reply. All this time Langley had been, as it were, fencing with himself. His problem was should he tell Lawton about the men whom he had encountered when he had gone to the wrong house? In other words, should he attempt to link up the dead man with the "Professor" and his colleagues? Should he tell the entire story, starting with Priscilla and ending with the corpse? He couldn't very well mention his escapade of the previous evening, as it wouldn't tally with the story he had already told the Police when he had reported the fact from Colonel Schofield's house that his car was missing. Also, he felt strongly disinclined to bringing the Schofields into the arena at all. At the moment, therefore, he decided to hold his tongue with regard to the antecedents of the case until he had seen which way the cat was jumping. As this thought formed in his mind, the idea of Ahasuerus came to him and he grinned to himself at the reminiscence. Lawton happened to look up and caught the grin.

"Hullo?" he said to Langley, "thought of something?"

"No," replied Langley, "what made you ask that?"

"Thought you were smiling at something that had occurred to you."

"No," said Langley, "sorry if I misled you."

There was a silence for a time. Langley felt a little annoyed with himself. It seemed to him that he had already conceded—and entirely unnecessarily at that—a point to the man who was facing him. That, to an extent at least, he had given himself away.

"Will you want me any more, Lawton? Or have I satisfied you?"

"I don't know about the latter," replied Lawton, "but I take it you'll be stopping at your hotel for a day or two at least, if I should want to get in touch with you again?"

"Oh yes. You can rely on that. I shan't be moving until the end of the week at least. If then."

"That's all right, sir. That's what I wanted to know. Well—good-bye, Mr. Langley; for the present, that is."

Langley shook hands with Lawton and made his way out. On the whole, he was by no means pleased with the way that things had gone. From his own point of view, it seemed to him that he had one foot on sea and one on shore and was to one thing constant never. He was far from feeling sure that Lawton didn't definitely suspect him—if not of the actual murder, of a certain complicity therein, and even allowing for the possible weakness of such suspicion, he was annoyed to think that despite all his efforts to the contrary, the Schofields might be dragged into the pool of things. This was the very last thing that he desired, but as things stood at the moment he didn't see how it could very well be avoided.

As he made his way back to the hotel—it was much too late by this time to return to the Racecourse—he didn't see or hear the car which came up very quietly behind him and drew almost silently in to the kerb. It was dusk by now and the quieter streets of the town were almost empty. Langley, warned perhaps by the sudden activity of a sixth sense, turned his head quickly—but he was a second or so too late. The men who alighted from the car did their work silently and efficiently.

PART TWO
CENTRE STAGE

CHAPTER I

I

ANTHONY Lotherington Bathurst sat at ease in an armchair at his flat and looked up somewhat sleepily as Emily, almost on tip-toe, brought a visiting-card in to him.

"The lady would like to see you at once, Mr. Bathurst, if you can possibly make it convenient."

"A lady, did you say, Emily? A euphemism, or a mere *façon de parler*? Or even, perhaps, the exercise of an unusually charitable mind? Which, my dear Emily?" He smiled as he spoke.

"No, sir," continued Emily, "really and truly a lady. A Miss Schofield—Miss Priscilla Schofield. Very nice indeed, sir. Ever so nice. What my kid brother would call a lovely drop of homework, sir."

"Bearing in mind, then, Emily, the assessment of such an acknowledged connoisseur as you describe, I shall be delighted to see her. Show Miss Schofield up—will you, Emily, please?"

When Priscilla Schofield entered the room, Anthony found no cause to quarrel with Emily's appreciation of the visitor. Or even with that of her kid brother! The red hair, the dark blue eyes and the force of character so easily discernible on her face, made him realize that here was no ordinary girl—either physically or mentally.

"Sit down, Miss Schofield," he said, "and make yourself as comfortable as possible."

"Thank you, Mr. Bathurst," said Priscilla. She took a seat.

"Now tell me," said Anthony, "what it is that I can do for you."

"Mr. Bathurst," said Priscilla, "I've been recommended to you by Lady Fullgarney. That's my primary excuse for coming to you. Pauline Fullgarney is my father's cousin. She has often told me how you helped her solve the 'Mystery of the Peacock's Eye', some years ago."

Anthony smiled. "To be exact, Miss Schofield, nearly fifteen. How time does fly, to be sure! When I was a callow youth—or something like that."

Priscilla smiled. "That's rather difficult to believe—as I look at you now. Anyhow, Pauline never seems to be tired of singing your praises, and when I was first in this trouble and told her all about it, she urged me to come to see you without wasting a moment. So here I am."

"I'm afraid," said Anthony, smiling, "that Lady Fullgarney is apt to over-value me in respect of the small service I was able to render all those years ago. But we will let that pass. I still retain the most fragrant memories of her and I am flattered to think she still remembers me. Now tell me of your trouble, Miss Schofield. Make yourself thoroughly comfortable and omit nothing, please, no matter how unimportant it may seem to be. But you probably know all about that and require no prompting from me."

Priscilla Schofield recounted to Anthony the story of her first meeting with Richard Langley and of the various contacts with him until the summary closure during the afternoon at the Angel Racecourse.

"That afternoon, Mr. Bathurst, a Detective-Sergeant named Lawton came with another man from the police-station and asked him to identify a man who they said had been found dead in Mr. Langley's car. He went along with them and—so we are told—they interviewed him. Mr. Langley left the police-station at Angel after the interview about half past four in the afternoon. That was a week ago today. Since then he hasn't been seen. He's simply vanished into thin air. That's why I'm here."

Anthony Bathurst looked up at her with keen interest shining in his eyes. "Extraordinary. What do the Police say about that, Miss Schofield?"

"According to what my father tells me, Mr. Bathurst, they're just as much puzzled as we are."

"Of course," said Anthony, "they would be . . ." and then he hesitated.

"Of course what?" demanded Priscilla.

Anthony answered her in another strain. "He may have cleared out deliberately, of his own free will, you know. That possibility, I suppose, must have occurred to you, Miss Schofield. Yes?"

Priscilla shook her head. "I won't entertain that idea for a moment, Mr. Bathurst. I've only known Mr. Langley for a few days, but I'm absolutely certain that he would never have done such a thing."

Anthony sat there silent for some seconds. The girl's answer had, as far as he was concerned, put a fresh complexion on the matter.

"There are many features of this case, Miss Schofield, which disturb me profoundly. And I fear that it's manifestly impossible for you to do justice to them in an interview of this nature. Many questions arise, too. For instance, who are these men that occupy the house you say Langley mistook for yours on the night the trouble seems to have started? Who stole Langley's car? Who is the dead man in the car and who murdered him? You indicated, I fancy, that the Police were inclined to regard it as murder?"

"Yes. I don't think there's any doubt about that. My father says there isn't."

"Well, there you are. Also—other questions raise themselves in my inquiring mind. Who is this man Langley? What is he? That is to say—professionally? And what is he doing in Angel? You appear to think, Miss Schofield, that he's merely on an ordinary holiday. But unless you are positive of that, my reply would be—November's an unusual month of the year for a man to be holiday-making. There may be nothing whatever in my point—but all the same I feel compelled to make it."

"I agree," said Priscilla, "with almost everything you've said. But still, I am bound to repeat that I have the utmost confidence in Mr. Langley, and I'm certain that you can start from that position without the slightest chance of the principle proving to be unsound. That statement of mine should help you."

"It does. It must do. Now tell me. How many men were in that house, according to Langley's story?"

"Five, Mr. Bathurst. He mentioned that, when he was shown in to the room, there were five men there. That includes the man who conducted him."

"Have you heard him refer to any of them by name?"

Priscilla reflected on the question. "Yes. I can give you two names. One Layman, the other Webber. And the last time he came to our house he mentioned another by name—at least I think it was the last time. He referred to a man named Newman. This Newman's connected with a shop or shops in the town of Angel, and according to Mr. Langley's story he must have run across him somewhere in the town and recognized him as one of the men he had met in the house. In fact, I think he said that was so."

Anthony made a careful note of the three names. Another spell of silence ensued. Anthony broke it.

"Please answer me a direct question, Miss Schofield. You know the missing man. I don't. I've never met him. What do *you* think has happened to him?"

Priscilla Schofield sat there quiet and thoughtful, and for some moments, before she replied. She clasped and unclasped her fingers on her lap.

"Candidly, Mr. Bathurst, I think he's met with foul play. I cannot visualize any other possibility."

"As sensational as all that—eh?"

"Yes. You asked me. I've given you my answer."

"You mean—dead? Killed?"

"Yes, Mr. Bathurst, I'm prepared even for that. Now you know better why I've come to you."

This time it was Anthony's turn to remain quiet. "H'm," he said eventually, "that's a pretty bad show, isn't it? You don't think that he may be under some form of restraint somewhere? Kept a prisoner, for instance, against his will?"

Priscilla nodded. "That is a possibility—of course. And I have considered it. It wouldn't be true to say that I haven't."

"And—in the end—you repudiate it? You feel that he's much more likely to be dead than anything else?"

Priscilla nodded again. "Yes, Mr. Bathurst—as you say—much more likely—as I see it."

"Tell me then," continued Anthony. "Accepting for the sake of argument that your version of the situation is the correct one, what do you think has happened? Why, for instance, should this man

---

Langley be killed? What motive could there be for such a drastic procedure? Murder, you know, Miss Schofield, has a terrifying finality about it, and it's a crime that our English law never forgives. I mean by that that it's seldom undertaken wantonly. Even by the most hardened criminals. Why, then, should Langley be killed?"

"I've asked myself that question, Mr. Bathurst, many times during the last few days. And I've been forced to this conclusion. Mr. Langley in some way had got on the track of something. Something evil and something to do with those men in the house. They got to know about it—and, in order to preserve their own safety and, shall we say, to avoid punishment, they took steps to remove him."

Anthony made no reply. Priscilla followed up. "Is that opinion so very absurd, Mr. Bathurst?"

"No-o, Miss Schofield. I'm bound to admit that it's an eminently reasonable opinion. All the same, I hope you're being too pessimistic. I do indeed."

"Will you take the case, Mr. Bathurst? That's the important point. Or are you going to send me empty away?"

"You need harbour no doubts, Miss Schofield. Where I know help is needed, I never refuse that help."

Priscilla Schofield rose from her chair impulsively and held out her hand to him. "Thank you, Mr. Bathurst, from the bottom of my heart. Now is there anything I can do for you in the matter or will you map out your own plan of campaign?"

"I must come down to Angel immediately. In all probability, from Paddington tomorrow morning. Can you give me a good train from memory?"

Priscilla's response was immediate. "Is the 9.10 too early for you?"

"No. I'm an early riser when there's work afoot. And I can call at the 'Yard' later on today. Expect me, then, on that train."

"Will you come to us first?"

Anthony considered the question. "No, I don't think I will—if you don't mind. Having heard your story, I've a strong inclination to go straight to the 'Bear and Ragged Staff'. There might be some scent still there for me to pick up. From there, I shall be able to scout round a bit. But I expect, nevertheless, you'll find me turning up at your place before many days have slipped by."

"I'll tell my father what you say," said Priscilla; "he knows I've come up to see you and also what I've come about. And the venture has his complete approval. So that he won't be in any way surprised when you do put in an appearance. There's the address and that's the 'phone number." She handed him a card.

"That's satisfactory, then," replied Anthony. He shook hands with her again. "We shall meet at Philippi. And in the meantime, Miss Schofield, avoid the depths as much as you possibly can."

II

When Priscilla Schofield had gone, Anthony jotted down an assessment of the various data with which she had supplied him. When he had done so, he realized somewhat ruefully that they were sparse in the extreme. As far as he could see he had (a) Langley's encounter in the wrong house with a bunch of five men, (b) the further contact with the fellow in the lounge at the "Bear and Ragged Staff", (c) the suspicions that Langley had felt with regard to Newman, the man with the two shops, and (d) the dead man found in the car. Which was the incident that seemed to have rung down the curtain!

"Pretty thin," remarked Anthony to himself, "or, in other words, a complete start from scratch."

But surely, he thought, Langley must have relations, or certainly connections, and he should be able to pick up some threads from them when the news of Langley's disappearance became more widely known. He saw, though, that it was there that he must leave the matter at the moment. When he arrived in Angel, with luck, things might clarify considerably.

With this thought uppermost in his mind, Anthony alighted from the 9.10 when it reached Angel at a quarter past one on the following day. A convenient taxi took him to the "Bear and Ragged Staff", where he was able to fix up satisfactorily. After the midday meal, he decided to walk round to the police-station and have a chat with Detective-Sergeant Lawton.

When Anthony was shown into Lawton's room, his first step was to produce his card, countersigned by Sir Austin Kemble, the Commissioner of Police. Lawton raised his eyebrows when he saw the Commissioner's signature.

"Good afternoon, Mr. Bathurst," he said, albeit a little frigidly. "I'm honoured to make your acquaintance. Although I must say I'm surprised to see you. Er . . . you know . . . wasn't exactly expecting you."

"No," said Anthony cordially, "I don't suppose you were."

"What's brought you to this part of the country, Mr. Bathurst? Something urgent, I take it?"

"The need for certain information, Detective-Sergeant Lawton. Which I'm hoping you'll be able to give me."

"Concerning what, Mr. Bathurst?"

"The recent disappearance of a certain Richard Langley. From an hotel in this town of Angel. To be precise—the 'Bear and Ragged Staff'."

Lawton spread out his hands with a gesture of resignation. "Information from me! There's a certain amount of unintentional humour about that. Can the blind lead the blind?"

Anthony looked up with interest. He hadn't expected an answer of that kind from this provincial officer. It added, he thought, a certain spice to the proceedings.

"Like that, is it?" he remarked. "Well, at any rate, what *do* you know?"

Lawton tapped on his desk with the end of a pencil. "In a way, I suppose, you couldn't have come to a better man. As a matter of fact—I interviewed Langley here in this very room on the afternoon that he disappeared. I had asked him to come along here. He came quite willingly. A man had been found dead in his car. I picked up Langley on the Racecourse. He was there in the company of some friends of his. Some people named Schofield, I believe. Langley went out of here after the interview and hasn't been seen since."

"Not even at the hotel where he was staying? Am I to understand that he didn't return there?"

"No. Nowhere! Whatever happened to him must have come along very quickly after he left here. And up to the moment, I regret to say, we haven't succeeded in picking up a single clue in connection with the disappearance. Not the vestige of a clue. We haven't, of course, given up hope yet. We're still trying, and at any moment, naturally, we may strike lucky and snatch at something."

"Where did Langley come from?"

"Same answer, Mr. Bathurst. Don't know! That's not the least puzzling part of the matter. So far, nobody has shown the slightest interest in his disappearance or in the problem of what may have happened to him. But personally I've formed the definite opinion that he was in Angel for a specific purpose. What that purpose was—search me!" Lawton made another eloquent gesture as he concluded his sentence.

Anthony rubbed the ridge of his jaw. "H'm! So that's how you feel about it, is it? I'm afraid none of it's very encouraging from my point of view. As I feared when I came down here, I'm starting at scratch—or even worse."

Lawton grinned at him. "Not a bad way of putting it. By the way—whose interests are you representing?"

"I don't know that I'm bound to answer that question. But I'll be frank with you from the beginning—just as I hope you'll always be frank with me. I am looking into the case in the interest of Miss Schofield—daughter of Colonel Schofield."

Lawton drummed again with his pencil butt. "I find that a little surprising," he remarked. "And I'll tell you why. According to the information that has reached me, the Schofields had only known Langley for the matter of a few days. I presume you're aware of that fact, Mr. Bathurst?"

"Oh, yes. Miss Schofield volunteered that piece of information. But let me digress for a few moments. I'd like to have a glance at the case from the other angle."

Lawton raised his eyebrows. "The other angle? I don't quite—"

"The dead man. You mentioned a dead man just now. The dead man in the car. Surely we must regard that as the other angle?"

"I suppose we must." Lawton's mouth shut like a trap. That wasn't the line he had expected Anthony to take. Anthony waited for him to go on. In this intention he was doomed to disappointment. Lawton sat tight and said no more.

Anthony prompted him. "What can you tell me about him?"

Lawton's face looked a little ugly. "Just about as much as I've told you about Langley."

"Bad as that, is it?"

"Every bit. Up to now, the dead man is unidentified. There was nothing whatever on his person to indicate who he was or where he came from. In fact the one clue—or half-clue—that *is* in our possession came from no less a person than Langley himself."

"How was that? What form did it take?"

"Langley supplied it to me when he came here. According to his story, the dead man begged a ride in Langley's car a morning or so before the murder. On the way—and they drove into Angel together—he told Langley (again according to Langley's story) that he had walked all the way from Eden. That's the sum total of our knowledge of him. But again, as I said just now, in reference to Langley, there's still time, and at any moment a clue may come along and knock at our door. At any rate, we shan't fail through any lack of either hoping or trying, I can assure you of that, Mr. Bathurst."

Anthony considered what Lawton had told him. The two shelves of the cupboard which had been opened to him were certainly bare.

"Tell me," he said to Lawton, "have photographs of Langley been published in the Press? It was a question I intended to ask Miss Schofield, but it slipped me."

"The answer's in the negative, Mr. Bathurst. But it's not been neglected—as an idea, I mean. Remember that it's only a matter of a week that this man Langley's been missing. We felt for some time that there was no urgent necessity to take extreme measures as an immediate policy. So please acquit us of any charge of undue delay."

"Nothing, my dear sir, was farther from my mind."

Anthony rose, walked over to the window and looked out with his hands clasped behind his back. Lawton saw the movement and watched him critically. He put something of his thoughts into words.

"Pretty black outlook—eh?"

"I don't know," said Anthony, turning to him, "there's a patch of blue sky away there to the east."

Lawton shook his head and laughed. "I wasn't referring to the view. I alluded to the Langley case."

"The case?" repeated Anthony. "Oh, I don't know! Something's bound to turn up before very long. It always does." He walked over to a chair by the wall and picked up his hat and gloves.

"Oh, by the way," said Lawton, "there's something else I omitted to tell you. It should be of interest. When Langley brought the dead man into Angel"—Lawton grinned as he spoke—"before he was dead, of course—you know what I mean—the man asked to be directed to Paradise Street."

Anthony looked at Lawton critically. "What's the point in your telling me that?"

Lawton grinned again. "Just this, Mr. Bathurst. There isn't such a street in the town of Angel. That's the point I thought might interest you."

Anthony pulled on his gloves and stood there with his hat in his hands. "Thank you, Lawton. As you say—a most interesting detail. I'm indebted to you. If I run into anything, I'll let you know."

III

Anthony made his exit from the police-station at Angel and gave serious consideration to his next step. The visit he had just concluded had proved almost profitless. After some moments' meditation, he decided to pay his initial visit to the house of the Schofields. He felt now that the sooner he was able to establish contact there the better for him and also for the adequate tackling of the main problem confronting him. He knew, from what Priscilla had told him, the direction of the locality where the house lay, and he resolved to walk there. If he did that, it would give him additional time for thought.

When he arrived there, after a stroll through some most delightful country, Priscilla received him with unconcealed acclamation.

"Mr. Bathurst," she said, "I never expected that you would come to us so quickly. I thought it would probably be days before we saw you. But I'm more pleased than I can say. My father will be delighted too. Especially today—because something's happened. But come along and see him—and he'll tell you all about it."

Anthony was conducted into the presence of Colonel Schofield, who shook hands with him upon introduction with an excess of exuberance.

"Pleased to see you, my boy," exclaimed the Colonel, "and if I may say so without offence, you look a bit different from what I expected. Don't know why exactly—but you do. What school were you?"

"Uppingham and Oxford, sir. With apologies in advance if either of them don't suit."

Colonel Schofield burst into a roar of laughter. "Ha-ha! Not bad that, I must say! What do you take me for—a Cantab? Not on your life, Bathurst—Wellington and 'the Shop' for yours truly. And none better, what's more. So you need have no misgivings in that direction, my boy."

Anthony gave him a quick rejoinder. "That's all right, sir. I was afraid I might have committed a *faux pas* and gone to the wrong 'Varsity."

"Sit down," said the Colonel, "and make yourself comfortable. You've come at a most opportune moment. Priscilla and I have something to tell you. Concerning this Langley fellow. Something which, I must say, has caused me no little anxiety."

Anthony noticed that Priscilla was showing certain signs of perturbation at her father's remarks.

"Tell me, Colonel—please," he contented himself with saying.

The Colonel cleared his throat preparatory to launching out on his story. "I'll tell you, Bathurst, of a little piece of information which, strangely enough, has come our way today. In view of what we now know, both Priscilla and I have felt somewhat disturbed by it. I'll tell you all about it. You listen to it carefully. The evening of the day before Langley disappeared he called here. At this house. We weren't expecting him—but there's nothing in that point. My brother-in-law, Professor Ballantyne, was here at the time. Now Langley, after a few airy nothings, as it were, made inquiries with regard to a certain fellow named Newman who keeps a couple of shops in the town. At least—that was the gist of Langley's story. Well, as you may guess, conversation was mutual and desultory. We talked on most subjects under the sun—what are you shaking your head for, Priscilla?"

"Because I think you're giving Mr. Bathurst an entirely wrong impression—I've no recollection of talking to Mr. Langley in the way you say we did."

"Tut-tut, Priscilla. That's my way of putting things. A man would understand me. Bathurst knows very well what I mean, don't you, Bathurst?"

Anthony smiled and indicated that he did.

"There you are, Priscilla, Bathurst understands perfectly—just as I told you he did. Well, to cut a long story short, the evening wore on and the time arrived for Langley to make his departure. I asked Priscilla to go along with him to speed the parting guest, as it were. She did. A few minutes later he came back and informed me that his car was missing. That it must have been stolen from outside the door here. Bit thick, wasn't it? Well, to continue the story, and acting on my advice, Langley 'phoned the police-station at Angel and immediately reported the theft. Used my telephone. I told him that it was the best possible thing he could do. You know—to strike while the iron was hot. He used that very telephone over there."

Colonel Schofield raised a long, thin finger and indicated the instrument in question. Then he turned somewhat dramatically towards Anthony and, raising his voice, said, "You've heard all that, haven't you, Bathurst?"

Anthony replied that he had. "Yes, sir, and what's the point behind your telling me all this?"

"That's just what I'm coming to, my boy—that's just what I'm coming to. The milk in the coconut. You listen to the sequel which we've picked up today." He leaned further over towards Anthony. "What do you think we've heard? And from our own cook at that. Not from a stranger. A Mrs. Woffington. Been with us for years and absolutely reliable in every way. I can vouch for that. Mrs. Woffington says that when Langley arrived here that night—and she swears that she saw him approach the house—he had no such thing as a car with him. That he walked up to the house after having run for some part of the way and that his story of having come here by car is not only a cock-and-bull story, but absolutely a trumped-up lie." Colonel Schofield concluded his narrative triumphantly and thumped one fist into the other palm. "Now what do you make of that, Bathurst?"

"H'm," replied Anthony; "strange, to say the least of it."

The Colonel fixed him with his cold, ice-blue eyes. "I wonder," he said, "whether it's possible you're thinking what I'm thinking."

"I can't answer that, sir, unless you confess it to me."

The Colonel's voice took on its dramatic note again. "Don't forget, Bathurst, that on the following day a dead man was found in Langley's car. Surely you aren't blind to that fact? To me—it's most significant."

Anthony decided to let Colonel Schofield continue talking. "Go on with the development of your theory, Colonel. I can't deny that you interest me."

The Colonel rose to the bait in the manner of a voracious pike. Anthony thought that he detected a shade of censure on the face of Priscilla. He avoided her eyes, therefore, and kept his gaze firmly concentrated on the Colonel.

"My point is this," went on the last-named, warming to his work, "it's come home to me very forcibly that Langley *may* have come here on that evening that I've just described with the sole intention of creating an alibi."

He turned towards his daughter as though he half expected her to contest his statement. But Priscilla refused to be drawn and remained silent. The hint of criticism, however, showed on her features even more clearly than before. The Colonel proceeded.

"It seems to me that Langley may have killed this man and then deliberately come on to this house in order to manufacture an alibi and cover up his traces. What do you say to that idea. Bathurst?"

"Assuming your theory to be correct, sir, how did the car get back to the 'Bear and Ragged Staff'?"

"How?"

"Yes—who drove it back there, for instance?"

"Why shouldn't Langley have driven it back there himself?"

"It may not be impossible—but it's decidedly unlikely. Miss Schofield drove him back to the hotel in *your* car. At least—that's the story that has been given to me. I have her authority for saying so."

The Colonel seemed a trifle nonplussed by Anthony's answer. But he returned to the attack after a moment or so's hesitation. "What was there to prevent his going back from the hotel to the place where he had left the car and then driving it back afterwards? Seems feasible to me."

"When?"

Colonel Schofield frowned. "There are, it seems to me, three possible answers to that question. One—later on the same night. Two—some time on the following morning. And three—which I regard as being by far the most likely proposition—*before he turned up at this house.*" Again the note of triumph crept into the Colonel's voice.

"I consider the last," replied Anthony, "to be, as you say, the *most* likely. I would go even farther than that and assert that it seems to me the only serious possibility. But even then there are a lot of nasty knobs on it, Colonel, if you come to analyse the implications attached to it."

"Such as?"

"Well, if Langley did that, and parked his car in the hotel garage as we know it was parked, because it was subsequently found there, he must have walked all the way out here to you. And the time factor, if examined at all carefully, would almost certainly destroy the value of the alibi. Even as it is, the time elements can be explored. It can be readily established within a little when Langley left the hotel and at what hour he arrived here. Sufficiently certainly to test your theory."

The Colonel grunted. He switched round in his chair and spoke to Priscilla. "What time was it when Langley showed up that night? You can remember, can't you? You're good on times."

Priscilla nodded. "About ten o'clock, I should say, without attempting to be frightfully accurate."

"There you are, then," responded Colonel Schofield; "find out what time he came away from the 'Bear and Ragged Staff'—getting that information should present no difficulty—and see how much time there was in between. That he had to spare. Another thing . . ." The Colonel paused. Anthony felt certain from the expression that had crossed his face that he had thought of something. Anthony and Priscilla waited for him to continue. Eventually the latter's impatience mastered her and she translated her thoughts into words.

"What is it, Daddy? You've thought of something. What were you going to say?"

"Why—this. I've just remembered something."

"About Mr. Langley, do you mean?"

"Yes, my girl. That's just what I do mean. About Langley." He turned towards Anthony with an almost cunning look on his face. "I can't make out why I didn't think of this before. Not like me. It's evident to me that I'm not the man I was. Must be going down-hill. Years ago I'd have remembered it like a shot. But when Mr. Langley arrived here the other night—on *the* night"—the Colonel emphasized his point by tapping Anthony on the knee as a species of punctuation—"I distinctly remember now that I formed the opinion that he was very much out of breath. Now what do you make of that, Bathurst?"

"Out of breath?"

"That's what I said. Breathless! Panting a bit! You know—blowing!"

Anthony smiled. "And you deduced from that?" he inquired.

"That he'd been running! Running hard. Do you recognize the possibility then, Bathurst?"

"Which one, sir?"

"Why—not the more obvious one—that he'd been running hard away from somebody or something—but that he'd been running to cut the time period down. For the alibi that he was deliberately trying to manufacture. There's one thing about it, you must admit—it pairs up satisfactorily with our Mrs. Woffington's story. Get the idea, my boy?"

The Colonel leant over and pushed his face close to Anthony's.

Anthony thought things over. There might be something in Schofield's suggestion. It would be wrong to treat it too lightly. Especially bearing in mind Mrs. Woffington's story that Langley had not arrived by car. But he had too little data by far to form any theory, and he knew that he must keep a perfectly open mind on the matter until more data were presented to him. He tacked, therefore.

"With the exception of Detective-Sergeant Lawton and his assistant you seem to have been the last people to speak to Langley before his disappearance."

"That's right," replied the Colonel. "I ran into him on the Racecourse on the following morning. Invited him to join me in the Members' Enclosure. And put him on to a thunderin' good thing! So he couldn't complain on that score, could he?" The Colonel chuckled boisterously at the savour of the reminiscence.

"Was he in good spirits that morning, would you say?" asked Anthony.

The Colonel's chuckle became a guffaw. "He was in good spirits *before* he backed that tip of mine. And, naturally, in damned sight better spirits afterwards. What do you think, Bathurst? Wouldn't you have been?"

Anthony ignored the side issue.

"He wasn't worried over anything?"

"Not on your life—if I'm any judge."

"And yet, on his own admission, on the previous evening he had had his car stolen."

Colonel Schofield shook his head. "H'm! I don't know that there's too much in that. He wasn't the sort to lose sleep over a thing like that. No, sir, you can take it from me that Langley was O.K. when he left Priscilla and me on the Racecourse that afternoon."

"You're reasonably sure of that, Colonel Schofield?"

"More than reasonably, Bathurst. Absolutely sure!"

Anthony nodded. "Thank you. I regard that as important. Now I'm going to ask you another question in connexion with Langley that perhaps Miss Schofield may be able to answer with less difficulty than you yourself, Colonel Schofield."

He saw that Priscilla's eyes were fixed on him. "Have you any idea, Miss Schofield, what brought Langley to Angel at this time of the year? I'm sorry if I seem to press the question. The Police have formed the opinion that he had come to the town for a specific purpose. But they'll go no further than that merely general expression of opinion." He turned to Priscilla. "I am aware, of course, Miss Schofield, that I asked this same question of you when you first approached me. But I'm wondering whether you are now able to amplify your previous answer. You've had, shall we say, since yesterday to think it over."

Anthony waited a moment or so for Priscilla to reply. When she did, however, he was doomed to disappointment. For Priscilla slowly shook her head.

"I'm frightfully sorry," she said, "but I can't add anything at all to what I told you before. I never discussed with Mr. Langley, at any time I was with him, the reasons that had brought him to Angel. And I can form no opinion that would be worth paying the slightest attention to. I'm sorry to let you down, Mr. Bathurst—I wish I could help you—but there it is."

"There you are, Bathurst," supplemented Colonel Schofield—"that's how it is. Pity! But if my girl says she can't help you, you can rest assured she can't."

Anthony nodded and smiled. "I accept that, Colonel Schofield, without the slightest reserve. Although, actually, I must confess to a certain amount of disappointment. I had hoped for some progress in that direction. It would have given me something like a starting-point. As it is, I must confess that I haven't yet been able to find one." Colonel Schofield twirled his white moustache. "Yes. I see your difficulty, Bathurst. I see it quite definitely."

Anthony sat there in deep thought. His meditations were disturbed eventually by Priscilla Schofield.

"A question from me now, Mr. Bathurst. And one that I hope and trust you will answer absolutely truthfully."

"I will endeavour to, Miss Schofield. What is the question?"

"It's about Mr. Langley. Now that you know just a little more about the case than I was able to tell you at our first meeting, do you still think that he's in danger? Serious danger? Frankly, now."

When Anthony's answer came it was grave and deliberate. "Frankly, Miss Schofield—I do. Although I've but little more to go on than I had."

Priscilla stood mute at his answer. Then she turned to her father. "I was afraid I should hear that. Sorely afraid. I even delayed asking Mr. Bathurst because I was so afraid. And it's all my fault. If it hadn't been for me he would have had nothing to do with any of it. I dragged him into it. I feel that I shall never forgive myself."

She clasped her fingers and sat down. Her genuine distress was evident. Anthony felt that to deal with this situation was just a little outside his province, and the Colonel was quick to see how Anthony was feeling. Anthony rose.

"Well, sir," he said, "I think that, taking everything into consideration, you won't mind if I—"

Schofield cut in. "Not at all, my dear Bathurst—not at all. I understand perfectly. You've got to get back. You'll have a little drop of something before you go? Which? Beer—or a short one?" Anthony nominated the latter, and when he left a few minutes later he had the satisfaction of thinking that Priscilla was looking a little better. On his way back to the hotel he churned the problem in his mind—but little inspiration came to him as a result.

CHAPTER II

I

ANTHONY Bathurst always contends that it was when he returned to the "Bear and Ragged Staff" after his visit to the Schofields that he first got to real grips with the Langley disappearance problem. It happened thus, and he is always the first to admit that he owed everything to the goddess of Fortune.

When he got back to the hotel, he walked into the smoke-lounge. He at once saw that the room was graced with several new faces. Faces that belonged to people who patently betrayed the somewhat arrogant fact that they were staying at the hotel and hadn't merely dropped in for a casual drink. There were a rather portly Naval Commander with a young blonde who showed a pair of unusually graceful legs and who was obviously not his daughter, and a little thin fellow with a sharp, perky sort of face who regarded Anthony when he entered with a glance that most certainly held a good deal more than ordinary interest. The Naval Commander, whom the blonde addressed as "Binky", was in rather boisterous shape and telling stories that were more vulgar in quality than anything else, and the blonde was receiving them with a regular punctuation of giggling appreciation.

Anthony, however, caught the thin chap stealing sideways glances at him with some degree of regularity. A waiter brought

Anthony the drink he had ordered and when Anthony replaced the glass for the first time a definite thought came to him that he had seen this thin chap before somewhere. Point now to be considered was when, where and in what circumstances? Anthony thought the matter over—hard and long. For a considerable time he travelled a barren road. It took him twenty-two minutes exactly to establish the desired connexion. When that did come, it surprised him. He had seen the man in the Court of Appeal one foggy, wintry morning about a year previously when an unusually interesting appeal case had been down for decision. The conclusion, therefore, to which Anthony came, after this interval of pondering, was that the fellow was in some way—direct or indirect—associated with the process of the Law.

"Interesting," said Anthony to himself—"decidedly interesting. Something may come of this." He looked up from his glass again just in time for the fellow to avert his eyes. "Trying to place me," he summed up to himself, "just as I've been endeavouring to place him. Wonder whether he's pulled it off."

At that precise moment a waiter came in and walked straight over to the thin man, and the two of them at once became engaged in close conversation. Anthony flung courtesy and convention to the winds and endeavoured to listen to what they were saying. Within a few seconds of the inception of the effort he felt both rewarded and justified, for his ears clearly caught the name of Langley. Beyond that, however, he could hear nothing distinguishable for some time afterwards, for the reason that the waiter got closer to the thin man and each of them, when this happened, dropped his voice a little. After a time the waiter fellow drew himself up and Anthony heard him say to the thin man—

"I'll see the manager, sir, and no doubt he'll make arrangements for you to have a word with him. That'll be the best thing. I'll tell him you'd like the interview to take place as soon as possible."

The waiter then collected glasses from a number of the tables within his orbit and made his exit. Anthony pondered over what he had just heard. For herein, he could see, lay another problem. What was this thin man to do with the missing Langley, and why was he here making inquiries concerning him? Also, what was the best direction that he himself could take? Should he lie doggo as far as the thin fellow was concerned and avoid contact with him or should he attempt to join forces, as it were, *with* him and regard him thus as an ally, as distinct from an opponent? He felt that it was a problem which could not be disposed of with an immediate solution, and that he would be compelled to wait for a time before he embraced a really definite policy. In the meantime he would hang around pretty generally in an attempt to pick up anything important which might be floating about or even stray, as it were, towards him.

But then he decided that there was still another possibility. The thin man had most patently evinced a certain interest in *him*. It was logical, therefore, to assume that this interest might be developed and amplified to such a degree that the thin man might, in time, make deliberate contact with him. This condition, Anthony felt, would be the rather more satisfactory, and he determined, therefore, to adopt a temporary policy of "wait and see". Scarcely had he arrived at this conclusion when there came a surprising occurrence. The thin fellow whom he had been watching since the waiter had taken his departure rose suddenly from his seat at the table and walked straight over to him. It seemed that he might have been reading Anthony's thoughts. Anthony looked up as the man drew level with him. He saw that the man standing at his side was smiling at him.

"Excuse me, sir," said the thin fellow, "and I hope I'm not making a mistake—I shall feel frightfully embarrassed if I am—but aren't you Mr. Anthony Bathurst?"

Anthony nodded. "Quite right, first time. You've no objection, I take it?"

The thin man's face creased knowingly and then slid, as it were, into a familiar grin. "I like that—I do indeed. That's a good one, I must say. No, Mr. Bathurst, to come to the point—quite the contrary in fact. Very pleased to think you're down here."

"Nice of you," murmured Anthony.

"Do you mind if I . . ." He pulled a chair a little distance from the table and sat down at Anthony's side. The latter suffered the intrusion in silence.

"As a matter of fact," the thin man went on airily, "I'm almost shaking hands with myself at what I'm calling my good luck in running up against you. I'd begun to think very seriously that the job I'm on wasn't exactly my particular cup of tea, but seeing you sitting here has caused me to revise my ideas and think a bit differently."

The thin man paused at this as though he were expecting Anthony to say something. Mr. Bathurst, however, still refrained. The man had started to make the running, and as far as Anthony was concerned he should continue to make it. For some time at least. The thin man, after a moment's silence, appeared to appreciate the position. He sensed that it would be necessary for him to delineate his own position in a considerably fuller degree before he got anywhere. He thereupon completely reversed his previous tactics and seized the bull by the horns. Putting his elbows on the table, he leant well over towards Anthony and said, excessively confidentially—

"I suppose—if we get down to brass tacks—that you're here on exactly the same lay as yours truly? Pretty safe bet, isn't it?" He pulled himself back and cocked a sapient eye in Anthony's direction. "Eh—what do you say to that, Mr. Bathurst?"

Anthony replied in even tones, "I find the question almost impossible to answer—seeing that I haven't the slightest idea as to what your 'lay' is."

The thin man eyed him doubtfully. Anthony bore the scrutiny imperturbably.

"Straight up?" inquired the man.

Anthony shrugged his shoulders. "Why should you think otherwise?"

"All right," replied the thin man, "you win—I'll come clean if that's what you're insisting on. Perhaps you've got the right to do so—after all, it's in your hands to dictate policy. The truth is I'm down here in Angel with regard to the disappearance of a certain Mr. Langley. Now what have you got to say, Mr. Bathurst?"

Anthony smiled. "You've cleared the air by your last statement, Mr.—er—I don't think I know your name."

"Maddison," replied the thin man, "Percy Maddison—representing Kenneth Smith, Livingstone and Luttrell, of Chancery Lane. You can place me now, can't you?"

"Inquiry agents, I fancy," admitted Anthony.

"You've hit it, sir. Bang on the target. One of the oldest-established firms in the little old village of London. Reputation unsullied. And I take it from your last remark that we now do understand one another?"

"Meaning?" said Anthony.

"The Langley business, of course. We're both in on it—eh? You and I."

Anthony decided to finesse no longer. "Yes. You may take it that way."

"And you're representing—"

"Say—friends of the missing man, Maddison. Nothing more than that."

Maddison let go a soft whistle. "Definitely not the 'Yard', then?"

"Definitely not the 'Yard', as you and Kenneth Smith, etc., would ordinarily understand the expression."

"I see. That makes a bit of a difference." The thin man puckered up his face, as though calculating the full implications of Anthony's answer. "Ah, well," he continued after a brief interval. "Now I've thought it over I don't feel I'm in any way disappointed to hear what you've just said. No—I think, on the contrary, that I'm more pleased than anything else."

"You're doing most of the talking," interposed Anthony. "Suppose I take a turn? You asked me whom I represented. I was frank with you and told you what you wanted to know. Let me put the boot on the other foot. What interest do you represent?"

The thin man simulated a mild form of indignation. "Come, come! Now that's not like you, Mr. Bathurst. According to the reputation that I've always heard given you. I was just as frank with you as you were with me. I told you just now I'd been sent down here by Kenneth Smith, Livingstone and Luttrell, of Chancery Lane. Now—didn't I? You can't deny the truth of that."

Anthony shook his head. "Oh no, Maddison. I can't have that. I wasn't born yesterday. You're not putting that one past me. The fact that Kenneth Smith, Livingstone and Luttrell, of Chancery Lane, sent you down here is one thing. I accept it as such for just what it's worth and no more. But you're in their employ. They cried go and you went. What I desire to know is who briefed them? For whom are *they* working? That's my point. And a very different proposition from yours—as you must readily admit."

He watched the man carefully as he made this last statement and went on before Maddison could frame a reply. "You've only told me part of the story, Maddison. The more important half of it you've kept back. And that's the part I'm after. Who briefed K. S. L. and L.?"

He leant back in his chair and continued to watch Maddison. Several seconds went their way in silence. Maddison, after considering Anthony's question, decided evidently to come to the point.

"If I told you that I didn't know I suppose you'd have a difficulty in believing me, wouldn't you?"

Anthony eyed him curiously, but made no answer. Maddison thrust a hand forward across the table.

"But I swear to you, Mr. Bathurst, that I don't know! It's God's solemn truth. If I did know, I'd be pleased to take you into my confidence. As I don't—I can't."

Anthony spoke slowly. "I don't know that it would be wise of me to believe you."

Maddison grew a trifle heated in his endeavour to justify himself. "I swear I'm telling the truth, Mr. Bathurst. Surely you can see that? Wouldn't it be to my advantage to let you in on it if I could, so that I could rely on your help and we could work together?" Maddison saw that his argument had carried some weight at least. He proceeded, therefore, to follow up at once the advantage he had managed to establish. "You can't gainsay the truth of that—now can you, Mr. Bathurst?"

"It's a point—I agree. And a good point, too. Your contention is that all you know is that your employers have sent you down here to find Langley—if he is to be found. Am I right?"

Maddison nodded. "You've got it, sir. That's the position absolutely. And no more than that. I've no more idea than the dead who's employing K. S. L. and L. I got sent for yesterday afternoon by Mr.

Clement Luttrell—I always look on him as my particular boss—received my orders and got packed off down here. But there is one thing I'd say, Mr. Bathurst. One thing additional, that is. There's pretty big money behind the job. I could tell that by Mr. Clement's general manner towards me when he commissioned me. He was sort of rubbing his hands over it, as you might say."

"I should have said your firm was extremely wealthy and not affected by isolated engagements or outside commissions—if I can call them that."

"So they may be, Mr. Bathurst—but they like a bit of fat when it comes their way—believe me. What firm doesn't? Not half they don't."

Anthony smiled at Maddison's expression. The latter was quick to perceive it and endeavoured to capitalize on it immediately. Putting his face very close to Anthony's he said—

"Well—what do you really know, Mr. Bathurst? Let's see if we can't compare notes. I'm ready to exchange—fifty-fifty."

Anthony shook his head. "I know practically nothing. Langley was interviewed by the Police here at Angel with regard to a matter that concerns his car, in the early afternoon of the day he disappeared. He hasn't been seen again. That's about the sum total."

"Is that so? Now that's very interesting. Disappeared just after the Police had entertained him—eh? Put the mockers on him properly? Now I wonder why, Mr. Bathurst? If we knew that . . ."

Anthony shrugged his shoulders. He wasn't telling Maddison any more than he had told him. He'd see first of all how Maddison reacted to that information. Maddison came again.

"First question's obvious, of course. What did the Angel Police interview Langley over? Any idea?"

"Langley's car was stolen the night before when he was visiting friends just on the outskirts of Angel. He reported the loss directly he knew of it. The car was returned to the hotel garage—that's here, of course—with something in it that wasn't there when Langley lost it. That's the part the Police were more than a little concerned about."

"How do you mean?" asked Maddison curiously, greedy interest in his eyes.

"Just this. The extra in Langley's car happened to be a dead man."

"Eh?" Maddison almost jumped in his chair. "A dead man, you say?"

"Yes. And probably murdered at that. Now, my dear Maddison, you see the point."

"By Jiminy! that's a different proposition altogether! I say, do you mean that Langley's suspected of the murder—by the Police? Is that what you're getting at?"

"Couldn't tell you. I haven't enough knowledge of the official point of view or insight into the official mind. I make a rule never to conjecture on matters of that kind."

"Yes—I know all about that. And I don't disagree as a broad principle. Pretty sound rule. Often stick to it myself. But what do you *really* think? About Langley, I mean?"

"I've a perfectly open mind. And until I get my claws deeper into the case generally, I couldn't go an inch beyond that statement. Now will you tell me what *you* know, Maddison?"

The thin man spread out deprecating hands. "When you spotted me, Mr. Bathurst, in this here lounge, I'd been on the job in Angel almost exactly one quarter of an hour! Or, in other words—I'd just arrived at the starting-post. So I haven't had much time to get busy, have I?"

"And you came down here with no preliminary priming?"

"To all intents and purposes—yes. What I had given to me to start with was that Langley had come to Angel and fixed up to stop at this hotel—the 'Bear and Ragged Staff'. Soon after he had come—he had disappeared. That's the sum total of the knowledge I started off with."

Anthony leant over to him. "Tell me this, Maddison. Who was Langley?"

"Search me! Haven't the foggiest."

"Where did he come from?"

"Same answer, Mr. Bathurst—with knobs on."

Anthony frowned. This was both disappointing and disconcerting. The proximity of Maddison, originally promising, looked like proving but little help. Anthony made one more attempt to delve into Maddison's knowledge.

"What was his profession—if any?"

"Still the same answer, Mr. B. Nothing doing. And that's the hat trick."

Then Anthony had an idea. "Got a photo of him—by any chance?"

Maddison grinned. "You've rung the bell at last. That's something I can supply."

Maddison's hand dived into his breast-pocket and produced a picture-postcard photograph. Maddison handed it to Anthony. The latter saw that it was the photograph of a group—to be precise, of a Rugger XV. "Mosslyn Park". Maddison's finger shot over the table to help towards identification.

"That's friend Langley," he said, supplementary to the indication of his finger—"the third chap from the right in the back row. Got his arms folded. Useful-looking customer in a rough-house—eh?"

Anthony looked at the photograph of the man that Maddison had described as being Langley. He agreed at once mentally that Maddison's opinion of Langley's physique was an eminently sound one.

"A forward," he said to himself, "and very useful in the tight. And—from a purely social standpoint—definitely not a man to get at variance with. Somewhere round six feet and in the region of fourteen stone. Fit and as hard as a bag of nails. Should have been able, with anything like an even break, to have held his own with most corners. Perhaps he didn't get an even break."

Anthony handed the postcard back to Maddison. "Thank you. That has given me a much better idea of the man than the picture I'd created in my mind."

"No doubt about that, Mr. Bathurst. There's nothing like having the authentic. Well, and what's your next step?"

Anthony sidestepped the question. "When I came in just now, I saw you talking to that waiter chap. I can guess you were on a spot of inquiry. Did you get anywhere with him?"

"Lord, no! Not an inch. But I'm going to have a chat with the manager. He's arranging it for me. May be able to find out something that way. How Langley fixed up here in the first place and so on." Anthony nodded approval. "Not a bad idea." He rose from his chair and stretched his arms. "As for myself—I haven't quite made up my mind regarding my next step. I think I'll sleep on it for tonight at least. I've known that help a man considerably before now."

"Me too, Mr. Bathurst," responded Maddison; "a spot of shut-eye often works wonders. I'll follow your example."

II

Anthony carried out the plan that he had indicated to Maddison. That night he went to bed comparatively early and slept on his problem. When he awoke next morning, he was undecided as to two moves only. The first was, should he interview Lawton again that morning as to whether any news had come through relative to Langley and concerning those inquiries which Lawton was superintending, or should he make the next move in the game entirely on his own initiative? Lawton's inquiries in the main were with regard to the normal transport channels—trains, long-distance coaches and taxi-cabs. The ordinary bread-and-butter routine invariably employed in cases of this nature. After breakfast had been served and consumed, Anthony made his decision. He would make the next move off his own bat—and be hanged to both Lawton and Maddison!

Leaving the "Bear and Ragged Staff" immediately after breakfast by the front entrance, he walked to the outskirts of the town and to a spot where he had previously noticed a telephone kiosk. To his satisfaction, upon arrival, he found it empty. Slipping in quickly, he closed the kiosk door behind him and dialled the "Yard" number. After an irritating delay of some minutes, he was able to establish communication with Chief Det.-Inspector Andrew MacMorran.

"Good lord," said the latter, "Mr. Bathurst of all people! I've been wondering for some time now where it was you were kickin' up your heels. Now tell me that, before you tell me anything else. It's some months since I heard from you."

Anthony explained where he was and the bare bones of the case he had accepted via Priscilla Schofield. MacMorran listened with what Anthony thought was his special brand of silent sympathy.

"H'm," MacMorran commented at length. "According to all that, you haven't made much headway. If any! You'll be wantin' me down there to hold your hand, my boy—I can see that much already." Anthony humoured him and MacMorran went on. "Probably," the Inspector concluded, "the whole problem'll fizzle out into a flop and you'll find that you've been looking for a man who's been called away suddenly to pay for a dog licence. I've had cases like that before, my boy, and when they've eventually sorted themselves out I could have kicked myself from Dan to Beersheba for wasting my time on them. So now you know what I'm inclined to think about your present case."

"Well, Andrew," Anthony replied, "that's as may be. Time will tell. In the meantime I'm ringing you because I want you to do something for me. I want you to get busy—pure official 'Yard'—you know what I mean—at the Kenneth Smith, Livingstone and Luttrell end. Their address is Chancery Lane. I want to know who commissioned them to find this man Richard Langley. To get that information will mean—with anything like ordinary luck—a great deal to me. In other words, who is it that's so frantically interested in the man? That's what I'm desperately keen to know. Get that for me, Andrew, there's a good scout—as soon as you possibly can, will you?"

"Just a minute, Mr. Bathurst, while I get that down. You've been going a bit on the fast side for me. Just give me that name and address you mentioned again, will you?"

Anthony did as MacMorran asked him. The Inspector grabbed a pencil and made the necessary entries on the pad in front of him.

"That's all right," he said; "I'll do what I can for you, Mr. Bathurst. Leave it to me."

Anthony elaborated. "I rang you, Andrew, because I felt that you had far more chance of getting it and getting it quickly than I should have had, working on my own. You can use more resources than I can."

"Oh yeah?" MacMorran returned down the telephone. "There's one thing—you don't change much. Just the same old kid stakes as always. Anyhow—I'll see what I can do for you. You usually get your own way."

Anthony ignored the subtle thrust. "When will you ring me—or what do you think—shall I ring you? Would you rather?"

"Yes. I think it would be sounder policy for you to ring me, if you don't mind. The point that we have to settle is 'when'?"

"That's more up to you than to me, Andrew. Depends how you get on with the particular job. What do you think are the prospects?"

"Let me see," replied MacMorran, "what's today? Friday. Give me a ring midday tomorrow. Say about a quarter past twelve. Ought to be able to have something for you by then. Anyhow, we'll see. That suit you?"

"Admirably, Andrew. Couldn't be better. That's settled, then. I'll ring you at the 'Yard' at 12.15 tomorrow. Thanks a lot, Andrew."

MacMorran mumbled something at the other end and Anthony rang off.

III

After he had 'phoned MacMorran, Anthony walked round to have another chat with Lawton. He found the latter in. The local detective received him cordially.

"Good day to you, Mr. Bathurst. Pleased to see you. Also your arrival is not ill-timed. We've had some news this morning of the highest importance."

"Of Langley, do you mean?"

Lawton shook his head. "No. Not exactly. Not of your friend Langley. Nothing so good as that. No—with regard to the fellow who was found dead in Langley's car. He's been identified at last."

"That's interesting," said Anthony, "and who does he turn out to be?"

"Man named Trimmer. Edward Trimmer. Local chap. Or comparatively so. Comes from Edenfield. Little village just beyond Eden."

"Who identified him?"

"His mother. Old girl about seventy. Been missing some days. She picked up the trail from the local rag."

"Good. That's settled one of your headaches, then. What did the chap do for a living? Did she tell you that?"

Lawton scratched the side of his nose. "Well—to tell you the truth—that's rather an awkward one. I questioned her, of course, but didn't get a lot out of her. If you ask me, the chap was a bit of a waster. Lived more or less by his wits, I should say would be the best way of putting it. You know the idea. Horses, dogs, cards, etc. Anything but a real hard day's graft. Was often away from home for days. And there's thousands like him, I'm sorry to say."

"As bad as that," murmured Anthony.

"You know," retorted Lawton unceremoniously, "as well as I do. You're a man of the world if ever I saw one, and I'm not teaching you anything."

"Tell me," said Anthony quietly, "do you think Langley's disappearance is in any way connected with the death of this man Trimmer? I'd like to know how you feel about that."

Lawton was in no hurry to reply. "Well," he said eventually, "that's a bit of a problem. I'll admit that much candidly. When I saw Langley for the first time and interviewed him he impressed me as a man that was telling the truth. Now"—and Lawton shrugged his shoulders—"I feel bound to say I'm not so sure. If he's straight and aboveboard why has he cleared off like he has? I think now that the chances are that there is a connexion between the two things—somewhere! It'll be our job to find that connexion."

"Thank you," replied Anthony, "for a frank answer. I'm indebted to you. Just give me the full name and address of the dead man, will you?"

Lawton referred to a file. "Yes. I can do that. Here you are. Edward Louis Trimmer. Aged 39. Address, 11, Sheep Terrace, Edenfield."

"Thank you again," replied Anthony, as he jotted down the particulars. "I am doubly indebted to you."

"Not at all," said Lawton.

"There's one thing that does occur to me. And that's this. You told me yesterday that Trimmer, when he rode into Angel in Langley's car, had (according to Langley) walked from Eden. Your news this morning tends rather to confirm the statement. Do you agree?"

"Oh yes," replied Lawton. "I'd thought of that myself."

IV

That evening Anthony made a comprehensive round tour of the small town of Angel. He spent some time in every hotel to which he thought it was at all likely that Langley might have been attracted. Direct inquiries, indirect suggestions and much discreet listening in many bars yielded him nothing at all. More direct inquiries, too, of garages and all road transport agencies were similarly unproductive.

He returned to the "Bear and Ragged Staff" with the feeling that although several hours had passed since he had accepted Priscilla Schofield's commission, he had not yet got away from the mark even. By no means a pleasant or illuminating thought. The grass might well be flourishing under his feet and the green bay tree prospering in its appropriate meadow. And when he came downstairs to breakfast on the following morning, his keen appreciation of dire and abject failure was still with him.

Maddison, who had already started his meal, beckoned him to the chair at his side.

"I've absolutely nothing to trade, Maddison. Neither a bean nor a sausage! So that if you're relying on me, you're relying on a broken reed."

"That's too bad," returned Maddison. "I had high hopes when I saw you come into the breakfast-room that you were on to something. You looked sort of satisfied with yourself. Still—Rome wasn't built in a day." He leant over and confided something to Anthony's left ear. "I've picked up something. Not a lot—but something. Langley was at the Racecourse during the afternoon of the day he vanished—in the company of some people named Schofield. Local people at that. I'm calling on them this morning. They don't live *too* far from here."

Anthony shook his head again. "I shouldn't—if I were you," he said nonchalantly.

Maddison was surprised, and showed his surprise at that.

"What do you mean? Why on earth not?"

Anthony carefully placed some mustard on the edge of his plate before he answered. He performed the operation with extreme care, so Maddison perforce had to wait. "I've seen them," he said. "Both Colonel Schofield and his daughter. You'll get nothing from them. Beyond, of course, what you already know. Langley was with them on Angel Racecourse when he was called for the interview with the Police authorities. That's their particular fragment of information. Not an iota more. So I shouldn't trouble them further if I were you. Mightn't like it."

Maddison thrust out his lower lip. "Thanks—very nice—I must say. They seem to have put up with you."

"I'm different," said Anthony, with deliberate provocation.

Maddison sat quiet for a moment or two. "I'm getting interested in all this. What's this fellow to do with the Schofields?"

Anthony chose the path of caution. "How do you mean—exactly?"

"Well—are they friends, as you might say?"

"Presumably."

"How long has the friendship existed?"

"My dear sir," said Anthony, "who am I to presume to answer details of that sort?"

Maddison reached rather unceremoniously for the marmalade. "H'm! Not very helpful, are you?"

"Sorry," replied Anthony, "but I can't make bricks without straw any more than you can. I'm just doing my best."

"I suppose so." Maddison sat in thought for some little time and then, with a curt nod to Anthony, left the table.

Anthony hung round the hotel for the remainder of the morning until he judged it time to keep his telephone appointment with Andrew MacMorran. He walked out of the "Bear and Ragged Staff" to the kiosk he had used on the previous day. He arrived at the place at ten minutes past twelve and congratulated himself that the time was appropriate. On this occasion he was in touch with MacMorran after but slight delay. The Chief Inspector, doubtless, had anticipated the call and had made arrangements to be ready for it.

"Well, Andrew," said Anthony as he opened, "how do we go? Any luck on my job, you old ruffian?"

He heard the Inspector's chuckle at the other end. "I like your style. You ought to know by this time that the 'Yard' never functions on 'luck'. If you mean a combination of skill, superb organization, and the highest form of human intelligence—well, then I'm with you."

"All right," said Anthony, "skip it and take the plates away. What about it?"

MacMorran chuckled again. "Well—what do you think? We had got what you wanted at least an hour and a half ago. I'll read you what my report says. You listen and don't interrupt."

Anthony heard the rustle of papers as the Inspector pulled them towards him. "Here you are, Mr. Bathurst. Your man Maddison is acting for Kenneth Smith, Livingstone and Luttrell, who, in turn, have been commissioned by Angus Mount Ltd., of Old Burlington Street, London. There you are—now you've got the basinful. Satisfied?" Anthony repeated the name of the second firm concerned, after MacMorran. "Angus Mount Ltd.—eh? That's rather indicative, isn't it?"

"You know who they are, of course," said the Inspector.

"I'll say I do. What do you take me for? If I said the biggest commission agents in the South of England, should I be very far out, Andrew?"

Anthony could almost hear MacMorran thinking. The reply came at length. "No-o, I don't think you would. They're certainly pretty big Turf business, and at the moment I can't think of anybody bigger. Well, Mr. Bathurst, I shall have to ring off now. I'm due for White Hart Lane this afternoon, Spurs versus the Villa, and I haven't too much time. What a game—eh? The K.O.'s at 2.45. So here's all the best."

"Right-o, Andrew—many thanks for your kindness, and I hope the game'll be a blinder. It's on the cards that I may ring you again early next week—so be prepared for more trouble."

"Don't worry. Always the good little scout. Cheero!"

The Inspector rang off and Anthony turned away to a closer consideration of his problem. So it was no less a firm than Angus Mount Ltd. who were interested in the disappearance of Langley! And interested to the extent of employing a private inquiry agent to probe it. Not entirely unsatisfactory, thought Anthony, seeing that Langley had actually been on the Racecourse at Angel on the afternoon when the Police had chosen to question him. The incident certainly fitted into the general pattern. It gave Anthony what he had been wanting for some time—a definite starting-point. He was able now to visualize the genesis of the affair. It also cleared the way for him and he thought now that his next step was plainly indicated. He must get in touch with Angus Mount Ltd. as soon as possible. He considered this course of action definitely preferable to establishing contact with Kenneth Smith, Livingstone and Luttrell. The former firm was functioning, as he saw it, as a primary influence, whereas the latter was moving on a secondary basis. Angus Mount had entered the arena first. He considered, too, that he had a clearly defined way of approach to them. Langley had disappeared—in itself a matter for investigation, as evident by the Maddison entanglement—and, in addition to that, there was the much more serious contingency of a man having been murdered. At least, such was the opinion of the Police authorities. The more he thought over the problem as it had now been unfolded to him, the less he was inclined to think of the chances of Langley's survival. The fact of the dead man found in Langley's car was significant that the opposing forces, whoever they were, had no scruples in the contest. *If* it suited them to remove Langley from the cast, Anthony felt certain that Langley would be removed—and that would be that! Bad going for Priscilla Schofield. That was the worst of these sordid tragedies—they invariably spelled pain and distress to a charming woman whose normal lot in life should be nothing but pleasure and sweetness.

Anthony walked back to the "Bear and Ragged Staff". His mind was now made up and he took his time. He would call on Angus Mount Ltd. of Old Burlington Street, London, the first thing on Monday morning. And he wouldn't take Maddison into consultation, either. For the time being at least, Maddison could paddle his own canoe. And it might need all his skill to keep it afloat.

V

Anthony presented his card at the offices of Angus Mount Ltd. at punctually 11.30 on the following Monday morning. The intervening time had proved entirely barren and profitless as far as any further news re Langley or Trimmer was concerned.

As he entered the building, he was more than ordinarily impressed by the offices of Britain's leading Turf Accountants. "Palatial" would not have been an inappropriate word. The clerk to whom he tendered his card shook his head at Anthony, and the look which accompanied the shake spoke volumes.

"I'm sorry," he said somewhat lugubriously, "but clients can only be seen by appointment. Otherwise all business must be transacted by letter, telegram or telephone. If you refer to our rules you will see."

"I'm not," said Anthony in return, "exactly what you'd term a client. But of course I can't blame you for not knowing that. Allow me." He held out his hand for his card. The clerk—a little annoyed—handed it back to him. Anthony scrawled MacMorran's name in the corner and handed it back again to the clerk. The latter raised his eyebrows in surprise.

"Scotland Yard?" he queried.

"You may call it that," said Anthony.

"That, I suppose, makes some sort of difference."

"I suppose it does. It often has—anyhow—perhaps you'll be good enough to find out."

The clerk nodded and disappeared with the card. Anthony was kept cooling his heels in the outer office for some minutes. Just as he was becoming a trifle impatient the clerk made his belated reappearance.

"Come this way, sir—if you please."

He followed his guide down a beautifully decorated and thickly-carpeted corridor into a room equally tastefully furnished. A man sat at a roll-top desk with no less than three telephone instruments within easy reach.

"Come in, Mr. Bathurst," he said, with some show of cordiality—"and sit down, will you? Thank you, Franklin—that'll do."

The clerk bowed and disappeared. Anthony took the most convenient chair and seated himself. The man who faced him wore a double-breasted suit which was smart in the extreme and generally he exuded the suggestion of opulence. He pushed a cigarette-case in Anthony's direction. "Smoke?"

"Thank you," said Anthony.

"Now what can I do for you, Mr. . . . er . . . Bathurst? And you'll permit me to express the hope that you won't take up too much of my time. Without offence, of course."

"Just a minute," said Anthony—"I'd like to start right, as it were, so that there's no misunderstanding. You know who I am. Whom have I the privilege of addressing?"

The man at the roll-top desk smiled. "I'm sorry. I forgot that Franklin hadn't told you. My name's Monkhouse."

"A director of the firm?"

This brought a smile of stiff superiority. "Junior partner."

"Thanks. Well, that's very satisfactory. I'll explain what I've come to see you about."

"That's the idea. That's what I'm waiting for. And, as I said, time's valuable."

Anthony took him at his word and came to the point at once. "I'm here in relation to the sudden disappearance, in the little town of Angel, of a man by the name of Richard Langley."

Monkhouse stopped drumming with his fingertips and favoured Anthony with a fixed stare. "I see. Langley. Yes—I follow. I've been slow. Well?"

"Your firm is interested in the matter, Mr. Monkhouse?"

"Er . . . yes . . . I suppose we are."

"May I inquire why, Mr. Monkhouse?"

Monkhouse didn't answer for some little time. He tapped his front teeth with the butt of his fountain-pen. Anthony waited for his reply.

"H'm," said Monkhouse, "bit of a teaser, this. You've caught me on one leg, rather. Don't quite know what I should tell you. Or how much. Afraid it's a job for our Mr. Hoare. Still—you seem to be knowledgeable of quite a good deal, so I can't pretend to stall you off. Wouldn't do at all. Not the thing." Here he changed his tone and began to speak in a much crisper manner. "Langley was employed by us. At the time of his disappearance, I mean. He was a private inquiry agent. Worked on his own account. Never on any account with a partner. We sent him down to Angel."

"In what connexion?" cut in Anthony relentlessly and without hesitation.

Monkhouse's fingertips resumed their drumming. After a time he looked up deliberately and shook his head. "Look here—I'd much rather not answer that question, if you don't mind. I don't have to answer, do I?"

"No—you don't have to answer. But I'd very much like you to. And I need scarcely point out that it will be entirely to your advantage." Monkhouse smiled at Anthony's frank statement. It was an attractive smile, and Anthony liked him all the better for it.

"No doubt you would and it would. All the same, you've given me a bit of a headache as it is. Don't mind admitting it. And I don't know that I've been altogether wise in telling you what I have told you." Monkhouse paused again. After a time, devoted evidently to a more serious consideration of the matter, he continued, "Look here, I'll content myself by saying this. We—that's the firm—have four clients in Angel. On our books. I don't mean by that that we have only four. As a matter of fact, our clientele in that part of the country is pretty extensive. Down there it's pretty thick, you know, with the huntin', fishin' and shootin' crowd. But that's by the way. The names of the four clients in Angel that are concerning you and me at the moment are Gunter, Webber, Layman and Miller. Langley was engaged by us in the matter of their respective accounts. I'll make you a present of that much information. But I don't know what his exact terms of reference were. And that's all I feel I can tell you at this stage. I'm not *refusing* to tell you any more. But that's as far as I'm going. Any more that you want must come from Leopold Hoare—my chief."

Monkhouse sat back in his chair and placed his fingertips together. "And that's where I must leave it," he added. "I'm sorry—but that's how it is."

Anthony looked grave. The names given to him were significant. "I see." He took out his diary. "Let me make a note, then, of those names you've given me. Gunter, Layman, Webber and Miller you said. Miller, eh? Will you be good enough to tell me their addresses?"

Monkhouse shook his head. "No. I'd much rather not. Don't ask me any more—please. If you must have additional information I suggest you make an appointment with Leopold Hoare. That's the only way you'll get it."

"When could I fix that?"

Monkhouse pursed his lips when Anthony put the question. "Well—leave that to me. I'll see what I can fix up for you. Leave me your address."

"It's on my card," returned Anthony, "you have it there by your elbow."

"That's right. So it is. Well—is that all for now, Mr. Bathurst?"

"According to you it is, I'm afraid. But many thanks all the same for what you have told me." He stopped. "One thing does occur to me, though, Mr. Monkhouse, and that's this. I did my best to tell you just now that it's in your interest that Langley be found—otherwise you wouldn't have gone to another firm of agents to do that job for you. Well—that being so—why not help me in all your power to find him? That's how the job appeals to me. And it's sheer common sense."

Monkhouse fingered his chin reflectively. "I grant you all that—willingly. But, as I see it, it's not quite so simple and clear-cut as all that. You see—you aren't aware of all the circumstances. Let me say there are—how shall I put it?—certain complications, that I'd very much rather Hoare dealt with than I myself. After all—he's my chief, and this is his responsibility. He's handled the affair right from the word 'go'. If you knew exactly what they were—these complications, I mean—you'd understand the position immediately."

"Perhaps I'm beginning to understand, Mr. Monkhouse. You'll let me know about your Mr. Hoare, then, as soon as you can?"

"Oh, yes. As I said I would. I promise not to let you down. I shall see Mr. Hoare late this afternoon. If things go all right, I'll give you a ring some time tomorrow and let you know what I've been able to arrange for you. You may rely on that—absolutely."

Anthony rose. "That's O.K. then. Again—many thanks. I'll wait until I hear from you tomorrow."

Monkhouse nodded. "That's the idea, old chap. Just a spot of patience."

Leaning forward, he knocked the ash from his cigarette into the tray in front of him.

VI

Back in his flat, and to an excellent dinner which the good and faithful Emily had prepared for him, Anthony followed his wont and began to toy with several theories, which he considered held intriguing possibilities. For he had certainly, through this visit of his to the firm of Angus Mount Ltd., made definite progress.

He had got so much nearer to the real Langley. He had established what he was and—almost—the reason why he had gone to Angel. The slight doubt which still existed in that respect he hoped to eradicate on the following day when he had a talk with this man of Monkhouse's nomination, Leopold Hoare. In the meantime, what was likely to have been the real reason underlying the commissioning of Langley by Angus Mount? It had been to do with four credit accounts held with that firm by four people resident in Angel. Monkhouse had definitely made a statement to that effect. Anthony considered the four names that had been mentioned to him. What were they now? Gunter, Layman, Miller and Webber. Yes—they were the four. And the names Layman and Webber had been in Priscilla's story.

Almost immediately, Anthony's questing mind seized on one point. All four names might well be German in origin—but thinly disguised. He took them one by one—this time in reverse order. Webber might well have been originally Weber. Miller in all possibility was Müller. Layman—this one pleased Anthony immensely, because he felt that it gave real point to his theory—might certainly have been Lehmann in earlier days, whilst it remained moderately obvious that Gunter could easily be a more British substitute for the Teutonic Gunther. "All extremely interesting," mused Anthony to himself, "but where do I go to from there?" As far as he could see, there seemed something wrong somewhere. There was inappropriateness. Where did this German conspiracy, as he had manufactured it, fit in with a famous firm of Turf Accountants? Angus Mount Ltd. were scarcely likely to be concerned with anything to do with international espionage. They were, on the other hand, much more probably interested in matters to do with those three familiar letters, L.S.D. And at any rate they had been sufficiently concerned to send a second emissary after the vanished Langley. Which fact argued that there were probably more than everyday issues at stake.

By this time, many trains of thought had begun to run through Anthony's mind. Why had Monkhouse elected to tell him this much and no more? Monkhouse, when he had been pressed, had certainly shied at something. What was it? Why had he been determined to throw the final responsibility on to his senior partner, Leopold Hoare? Anthony's thoughts went back to his first interview with Priscilla Schofield. To her story of Langley's chance encounter with a certain five men when he had returned the cat, Ahasuerus. Five men! Monkhouse had mentioned four men. But—and Anthony remembered this fact with relish—Priscilla had mentioned another name to him. What was it, now? Anthony thought. The name of a man who kept two shops in the town of Angel. It came to him quickly. The name was Newman. And again the coincidence hit him hard. Newman, according to his recently-born theory, could so easily be Neumann!

In that case then there would be five names every one of which was of German origin. Strange—to say the least of it. Again Anthony reverted to what Monkhouse had said. He had used a somewhat unusual phrase in relation to Langley's employment by Angus Mount. Monkhouse wasn't sure "what Langley's exact terms of reference had been". What did that mean?

Anthony turned it over several times in his mind and he came to the conclusion that what Monkhouse meant was this. That he wasn't sure whether Langley had been sent to Angel by Hoare, acting for Angus Mount, and had been equipped with the full story. It was just on the cards, he thought, that Langley might not have been told *why* he was to do certain things. This might well have been, judging by Monkhouse's own attitude towards Anthony himself. It had been guarded, and excessively careful, and might well indicate that Angus Mount Ltd. were inclined as a general rule to play for safety. He would wait until the morrow before he came to any really definite conclusions. What Hoare told him should clear the air in every way and put an end to the labyrinthine meanderings of conjecture.

VII

Anthony's telephone rang, shrill and insistent, at twenty-two minutes to twelve on the following morning. When he answered it, he heard the welcome voice of Monkhouse at the other end.

"Bathurst speaking," he said quietly.

"Oh—good morning, Bathurst—Hilary Monkhouse this end. Re your call here yesterday. You were probably expecting me?"

"Good morning. Yes, I was. You're punctual! But I was hoping you would be."

"Good man. Both rugged and noble of you. Well—I'm frightfully sorry—I hardly know how to begin—but you're on a 'stumer'. It's damned bad luck, but you can't help it—it goes that way sometimes."

Anthony replied in quiet tones. "How do you mean, Monkhouse? I don't know that I quite understand you."

"Well—it's like this. Hoare hasn't been into the office for a couple of days, and we've heard this morning from his place at Hassocks, in Sussex, that he's in the throes of a nervous breakdown and mustn't smell the whiff even of business for at least six months. Which is distinctly 'no bon' from your particular point of view. See what I mean?"

Anthony received the bombshell with the dignity of silence. "I see," he remarked eventually. "Rather puts the lid on it, doesn't it?"

"Does rather, old man. If you look at it sensibly. As I feel sure that you will."

Anthony attacked again. "There's nobody else at your place, I suppose, whom I could see in your Mr. Hoare's stead?"

He could almost hear Monkhouse rejecting the suggestion at its birth. "H'm," came the reply, "afraid not, old chap. No—we couldn't manage that. Everybody else here would feel exactly as I do about the matter. That it's Hoare's particular cup of tea and only his. So you see there's nothing more I can do about it for you. Much as I should like to. No—it's the bundle, old man. You've 'had it', in other words."

Anthony realized that it was time to accept the inevitable—with inward irritation but outwardly with as much grace as he could muster in the circumstances. He translated this realization into effect. "In that case, then, I must thank you for your kindly intentions, accept the will for the deed and retire from the arena. Thank you, Monkhouse."

Anthony thoughtfully replaced the receiver and retired to his big armchair to consider this new aspect of the problem. So Hoare wouldn't play ball—eh? That was how the situation appeared to him at first blush. Hoare wouldn't play—yet awhile—and, like many other people caught in similar circumstances, had deliberately taken refuge in that popular asylum, *"hors de combat"*. The more Anthony thought over these new features of the problem the more he came to the conclusion that Angus Mount Ltd. were deliberately steering clear of the case directly it threatened to become open warfare. They were content to rely on the work done by Kenneth Smith, Living-stone and Luttrell's agent, privately—and more or less under cover.

After a period of intensive thought, Anthony knew that he must now return to Angel by the first convenient train and see the Schofields immediately he got there. There was this about it—his journey to London hadn't turned out entirely profitless. Although he had not gained as much information as he would have wished, he had gained *some*, and from one point of view at least, had progressed in the right direction.

CHAPTER III

I

MADDISON met him in the vestibule as he entered the "Bear and Ragged Staff". From the celerity of the contact, Anthony formed the opinion there and then that Maddison had been waiting for him with deliberate intent.

"Hallo, Mr. Bathurst," he said, with a somewhat unusual cheerfulness, "didn't know you'd been away. It wasn't till dinner last evening that I missed you."

"Yes. I had no option. Great nuisance—interrupting a case—but there you are—you get it sometimes, and what can't be cured must be endured."

"Oh, quite. I've been in the same position more than once. Any luck?"

Anthony flashed a quick glance at him. He thought that he detected a note of confidence in Maddison's tone.

"No," he replied, "nothing to wave flags about. You?" Maddison shook his head. "Same as you, Brother Smut. Taking one pace forward and two back. Nothing pleasin' at all." Maddison stopped. But continued almost immediately. "By the way—you've been in demand while you've been absent—somewhat. You've been wanted, as a matter of fact. That's how I knew you weren't here." Anthony's brows furrowed. "Wanted? Whom by?"

Maddison winked at him. "Ah—that's the point! The *interesting* point. The inquiries for you were made by a lady. An authentic lovely, too. A very satisfactory piece of homework indeed. I couldn't help feeling how unlucky you were not to be in when she called."

"Kind of you, I'm sure," murmured Anthony, "and in the midst of all this sympathy, did you happen to hear the lady's name?"

"No—I didn't. And that wasn't my fault, I assure you, Bathurst. Because I craned my ears to catch it and failed. I may as well come clean." Maddison grinned as he made his confession.

"Ah, well," remarked Anthony, "it's not of any great consequence. If she really wants to see me, no doubt she'll call again."

He turned away from Maddison and made his way to his own room. He wasn't at all mystified by Maddison's announcement. The inquirer had been Priscilla Schofield without a doubt. And he felt that the odds—and fairly heavy odds at that—were that she had important information for him. A condition which entirely fitted the resolve he had made to return to Angel and which he had already put into practice. Anthony thrust his hands into his trouser-pockets and began to pace the room. But not for long. He decided to stick to his original intention to visit the Schofields after dinner that evening.

When the time came he put this decision into execution after previously telephoning to Colonel Schofield to expect him that evening. The Colonel was delighted to hear that he intended coming.

"If you can manage to make your way out here, Bathurst, Priscilla will be able to run you back later on in the car. I'm sorry I can't send her in to Angel for you, because she's taken herself out for the day and I very much doubt whether she'll be back in time to come for you. She warned me when she went that she'd be pretty late."

Anthony accepted the situation as Colonel Schofield outlined it and arrived at the Schofield residence at about a quarter to nine. Priscilla, to his satisfaction, was in. She came to him with glowing eyes.

"Mr. Bathurst, I can't tell you how pleased I am that you've come this evening. In a way it's an answer to my prayers. Actually, I've been trying to get in touch with you since yesterday afternoon. I even went to the 'Bear and Ragged Staff' to see if I could find you. But even there I missed fire. You weren't there. I've been frightfully worried about it."

"I'm sorry, Miss Schofield, to think that I've been so elusive. As a matter of fact I've been in town making certain inquiries with regard to your friend Langley. And it's in connexion with that visit that I've come to see you this evening. What it means is this. We shall have to exchange our information."

"That's right. I shall love to." Her eyes were still shining. "Tell me yours first, Mr. Bathurst—will you, please?"

"Of course. I intended to. First of all, I desired to know as much as I possibly could of the genesis of this affair. So to that end I used the 'Yard'. The 'Yard' has amazing resources which it can call upon— as you probably know."

Priscilla nodded. "Yes. I do understand that. Daddy always insists on it as a solid and solemn fact. He rubs it into me almost as a matter of course. Well—how did you get on?"

"Well—I found out certain important facts. About Langley, I mean. Without anything to go on. I was working, you see, so much in the dark. Langley was a private inquiry agent, who invariably worked on his own. In this instance he was employed to come to Angel by a firm who trade as Angus Mount Ltd." Anthony broke off to ask Priscilla a question. "Does the name convey anything to you."

Priscilla shook a puzzled head. "Not a thing." She turned to her father. "Angus Mount Ltd. Does that name strike any familiar chord with you, Daddy?"

The Colonel coughed. "What name was that?"

Priscilla repeated the name. The Colonel's face took on an expression of seraphic joy. "Angus Mount! I should say so! Good lord—rather! One of the biggest bookies in London Town. Angus Mount—eh? Household word in sporting circles. 'Angus always pays.' So that's who friend Langley was connected with—eh? Ve-ry interesting. Very interesting indeed! Ah, well—so we're just beginning to learn things. Go on, Bathurst. You've whetted my appetite."

"I'm afraid that's easier said than done, sir. Because I haven't very much more to tell you. All my subsequent attempts to obtain further information failed. Why exactly Angus Mount sent Langley down here—I don't know. I endeavoured to find out by a series of questions, but they stymied me. All I can say with any degree of confidence is this. Down here in Angel, Angus Mount did have certain customers. They describe these people as their clients. You know of course what I mean. People who have credit accounts and who are in the habit of betting with Angus Mount Ltd. at S.P. or Tote prices just as they choose. Langley was sent down here on some errand or investigation which in some way touches all or some of these Angel people. There's little doubt that Angus Mount Ltd. are seriously concerned with regard to some particular aspect of them. That's the sum total of my knowledge, sir. Not a lot, perhaps, but definitely a starting-point."

"H'm," said Colonel Schofield, "might be anything, mightn't it? Anything from common or garden bad debts to a case for Tattersall's Committee. H'm—not much there for us to discuss that I can see."

Anthony addressed himself to Priscilla. "So much for what I've discovered from my jaunt to town. And before you tell me *your* news, please answer me one question. You told me, when you first saw me, of Langley's encounter with certain people. People who live, I believe, not very far from here. At least, that condition would apply to some of them. Would you be good enough to repeat their names—such as he told you?"

Priscilla puckered her brows. "Yes, I can do that. He picked up some of the names. I think I shall be able to recall them. One was called the 'Professor'—that's not much good to you, is it? Although, personally, I think his real name's Gunter. Another Layman—and another Newman."

"Thank you," said Anthony. "Gunter and Layman were among the names mentioned to me by Angus Mount. Significant, isn't it?"

But Priscilla was adding to her previous statement. "Newman was the man who had two shops in Angel. One, a sort of pastry-cook tea-shop, and the other—I *believe*—was a baker's near the Racecourse somewhere. Didn't I tell you that before?"

"You mentioned the man's name, Miss Schofield, and the fact that he had two shops in Angel. But I don't think you mentioned the proximity of one of them to the Racecourse. But now I'm delighted to say that I find that last fact both interesting and illuminating. Well—that's that! And now its over and done with I'm prepared for your item of news."

"My news is good." replied Priscilla—almost mischievously.

"Good?" echoed Anthony queryingly.

"Yes, good. Or at any rate, relatively good. Isn't it, Daddy?" She turned appealingly to Colonel Schofield.

"You say so, my dear. Though I'm hanged if I can see what proof you have of it. See what Bathurst thinks."

"I haven't any proof—as proof goes. I merely trust my womanly instinct. And you know that you can always bank on that as a safe bet. You wait a moment, Mr. Bathurst, and I'll show you something."

Priscilla walked out of the room as she spoke. Anthony, interested to hear what was coming, waited for her return. Colonel Schofield filled in the interval.

"I think you'll find what Priscilla has to show you—interesting. There are no two ways about that. But whether you'll invest it with the importance that she does, I take leave to doubt. Personally, I don't think you will. Still—you'll be able to judge for yourself." The Colonel subsided.

But the silence which followed was not for long. Priscilla entered again waving a sheet of paper. It seemed to Anthony's eye, as he caught his first glimpse of it, to be a fairly large sheet of paper.

"This," announced Priscilla, "is a proof to me that Richard Langley is not dead—but alive. Or, at the worst, was alive a few days ago. Which, you must admit, is relatively good news, as I said."

Anthony raised his eyebrows. "Explain, please, Miss Schofield. I'm all attention. But I warn you, I shall take a fair amount of convincing."

"All right, Mr. Bathurst—I'll accept your challenge gladly. Look at this, if you please."

Priscilla took the sheet of paper she held and placed it on a small Sheraton table close to Anthony.

"Look at this, Mr. Bathurst, will you, please?"

Anthony went over at her invitation and leant across the table. Priscilla spread the paper in front of them both.

"Torn," said Anthony, "from an old magazine. Bound copy, I should say, in all probability. It was a common practice in our parents' time to have magazines bound into annual volumes. My own people had many bound copies of the old *Strand Magazine*."

"Read this," said Priscilla simply.

Scrawled along the margin was a string of words. They had been scrawled in pencil in such a manner that they were only just legible. Anthony read it. *"Miss Priscilla Schofield, c/o Colonel Schofield, Eden Road, Angel."* He looked at Priscilla. "Well?"

She nodded. "That," she declared, "was written by Richard Langley."

"Certain of that?"

"Um! Positive!"

"Recognize the writing?"

"No-o. Can't say that. Never seen Mr. Langley's writing in my life. But I know it's his all the same. Instinct, Mr. Bathurst. My womanly instinct that I referred to just now. Besides—who else would want to write to me in such extraordinary circumstances, knowing what we do know?"

Anthony made no reply. He leant over the table, gazing at the torn-out magazine page. Priscilla came across to him again and turned it over in front of him.

"Now look at the reverse side, Mr. Bathurst. I think you'll find it even more interesting."

Anthony gazed at the other side of the printed sheet. He was utterly and entirely surprised at what he saw there. The page was headed. "Confessions". Anthony, after a moment or so's consideration, recognized it for what it was. It was typical, he knew, of an old-fashioned feature of magazine production for a celebrity of sorts to be invited to list his "favourite" choices with regard to many matters such as food, drink, literature, music and kindred things. This page of confessions had been originally completed by Danny Maher, the onetime famous jockey. Here were the questions with the original answers as they purported to emanate from the American horseman, and this is how Anthony saw them.

He first of all counted them. There were sixteen of them. Danny Maher had answered the questions that follow, presumably in his own handwriting. But with one exception his choices had been struck through subsequently and alternatives substituted.

What is your favourite meat? ~~Beef~~. Lamb.
What is your favourite vegetable? ~~Green Peas~~ Asparagus.
What is your favourite fruit? ~~Melon~~. Nectarine.
What is your favourite poultry? ~~Chicken~~. Goose.
What is your favourite flower? ~~Carnation~~. Lily of the Valley.
What is your favourite English watering-place? ~~Brighton~~. Eastbourne.
What is your favourite season of the year? ~~Summer~~. Yuletide.
What is your favourite day of the week? ~~Sunday~~. Saturday.
What is your favourite tree? ~~Oak~~. Plane.
What is your favourite name for a girl? ~~Helen~~. Iris.
What is your favourite month of the year? ~~June~~. December.
What is your favourite name for a boy? ~~Charles~~. Eric.
Who is your favourite author? ~~Dickens~~. Reade.
Who is your favourite musician? ~~Handel~~. Wagner.
What is your favourite novel? *~~Uncle Tom's Cabin~~. Esmond.*
Who was your favourite race-horse? Bayardo.

As previously stated, Maher's choices had been struck through in pencil scrawl, scarcely legible—as the marginal address had been—and other choices substituted, as shown by the amendments. With one exception, however—that of the last-named selection. For some reason or other the choice of the mighty "Bayardo" had been allowed to remain unaltered. Anthony frowned at what he saw in front of him and looked in wonderment from Priscilla to Colonel Schofield.

"First of all," he said, "and before I make any serious comment on this matter, may I ask you from where you got this?"

"Yes, you may," answered Priscilla—somewhat proudly, Anthony thought. "I expected you to ask me that. That was brought to me yesterday afternoon by a messenger from the Snow-white Sanitary Steam Laundry, of High Street, Angel! That causes you some surprise, Mr. Bathurst, doesn't it?"

Anthony thought it over. "Well," he remarked eventually, "I suppose I can assume it was accompanied by some sort of explanation?"

"Yes, I suppose you could call it that. One of the roundsmen employed by the laundry brought it. His story was as follows. It had been picked up yesterday morning on the floor of the laundry's 'sorting-of-delivery' room. What have you got to say to that, Mr. Bathurst?"

Anthony countered with another question. "How had it come there? Any explanation of that particular point?"

"No. That's the rather disappointing part about it. I'm ready to admit that. It was just picked up off the floor. One of the girls who were engaged in the sorting of the dirty laundry that had been brought in from that day's collection noticed it, picked it up and scrutinized it. Then she saw my name on it, and as we happen to send our stuff to the Snow-white, she asked one of the roundsmen to bring it to me."

Anthony considered the statement. "Interesting—without a doubt," he commented—"exceedingly interesting. And now that you've dealt with the 'exhibit', as I'll call this paper, may I ask you what you make of it yourself?"

Anthony waited for the reply to be forthcoming. Priscilla spoke to her father.

"Well, Daddy, what do you make of it? You have first go at Mr. Bathurst and leave me to take second innings."

Colonel Schofield shook his head. "I'm sunk! Absolutely sunk! Scuppered! So it's not the slightest use appealing to me. Your lead, Priscilla."

Priscilla pursed her lips before she answered. When she spoke, she spoke slowly, calmly and deliberately.

"I believe—and my belief is firm and unshaken—that this message came to me from Mr. Langley. That in some way it's been directed to me, because he needs my help. That he desires me to know where he is. That's all—but it's enough in its way, isn't it? Don't you think so?"

Anthony heard her out and remained silent. Priscilla attacked again.

"Well, Mr. Bathurst—and what's your reply to all that?"

Anthony smiled at her. "There's one thing, Miss Schofield—I haven't contradicted you, have I?"

"I know you haven't. That's the thought that's uppermost in my mind. But does that necessarily mean that you agree with what I've said?"

There was a twinkle in Anthony's eye. "It might, mightn't it? There are more unlikely contingencies."

"Don't tease! It's not worthy of you. Besides, this is far too serious a matter for anybody to joke about."

"Miss Schofield—your reproof is just. I stand abashed. Angel shall be my washpot and over Eden will I cast my shoe. I'll come to the point. That's what you want me to do, isn't it? I *do* think this page of stuff came from Langley—but before I say any more in support of this contention I'd like to ask you one more question. May I?"

"Ask on," said Priscilla demurely.

"Do you think that Langley himself actually wrote anything that we can see on this old page?"

"Yes. I do. Most certainly! Why?"

"I just wanted to see which way your thoughts were travelling."

"I see."

"Yet another question, Miss Schofield. Which words of these we have here do you think were written by Langley?"

Priscilla pointed one by one to the words of her selection. "This address—my name, etc.—and these words in pencil that have been scrawled on top of Danny Maher's choices. I read them as *Lamb, Asparagus, Nectarine, Goose, Lily of the Valley, Eastbourne, Yuletide, Saturday, Plane, Iris, December, Eric, Reade, Wagner*, and *Esmond*. There isn't one for the last one. It seems to be missing."

"You must be Irish!" said Anthony; "you're as good as the chap who trod on the stair that wasn't there."

Priscilla laughed. "You know very well what I mean."

"Yes, I expect I do."

Colonel Schofield in his chair by the fireside was heard to mutter—"Fantastic—if you ask me—all of it! Lot of tripe. Doesn't mean anything."

"Well," said Priscilla again, "am I being so terribly absurd?"

"As a matter of fact, Miss Schofield, you're being far from absurd. On the contrary, you're dead right."

"I knew it," she said simply. "I knew it all the time in my heart."

The Colonel snorted his disapproval. "She knew it—in her heart! Admirable sentiments, no doubt, but they cut no ice with me. No, sir. I want something a good deal more concrete than that to convince me. What do you say, Bathurst?"

Anthony smiled at the Colonel's outburst. "I'm not expressing my opinion, sir, upon any dictation from my heart—you may rest assured of that. On the contrary, my statement that this message comes from Langley is based on what my brain tells me."

"Suits me," replied the Colonel with composure, "but please explain how you've arrived at that conclusion. Then I shall be in a position to criticize and perhaps attach more importance to the statement."

Anthony accepted the challenge. "I shall be only too pleased to do so, sir."

"Good. That's the stuff that suits me. Let's hear your reasons, then."

Anthony took the old magazine page, faded and almost brown with age, and passed it over to Colonel Schofield.

"You can see what this was originally, sir. It's obviously a page of so-called 'Confessions' by a famous jockey of the time, as to certain of his selections, favouritisms, likes and dislikes in various directions. Over each one of these original choices, with the exception of the very last one, there has been scrawled in pencil—some are scarcely legible, you will agree—an alternative choice. Have a glance at them for yourself, sir."

Colonel Schofield took the list and scrutinized it carefully. "Yes, Bathurst, I can see very well what you mean. There are three of them, as you say, almost illegible. But I take them to be respectively, Nectarine, Iris and Wagner."

"Quite right, sir. I came to the same conclusions myself. And Miss Schofield is also in agreement. Good! Then we've reached a mutually agreed starting-point. If you list them in order—*Lamb*, *Asparagus*, *Nectarine*, *Goose*, *Lily of the Valley*, *Eastbourne* and *Yuletide*, and then take the initial letters of those nouns, we shall, minus any difficulty whatever, arrive at the name of 'Langley'. The effort is simplicity itself!"

"By Jove!" said Colonel Schofield, "so we do. Very ingenious, I must say! Very neat indeed. And, of course, pretty obvious, when you come to give the matter a little serious consideration. Don't you agree with me, Priscilla?"

Priscilla nodded—her eyes sparkling with excitement. "Why, yes, of course. And I hadn't the intelligence to see it. I must be the world's prize mutt. And if I looked at that list once, I must have looked at it a hundred times at least."

"So far, then," went on Anthony, "we've established the link of Langley. We'll proceed, then, from there. Following the same plan, and taking in order these choices, *Saturday, Plane, Iris, December, Eric, Reade, Wagner, Esmond* and *Bayardo*, we reach a second line of solution that adds up to 'Spider Web'. Why it should spell thus, for the moment I can't pretend to explain. All I can assert as a preliminary is that it does."

"Oh—but I can explain," burst in Priscilla impetuously, "and I know the allusion. The 'Spider's Web' is a tea-shop in Angel. Its called the 'Old Spider's Web' actually, but that's near enough. Mr. Langley went in for tea one afternoon."

"In that case, then," said Anthony, "we can say with confidence that we've very definitely got somewhere. Thanks to you and to your laundry, Miss Schofield. Please tell me more."

"I don't know that there's such a lot more for me to tell. Excited as I am, I mustn't exaggerate importances. You know what I mean—I don't want you to get me wrong. But from what Mr. Langley told me I feel positive that he had been to the 'Spider's Web' for tea. One afternoon—about a week ago I should think. Not a lot in that perhaps. Just as a bare fact by itself. But it *might* mean something—and now I've thought of something else."

"Good," said Anthony—"a girl after my own heart. Please tell me what it is and put me out of my misery."

Priscilla didn't hesitate. She was eagerness personified. "What I've thought of, Mr. Bathurst, falls almost naturally into two halves. Two sections or categories, rather. The first category is factual. The second is merely conjectural."

"Let's have the factual first. It's more important by reason of its being factual."

"Of course. I saw that myself directly I started to speak. The 'Spider's Web' is kept—or shall I say belongs to—that very man, Newman, whom we've already discussed."

"The two-teashop man, you mean?"

Priscilla nodded. "Exactly, Mr. Bathurst. That's the man."

"Excellent! Now let's have the second section—what you term conjectural."

"It's this. That I'm definitely of the opinion that Mr. Langley went to the 'Spider's Web' *deliberately*. In fact, I know he did."

"Why?" cut in her father.

"Well—don't you remember that he told us that he felt pretty certain in his own mind that Newman was one of the men he'd met in the house over the way?"

"Damn it—so he did! Yes—you're quite right, my girl. I do remember it now you mention it."

Anthony concentrated on Priscilla. "Miss Schofield, answer this, please. Did Langley definitely *tell* you he'd been to this shop?"

"No. I don't think so. He didn't get quite so far as that. But from what he hinted to me, I feel pretty certain about it."

"Your idea was that he was on to something?"

"Yes. That's just how I felt—and still feel—about it."

Anthony fell to thought. "As I see things—its tremendously important," he remarked eventually. He went on. "I'll try to explain what I mean. Does the inclusion of the 'Spider's Web' term in the message mean that it has a *new* and *sinister* significance, which Langley is trying to convey to us, or is it but the mere confirmation, as it were, of this previous idea that you say he hinted to you? That, it seems to me, is the important point at issue."

He looked at Priscilla and the Colonel as he spoke. "You see the point?"

"Absolutely," said the girl.

The Colonel grunted non-committally and handed Anthony his cigarette-case. Anthony took a cigarette, lit it and drew the smoke down into his lungs.

"I'm inclined to think, myself," he declared slowly, "that there's something 'new' about it—something entirely new—and something pretty dreadful at that. I propose to proceed now, with your assent, on the assumption that that version of mine's the correct one."

"May I butt in?" asked Priscilla tremulously.

"Give me a couple of minutes before you do," said Anthony, "because I want to pursue something." He waited for a moment or so before he went on. Priscilla watched him almost as though she were fascinated.

"I want to ask you," he said—"to ask you both—why you think Langley chose this method of communicating with you?"

"That's just what I was about to ask you," put in Priscilla breathlessly, "because I find it just a wee bit puzzling."

"Tell me exactly, Miss Schofield," said Anthony, "what you're thinking."

"Well," returned Priscilla, "I look at it like this. If Mr. Langley could do what we *think* he has done, in connexion with this old book-page, why didn't he send me a letter? I mean a proper letter. I can't quite understand how the latter could have presented any more difficulty than the former."

"Exactly," said Anthony. "I was coming to that myself. I've been considering the point for some little time. But have you looked at it *carefully*, Miss Schofield?"

"How do you mean, carefully, Mr. Bathurst?"

"Well—let's assume as a starting-point that Langley is, or was, under some form of restraint somewhere."

She nodded.

"Agreed. I think he is. I don't think that there's any doubt about it."

"Right. And let me say at once that I agree with you. Certainly, as far as the past tense goes. What does that mean, then? Let's examine the possibilities. Firstly, I should say that in all probability he's well watched. Too closely watched and guarded to be able to write a letter—or anything in the nature of a letter—to you. To be able to do that he must be in possession of paper—some sort of writing-paper—and would undoubtedly be seen—that is to say observed—when writing to you. He would have a serious task to conceal the effort so successfully that his captors would know nothing about what he was doing. Is the point made?"

"Yes. I see that." Priscilla nodded again.

"Good! Let's proceed from there then. If Langley *is* under this restraint—that is to say kept a prisoner somewhere—he must be in an apartment of some kind. That goes without saying. Well, then, it seems to me that, in that apartment where Langley is, there is, or was, a bound annual volume of an old magazine which at this precise moment is minus a page. That's how I see things, Miss Schofield."

"And I think you're right," chimed in Priscilla.

"So do I," supplemented the Colonel—"I think you've hit the nail on the head, Bathurst."

"I'm gratified to hear your opinions. Now then! If Langley *had* access to this book, which, under surveillance, he could easily pretend to be reading, he could much more simply scrawl the keywords on that 'Confessions' page, and at odd moments, too, than he could write an ordinary letter without it being obvious to his captors what he was up to. And that, in my opinion, is what Langley has done, and the method by which he did it."

Priscilla sat silent as she considered the salient points of Anthony's argument, but she nodded her head assentingly from time to time.

"Granted all that," boomed Colonel Schofield—"and I'll concede that it's feasible enough—what I certainly *don't* see at the moment is how Langley got that tell-tale page *out* of his place of captivity. There's one thing in writing it and another in disposing of it. There's a poser for you, Bathurst."

"Yours is a good question, Colonel, and it opens up a wider field of conjecture."

"I'll say it does," remarked Colonel Schofield, chuckling to himself.

"Isn't it fairly obvious how he did it?" said his daughter.

Anthony smiled at this confident statement. "Well, Miss Schofield, and what's the explanation that you have to offer us?"

"Why, surely, Mr. Bathurst—that Mr. Langley hid it in his laundry! What other explanation could there be?"

Anthony shook his head and thrust a question at her. "What laundry could Langley send out—if our assumption that he's a prisoner somewhere is correct? I can't believe that he's a prisoner with all home comforts. H. and C. Fruit garden, well stocked, with use of library and study. If so—it's something different from anything in that line that has so far come my way."

Priscilla pursed her lips and flushed a little. "Yes—I see what you mean. I hadn't thought of it quite in that light. I'm sorry."

"Well—you see the point now, don't you?"

"Of course. But all the same I—" Priscilla stopped.

Anthony appeared to sense her difficulty. "Let me help you," he said. "I'll pick the argument up, as it were, from where you left off. I think you're only *partly* right about Langley and the laundry. The laundry point, of course, must be conceded. But it wasn't *his* laundry. From where it actually *had* come to the Snow-white Steam Laundry, I'll attempt to verify first thing tomorrow morning. In fact, events are crowding so thick upon us that I'm promising myself a busy day tomorrow in more than one direction."

"Don't you think," said Priscilla gravely, "that there's every indication from this communication we have here that Mr. Langley is being kept a prisoner at the 'Spider's Web' itself? Because I do."

"I think everything points that way, Miss Schofield, and that's also a matter upon which I intend to get busy tomorrow. The laundry inquiry may settle the point."

"If he's there," snorted the Colonel, "why wait, sir? Dammit—why wait an instant? Let's have action first and talk afterwards. Neither you nor I belong to the great parrot-house at Westminster, do we? Well then, sir. I say 'get busy'. To delay a day—or even an hour—might have fatal results."

The Colonel subsided after his impassioned outburst and breathed heavily down his waistcoat. Anthony replied.

"Possibly, sir. But I don't think it's probable. Had Langley's enemies been out to take drastic action against him—and by that I mean been out to silence him in the most effective way possible—I don't think that they would have delayed such action. I think it's a fairly safe bet that they would have acted at once—or certainly pretty quickly. That's why I think I shan't be risking *too* much by letting things remain as they are until tomorrow morning."

"H'mp," grunted the Colonel, "don't like it! Don't like it a little bit, sir. Why not turn it straight over to the Police?"

"What have I got to go on, sir?" asked Anthony patiently—"this old magazine-page with these scrawled pencilled words. What would the ordinary policeman think of it? No, Colonel Schofield, I must feel more certain of my ground before I trouble the Police with this."

"Bathurst," exploded the Colonel, unable to contain himself, "you're forgetting something. Something damned important, too."

"I don't think I am, sir—but to what are you referring? Please tell me."

"To the indisputable fact that there's already *one* dead man in this case! And it seems to me that before we know where we are we shall be faced with two."

"Langley himself, do you mean?"

"Of course," grunted the Colonel, "who else? I should have thought the fact was pretty obvious to you. It *is* to me, despite what you say about their delaying action."

Anthony meditated on what Schofield had said. Eventually he replied, but he chose carefully the words of that reply.

"I'll promise you this, sir. The moment that I feel Langley is in serious danger of losing his life I'll act immediately, and be hanged to everything else. At the moment, candidly, and as I explained to you just now, I don't think that that danger exists. No—I won't say that. I'll amend that to a statement that I don't regard the danger as imminent."

But Colonel Schofield stuck doggedly to his point. "Look here, Bathurst. I'm not satisfied. I'm a man of few words, but damn it all I like to say what I think. This is how it strikes me. If these scoundrels have already killed a man—and you'll admit that things look very much like it—and Langley *knows* something about that murder—then there's already a pretty good incentive for them to get rid of Langley. Dead men tell no tales, my boy. One of the soundest axioms you'll ever run across in your little trip down the ages."

"I agree to a point, sir. *If* Langley knows something! It all depends, as I see it, on what Langley *does* know. And how much. Personally, I don't feel that Langley was ever much more than 'on the track' of something. And it's on that assessment I'm measuring his chances of safety. Believe me—if he'd known much—he'd have been put out like snuffing a candle."

"Very well, my boy. Have it your way. I'll give way to you. Your experience of criminals is undoubtedly more extensive than mine. What's your next step in the matter—did you say?"

"That, sir," replied Anthony, "I haven't decided. I shall make up my mind on that first thing tomorrow morning. It may even depend on the weather."

II

Punctually at half past eleven on the following morning Anthony entered the tea-room bearing the sign of the "Old Spider's Web". As he entered, he gave a quick glance round, and seeing a knot of young people descending a stairway just to the left, he followed them. To his intense satisfaction he felt in good fettle. His telephone inquiry of the Snow-white Laundry had elicited the fact that the laundry had "collected" from the "Spider's Web" establishment a couple of days before Priscilla had received the scrawled communication.

This fact he considered of the highest significance, and it clinched his already formed intention of visiting the "Spider's Web" at the earliest opportunity. Anthony descended the staircase of the tearoom and his first reaction to the artificial decoration which confronted him was similar to Langley's. The counterfeit cobwebs, the imitation mildew, the pseudo-peeling crust of plinth and plaster struck him as distinctly unpleasing, but at least possessing some degree of originality. He took a seat at a small table, over which an old oak beam in the ceiling almost touched his head when he stood at his full height.

A young girl came to his side almost immediately and quietly accepted his order for coffee. When she had disappeared up the staircase, Anthony seized the chance to look round and to take stock of his surroundings. Three other tables were occupied. Three women of uncertain age were at a table in the far corner, the young people who had preceded him were at the next table, and at another table, almost in the middle of the place, a girl sat in the company of an engineer of the Merchant Navy.

Anthony then turned his attention to the apartment itself. It had obviously been originally the cellar of an old house before the latter had been converted into a shop. Its shape was unusual. Something like, Anthony decided, a grotesque design such as one cuts from strips of paper. It had odd corners and unexpectedly placed alcoves.

The young girl who was serving him brought the coffee and then Anthony noticed that the other customers in the room were being attended to by a thin, rather sullen-faced woman whom he at once classified as a foreigner. "French," he thought, "probably—but I wouldn't bank on it. Might be any thing. Probability, though, French or Belgian." He heard his waitress address the woman as "Madame", an appellation which fitted the conclusion at which he had just arrived. "Interesting," he murmured to himself. "Interesting place—the 'Old Spider's Web'—removed rather from the usual run of teashops. I wonder what's behind it all."

He sipped his coffee without hurrying and let his eyes travel round the room again. After a time, one of the alcoves in the far right-hand corner began to offer him a more than normal amount of interest. For one thing, its shape, to say the least of it, was odd. The angle of the wall was definitely much more acute than one would have expected, and Anthony began to think—and to think furiously. It occurred to him that this cellar in which he sat might well be but a part of the original cellar, which had probably extended for some appreciable distance under the original house or dwelling, whatever it may have been. This thought, although satisfactory from one point of view, was distinctly disturbing from another—that of Langley's ultimate safety. Anthony's eyes travelled to the particular alcove again. He measured as a mental calculation the height and the distance across the opening before finishing his cup of coffee. As he replaced his cup in the saucer, he heard a cough almost unpleasantly close to his elbow. Looking up, he saw the sullen-lipped woman whom he had classed as foreign standing at his side. He had an uneasy suspicion that she must have been there, or near there, for some time without his being aware of it.

"If you have finished—will you please vacate the table? There is not time for people to sit about. The gentleman should remember that there are other people waiting who have not all day at their disposal."

The accent and the phrasing were un-English. Anthony smiled and ignored the discourtesy.

"I'm sorry." He indicated two unoccupied tables. "You have other tables—not in use."

The reply came—chill and from thin, shrewish lips. "That is nothing. The tables are booked. The people for them will be here in a few moments. Please pay your bill at the desk upstairs."

Anthony bowed and made his way up the staircase, paid his bill and walked out of the shop thoughtfully. As he strolled back to the "Bear and Ragged Staff" he debated in his mind whether he had enough to take to Lawton for action. He had not seen the inquisitive Maddison for some little time now, and he considered that it was quite on the cards that the man had returned to London. Another thing—he felt pretty certain—and with some misgivings at that—that the woman of the teashop addressed as "Madame", who had stood at his elbow, had been more than ordinarily observant of his interest in the topography of the cellar. He knew now that it was a pity he had shown his hand, if only to the extent of that careful scrutiny he had given to the apartment. That part of it, however, was over now, and Anthony well knew that it was no use crying over spilt milk. The only clear plan that he saw in front of him as he walked along that morning was that of immediate action. Action, too, which he felt he alone could take. He could not expect Lawton to make bricks without straw or to envisage a serious fire minus even a thin column of smoke. Problem was—how could he contrive to nose round the "Old Spider's Web" and afford himself more tangible satisfaction? This must happen obviously after the shop had been shut for the day. How he was going to effect this tour of inspection he was entirely unable to see at the moment.

But he tossed the carking care over his shoulder and decided to return to the "Spider's Web" that same afternoon for four o'clock tea. After that—anything might happen. If he kept his eyes well skinned during that second visit his brain might hit on something— you never knew! Anthony went in to lunch, therefore, with hope running high in his breast.

III

Maddison made no appearance at the luncheon table. Anthony thought that his ante-lunch idea with regard to him might well be true. After lunch he spent a lazy time in the lounge, refused the offer of afternoon tea and at a quarter to four set out again for the "Spider's Web".

When he arrived there he varied his previous procedure. Instead of descending to the cellar to have his tea, he went to the extreme end of the main room and sat down at a table near a line of windows. These windows, he soon saw, commanded a sort of mews which seemed to end in a cul-de-sac. Anthony ordered his tea—this time from a waitress whom he had not encountered before. When she had taken the order, Anthony took particular care to notice where she went. He saw that she passed through a doorway about halfway down the room and which led, in all probability, he considered, to the kitchens. The waitress brought his tea. So far, there was no sign of the sullen-lipped "Madame"—which fact was not worrying him in the least. As the waitress placed the tea-things in front of him, together with bread and butter, a small pot of jam and an assortment of small pastries, he looked up at her.

"What time do you close?" he asked.

"Eight o'clock, sir."

"As late as that—eh? I didn't think that you kept open as late as that. I am rather surprised. Do you serve dinner, then?"

"Oh yes, sir. We serve a three-course meal between half past six and eight."

Anthony smiled at her. "So that if I'm hungry this evening, I shall know where to come—eh?"

"Yes, sir, that's right. It's quite a nice dinner, too."

"What do you charge for this evening meal?"

"Five shillings, sir—if you have the *table d'hôte*."

"Good," returned Anthony. "One of these evenings I'll pop in and try it out. You know—when I'm feeling really hungry. Is it served in this room?"

"Yes, sir. You must come in here. This is the only room in which dinner is served. We only use the place down the stairs for afternoon teas and morning coffee."

"I see. Many thanks for the information."

Anthony got through his tea with celerity after the girl had gone, paid his bill and cleared off. With the memory of his experience of that morning fresh in his mind, it was not part of his plan to remain on the premises for any longer than was absolutely necessary, and thereby, possibly, draw undue attention to himself. For in his brain there had been born just the glimmerings of a plan. Whether he had a reasonable chance of carrying it out successfully he was unable at that juncture to gauge. That chance he would be in a position to assess more accurately when he returned for dinner in the evening. But it had occurred to him as he had been sitting there that the doorway which presumably led to the kitchen might present certain moderately attractive possibilities. Possibilities, too, which he could measure later on without running any particularly minatory risks. In other words, Anthony, as he wended his way back to the "Bear and Ragged Staff", had definite designs upon that connecting door.

IV

Anthony came back to the "Spider's Web" at twenty minutes past seven. He had chosen this time deliberately. To his gratification, the waitress who had attended to him that afternoon was close to the table he selected and came across to him with a smile directly she noticed his arrival. He looked at the *table d'hôte* details she presented to him and declared for minestrone soup, fried halibut and a sweet. The quality of the food turned out to be considerably better than he had anticipated, and it was close on eight o'clock when he finished the third course and called for his bill.

When he had entered he had chosen a table which by reason of its position meant that he must traverse almost the entire length of the room in order to make his exit—and in that process of traversing would be compelled to pass the door which led, as he thought, to the kitchen. He knew, however, that herein would be his most ticklish moment, as it would be fatal to his plans should he collide with one of the waitresses on her way back from the kitchen to the dining-room. He had calculated, by observation, that there were five waitresses on duty in the dining-room, and if he could possibly arrange it, he would commence his move towards the door when he could see all the five of them busy round their respective tables.

At two minutes to the hour, and after he had waited for some little time, the condition for which he had been waiting prevailed, and Anthony moved off from his table and slipped quickly towards his first objective. It was his idea that by using this door which led from the main restaurant to the kitchen he might find a place of temporary concealment somewhere in another part of the establishment. He was in the passage in the twinkling of an eye, and, seeing no likely haven immediately to hand, made straight for a staircase which he saw ascending about half a dozen yards in front of him. Making quick decision, he padded up the flight of stairs almost noiselessly and softly turned the handle of a door immediately facing him. It was herein that he was taking one of his biggest chances, but for once the luck held and Anthony found himself standing in an empty room. A quick glance round it showed him that it was furnished as a bedroom. Realizing that the coast was temporarily clear, he stood for a few moments by the door, listening for any sound that might come from below. But none came—so Anthony looked at his watch, saw that the time was almost ten minutes past the hour, and then dived quickly and quietly under the bed. He knew that it might well be that he would be forced to spend some hours in this position, so first of all he took pains to make his posture as comfortable as possible in the circumstances. He had calculated that the shop portion of the establishment should be cleared up before the hands of the clock reached nine. Similarly, he reckoned that those who would eventually come upstairs for sleep would not do so until more like ten o'clock and past. It was his plan, therefore, to make his downstairs sally about a quarter past nine, that is to say round about the time when the majority of people at least would be somewhere between the dining-room and the bedroom in which he had concealed himself.

This, then, was the gaunt skeleton of his plan, deviations from which he knew full well might be rendered necessary at any given moment. Anthony, churning these matters in his mind, crouched beneath his bed and waited for his zero hour. The time passed on leaden wings, and several times he was compelled to shift to the support of his other elbow. At a quarter to nine, as his wrist-watch had just showed him, his heart raced to his mouth. For suddenly he heard the sound of steps outside the bedroom door, and then, to his consternation, the door itself opened. More footsteps told him that somebody had come into the room. It was a woman. Anthony was sure of that—from the light sound of the steps across the floor and from the soft swish of a skirt which accompanied that sound. He lay motionless beneath the bed and stifled his breathing as best he could. Heaven send that he wouldn't have to sneeze!

To his dismay—for he had hoped in his heart that the visit, seeing that time was yet comparatively young, would be but short-lived— he heard the woman seat herself but a few paces' distance from the bed. Certain noises came to his ears. For a time he found it difficult to identify them, but he rather fancied that the seated woman was brushing her hair. This might mean that she had it in mind to go to bed—a possibility which by no means fitted to the pattern of his plans. It meant, *inter alia*, that there would be an added risk for him when he attempted to make his exit from the bedroom. All the same, no benefit ever came to anybody through meeting trouble halfway, so Anthony decided to lie doggo for as long as he could and await imperturbably the course of events.

After a period of about five minutes, and which seemed almost endless to him as he lay there, he heard the hair-brusher replace the brushes on the trinket-tray of what was evidently the dressing-table, push back her chair and cross the room again to the door. When the door opened and was shut again and he also heard the sound of retreating footsteps, he knew that the visitor had gone and that he was once more alone in the room. The imminent peril had passed!

Anthony looked at his watch again. What he saw pleased him. It was just nine o'clock. He intended to make the vital move within the next quarter of an hour. He eased himself from under the bed, dusted his clothes, and crept out to listen again at the bedroom door. He knew what he was listening for—it was one of the pivots upon which his plan had been built up. He was listening for the sound of a radio somewhere in the house, broadcasting the nine o'clock news. For he had figured it out that the establishment was almost certain to possess a radio and that there was quite a strong possibility that the majority of the inhabitants of the household would be listening in at this particular time. After a wait of a few moments his ears caught the welcome sound for which they had been straining . . . it sounded to his ears something like "and this is Old Mother Hubbard reading it . . ." but he knew it wasn't that, and he was satisfied that, so far, all was going well for him.

He closed the door soundlessly behind him and without glancing back began to creep silently down the staircase. He reached the corridor by the main restaurant without mishap, and by now the words of the announcer broadcasting the news from another room moderately close at hand had become completely audible to him. All to the good, he thought, and now a straight journey for the tea-room in the redecorated cellar of the "Old Spider's Web". If he could only make it! He turned into the main room of the restaurant and to his intense relief saw that it was not entirely dark. One rather subdued electric light was burning at the far end of the room and showed him that the chairs had already been stacked for the room's cleaning before opening time on the morrow. He slithered into the restaurant proper, unchallenged and unseen, and made quickly for the stairs which descended to the cellar. If only he were lucky enough to find that place as quiet as the main room had been! Again the luck held, for as he entered he saw that the chairs had been stacked against the tables in the same manner that had been the case upstairs.

"Now," said Anthony to himself, "here I am and this is where I start to get to work." He walked straight over to the curiously-shaped alcove which had whetted his curiosity when he had drunk his morning coffee there but a few hours previously. In depth it was about two feet—barely any more than that. Anthony ran his fingers over the surface of the walls which formed its two sides. The unusual degree of the angle they formed with the back wall had stimulated his curiosity when he had first noticed them, and he was determined to put an idea he had in relation to them to the test. Nothing, however, rewarded his endeavours. There was no protuberance or knob and there was no unevenness on the surface. Anthony, therefore, having run his fingers up and down the surface of the wall two or three times, gave up the attempt and stood back a few paces to take another look at the problem which confronted him. Inasmuch as the light wasn't over-good, he took his electric torch from his pocket and allowed the light to play on the middle section of the alcove.

He grinned to himself as he did so. The imitation mildew and cobwebbed condition had been so artificially and so cleverly manufactured that it might well have been abandoned to desuetude for at least one generation by reason of this appearance. Then his eye caught sight of something which prompted him to look twice at it. At about a height of six feet—almost level with his own eyes—and across the angle of the right-hand wall, was poised a cunningly-executed imitation spider's web. The gossamer-like filaments were almost true to life. As Anthony looked at it, it occurred to him almost instantaneously that the position of this web—even though it had been artificially constructed—was peculiar. It looked strangely out of place. As though there were a definite purpose behind it, beyond the primary one of mere decoration. It wasn't quite in the position where one would have expected to find it.

Anthony went closer to it, scrutinized it even more carefully and then placed a fingertip against its centre. As he did so, he felt something yield to his gentle pressure, and with his heart exultant at this measure of success, he exercised a greater amount of strength. Without further ado, the back wall slid away gently and smoothly, as do the doors of certain trains, into a groove in the body of the wall, and he saw another apartment over the threshold. This was obviously part of the same original cellar as that in which he had recently stood. Before he crossed the threshold, however, Anthony, taking all the care he could, went back to the foot of the cellar staircase and listened intently. But all was quiet—no sound came to him from the regions above.

Anthony looked at his wrist-watch again. It was now twenty minutes past nine. He'd give the job another ten minutes. Not a moment longer. Beyond that time, he felt that he was seriously jeopardizing his margin of safety. Directly he crossed into the farther cellar he felt positive that this must be the place from which Langley had sent his message. It boasted a chair, a table with a few books on it and a mattress. The last-named article lay on the floor of the cellar in the extreme left-hand corner. But the place was empty now. Why was that? Also, following the same line of reasoning, where was Langley now? A chilling thought came to him. Had Colonel Schofield's fears been justified? Was Langley still alive? The assumption that he had been removed certainly brought with it no particular degree of comfort. But then Anthony began to reassure himself. It might be that, after all, he was barking up the wrong tree and that Langley had never been confined here. And as the thought was born in Anthony's brain, so, almost simultaneously, it died and he knew the worst. For his eyes caught the little array of books that lay on the table. He could see the title of the top one. His eyes read it from where he stood—*The Woman in the House, Annual Volume, 1908.*

"And I haven't the slightest doubt," he whispered to himself, "that page 277 of that annual volume is missing. I'll put the matter to the test."

Anthony walked over to the table and picked up the book. Yes—here was proof—absolute and counter-proofed. It was apparent to the most casual observer that page 277 had been torn out. Anthony realized now that there was nothing more that evening to keep him in the "Old Spider's Web". He knew what he had come to find out.

He replaced the annual volume of *The Woman in the House* for the year 1908 on the table, went back to the cellar tea-room, manipulated the sliding door of the alcove and prepared to leave the establishment. As he came out of the cellar room, he saw with a smile a heap of towels . . . it seemed that they had been flung carelessly across one of the larger tables . . . no doubt Langley had also seen them . . . or others similar. Yes—Langley had seen them!

V

Anthony came up the staircase from the cellar tea-room and found himself once again in the room of the main restaurant. The time now was half past nine, and there was still not a soul to be seen. The nine o'clock news with its supplementary reports, Anthony hoped, was still holding those of the inhabitants who had remained on the premises. He calmly walked to the door which opened out on to the street, unlatched it and stood there in the evening darkness. He carefully and quietly closed the shop door behind him, and as he stood there in the comparative gloom—because the nearest street-lamp was some distance away—he congratulated himself that his rather daring adventure had passed off so successfully and without the slightest interference. He had run several distinctly unpleasant risks, but had pulled the whole thing off as smoothly and comfortably as if he had been in the position of stage-managing the entire performance himself.

At that precise moment, however, a strange incident occurred, and Anthony realized that the bed was not all roses by any means. As he moved away from the door of the "Old Spider's Web" a man came from the kerb and walked straight up to him. When he came abreast of Anthony he deliberately stuck his face out and stared straight and direct into Anthony's eyes. The latter was taken aback somewhat by the suddenness and extreme discourtesy of the action, and before he could make any comment or remonstrance the staring man turned abruptly on his heel and swung impetuously away.

Anthony, for the moment at a loss, stood on the pavement and watched him. The man walked the length of the street under Anthony's surveillance and then sharply turned the corner and was lost to sight. As Anthony walked back slowly to the "Bear and Ragged Staff" he had much more food for thought on his journey than he had anticipated a short time ago. But his main problem remained the same. Where was Langley?

CHAPTER IV

I

As HE went into his hotel, he ran slap into Maddison. Bearing in mind his earlier anticipations, Anthony was a little surprised at the encounter.

"Hullo," said the agent, "how's tricks? Found the missing man yet? Or are you still running round in circles?"

"I haven't found him," replied Anthony, "and I take it by reason of your inquiry that you haven't been any more successful."

Maddison winked. The gesture was evidently intended to convey a great deal. "Shouldn't be surprised if I'm not on to something. At long last. Had a brain-wave yesterday and I fancy it's going to turn up trumps. Still—you never know—doesn't do to be too confident when you're working on a job of this calibre. But there's one thing I can say. I'm very definitely not running round with my tail between my legs and my tongue out. No, sir—I'm not doing either of those things. Not Percy Maddison. Not on your life! So you can draw your own conclusions, Mr. Bathurst."

"Good," returned Anthony. "Good for you. Delighted to hear it. I shall have to pull up my socks. All the same, I'm for bed now. I've had a tiring day. Night, Maddison."

Anthony went to his bedroom then for two purposes—one, for an exercise in concentrated thought and two—sleep. They were to be taken in that order. The point that worried him most now was the whereabouts of Langley. He felt this anxiety acutely apart from any serious interest occasioned either by Priscilla Schofield or by her father's forebodings. Where had Langley been taken? And if he knew, or thought he knew, the answer to this question, what was his best method of approach? The method which combined the maxima of telling effectiveness and bodily safety.

For a long time Anthony made no headway at all with his problem. If he brought Lawton into the picture—and he was strongly tempted to adopt this procedure—could they act swiftly enough to be consistent with Langley's safety? If he didn't bring Lawton into it and decided to play a solo hand in the game, how much could he accomplish himself before running into some sort of trouble—if not into actual disaster? His handicap was that he *knew* so little! Merely that a man named Langley, employed on a special inquiry by a firm of Turf Accountants, was missing and another man, apparently only on the outskirts of the affair—dead. And, no doubt, murdered. Precious little there for any investigator to collect and analyse. Anthony lay awake for a long time with his problem still unsolved, and when he eventually went to sleep it was in precisely the same condition. But he slept soundly for all that.

II

Directly after he had breakfasted on the following morning, Anthony went to the hotel telephone and got through to Priscilla Schofield. He told her of what he had discovered with regard to the "Spider's Web" and of certain more urgent fears that he was now harbouring in relation to Langley. Priscilla listened—a prey to burning anxiety. Anthony's next question surprised her.

"I've just had something of a brain-wave. You know those people opposite to you? Where Langley went the night you started all this business? Well—while I think of it, see if you can give me the 'phone number of the house—will you? Look for it under the name of Gunter—will you, Miss Schofield?"

He listened for her reply. It wasn't too audible. "G for George," said Anthony. "Gunter—not Hunter. Understand?"

Priscilla intimated to him that she knew the name, and soon came through with the 'phone number he wanted. "Nirvana 2288— it's in the directory under the name of Felix Gunter. What are you going to do, Mr. Bathurst?"

"I'm going to administer a shock, Miss Schofield—or at least I hope I am. That's certainly my intention. And if one administers anything in the nature of a shock—you never know what may follow. In this instance. I'm looking forward very confidently to a definite and highly successful reaction. Anyhow, I'll give you another ring tomorrow."

"Thank you, Mr. Bathurst, and till you ring I shall be eaten up with anxiety. I am now—but I shall be a million times worse until I hear from you."

Anthony hung up thoughtfully and walked back to the smoking-room. After fiddling about somewhat aimlessly with a succession of morning papers, none of which he found in the least interesting or instructive, he made his way back to the telephone and asked the operator for Nirvana 2288. As he did so he looked at the time. It was just ten o'clock. He approved that fact. Not a bad time by any means, he persuaded himself, for the type of message that he was about to send to friend Felix Gunter. The same Gunter who backed his fancy and had his playful Tote Double with no less a firm than Angus Mount Ltd.

While Anthony's thoughts were tangenting in this direction, he heard a voice speaking at the other end of the line.

"Nirvana 2288—Gunter speaking. Who is that, please?"

Anthony twisted his mouth into a crooked smile and replied airily, "May I speak to Mr. Langley, please?"

He could almost hear the tense breathing at the other end. But Gunter quickly pulled himself together and came back into the fight. "This is Gunter speaking, I said. What name do you want? Langford? I'm afraid you've got the wrong number. There's nobody here of that name."

"Shucks," retorted Anthony laconically, and with exactly the right intonation—"likewise nuts—you know what I said. You heard. I said Langley. Not Langford. Tell Langley I want him—Detective-Inspector Lestrade of Scotland Yard speaking. Tell him it's urgent."

"There's no Langley here," came down the telephone. Gunter's voice was deep-throated and guttural and vibrated with uneasiness. "You've got the wrong number, I tell you. What number do you want? This is Nirvana 2288."

"You're telling me," retorted Anthony, "and I know you, Gunter. You won't get away with anything. I want Langley. And Langley I'm going to have. So don't play the fool any more. I've an urgent message for him. I hoped to get him at the 'Spider's Web', but I was just too late. Not my fault. Circumstances over which I had no control. They tell me he's been moved—at least that's Newman's story. Says you had to move him."

But that was the end of the telephone conversation. Anthony heard Gunter bang the receiver down at his end, and he knew that spelt finish. "Never mind! He'll be damned careful what he does with Langley after that warning," said Anthony to himself. "I rather fancy I've placed a reasonable percentage of the fear of God in Mr. Gunter—which was just the condition I wanted to effect."

He returned to the smoking-room and looked out of the window into the street. Try as he would to persuade himself otherwise, he was still dissatisfied. He was not *attacking* the enemy sufficiently—he was merely frightening him—all that he had done so far had been to fight a series of delaying actions. Which from Anthony's own point of view was definitely not good enough, and if nothing vital happened before very long he knew that he would be compelled to change his tactics.

III

Before many hours had passed Anthony had occasion to alter his opinion. And, which is perhaps more, to alter it radically. For one thing it was a black night—and the blanket of blackness had descended on the town of Angel comparatively early. The time of the year, it must be remembered, was approaching the final days of November, and on this particular evening it was pitch dark and inclined to be foggy soon after four o'clock in the afternoon.

Anthony finished dinner before seven o'clock and decided to spend the remainder of the evening with the Schofields. By seven o'clock he had come out of the "Bear and Ragged Staff" and was surprised to find how black and uninviting the weather was. But he judged that things might well improve under either moonlight or starlight, so he shrugged his shoulders, turned up the high storm-collar of his overcoat and headed up the main street in the direction of the Schofields' house. He had not taken very many paces when he became aware that he was being followed.

After a minute or two his ears told him that he was being followed by two men. It didn't occasion him any supreme difficulty to become certain of the fact. The news was neither comforting nor reassuring, and Anthony was annoyed with himself at his carelessness at having come out that night without his revolver. It was too late now, however, to remedy that omission, so he decided to find out more. He dallied, therefore, by a shop window that showed some light and waited for the two men to come nearer to him. As it happened, they were quite unconcerned at his action and approached without any hesitation to within a matter of about a dozen yards. Anthony turned and deliberately walked towards them. They stood their ground, eyeing him almost truculently and certainly contemptuously. Anthony looked at their faces and recognized one of them without the slightest difficulty. It was the man who had come and stared at his face when he had made his surreptitious way out of the "Spider's Web". To Anthony's way of thinking, this must be the man named Newman. The other was a thin, weedy, rat-faced man, and now that Anthony had seen them at close quarters, and taken stock of them and of their physical capabilities he found himself feeling a trifle less apprehensive. He turned again, therefore, left the two men where they were standing and continued in the direction he had been taking prior to his voluntary halt. The two men waited for a brief period and then fell, almost mechanically, in his tracks again.

When he had moved on for a distance of about a hundred yards. Anthony noticed something else; by reason of which his original anxiety and apprehension not only returned but increased. On a half-turn, he had observed that one of the men following him had flashed a torch three times in rapid succession. This incident alone might not have perturbed him unduly, but the fact that Anthony felt moderately certain that the flashes had been answered by other flashes some distance *ahead* caused him to sit up very straight, as it were, and take infinite pains to notice. Yes—he had been right! Another succession of flashes had been followed by yet another set in answer. The idea, evidently, was some sort of encirclement. Anthony felt himself regretting the absence of his revolver more and more. Assuming the strength in front of him to be in similar measure to the strength behind, the odds were now four to one. Sufficient to give the best of men pause and by no means a comfortable proposition whichever way you looked at it. Unhappily, too, the next few moments brought Anthony an even greater degree of alarm. In addition to the flashes ahead and behind, his eye caught a third direction from which similar flashes were coming. This lay away to his right—that is to say in the direction of the river. The river! With black darkness everywhere! Anthony visualized perilous possibilities.

This latest discovery, and working on the same degree of calculation as regards strength of personnel, might well be the means of increasing the odds against him to sixes. Definitely—not so good! Anthony carefully adjusted his thinking-cap. This appeared to be one of those times, very certainly, when discretion would be much the better part of valour. He realized that he must act—and act quickly. There was no alternative. He took a lightning-like stock of the situation as he saw it. And he saw that it was imperative for him to break contact with the three aggression points as they converged on him and to remove himself from the orbit of their intended encirclement at the earliest possible moment. In other words—at once! Or, if not absolutely at once, at the first clear-cut second when conditions for that break-away became in the least degree favourable. Again, he knew that he must break away to the left, that is in the opposite direction to where the third centre of antagonism was—and *away* from the river. The hope surged in Anthony's breast that there would soon come to his aid a convenient side-turning on his left-hand side, because the space between the three fires in which he moved was becoming smaller with every pace he took. He would give no warning, though, to his stalkers— no suggestion of a warning—and sauntered along the pavement with entire nonchalance.

All the same, Anthony grew more and more worried as he saun- tered. For no break came in the buildings. No sanctuary side-turning showed in the roadway. By this time he could see the figures of two men coming towards him through the mist quite plainly. He assessed the distance they were away at approximately two hundred yards. Two hundred yards that would very soon be a mere hundred! That rapidly *became* a hundred! And then, just as that had happened, Anthony's long-looked-for turning came. It was a narrow, twisting, old-world side-street with a cobbled roadway, and Anthony, sauntering along at one moment had turned like a swerving three-quarter and was down it like a flash. Anthony ran hard, straight and fast as a wing "three" for the line, but the noise of running footsteps in his rear left him with no illusions as to his personal safety. As he ran—and it must be remembered that he didn't know towards what he was running—he knew all too certainly that it was incumbent upon him to find salvation somewhere within the next few seconds. It might be that he would come to a public- house. The publicity of the bar would protect him for a time only. At closing-time there would still be the same problem to face. Which meant that although a public-house would furnish a place of safety better than some establishments, there might be other havens which would be far superior to a public-house.

Anthony continued to run hard. But his pursuers, if anything, were closer on his heels now than they had been at any time since he had attempted to give them the slip. One of them in particular, and, from what Anthony could see of him, a big, powerful fellow, had outstripped his companions and had come to within about a dozen yards of Anthony. This fellow, too, from the manner in which he ploughed on, evidently knew the particular line of country far better than Anthony did, and he moved forward at an amazing speed for so big a man and also with the utmost confidence. Anthony knew beyond any shade of doubt that it would take him all his time to shake this fellow off, so he spurted sharply—mainly with the idea of finding out whether his pursuer was capable of pulling out a similar burst of speed at will. He soon had his answer. And from his point of view it was the wrong one. Far from being dismayed by Anthony's increase in pace, the big man in the rear actually improved his position, and Anthony knew that his already meagre lead had been cut down to something like nine or ten yards. It was at this critical moment that Anthony saw the movement of a door in the wall a few paces ahead of him. This door which he had spotted was swinging, which meant, pretty conclusively, Anthony argued to himself as he ran, that it gave access to somewhere and that—even more importantly—somebody had just used it.

He therefore shot his body straight towards this door as a runner breasts the tape, and to his intense relief it yielded to the sudden impact and gave him blessed entrance. He found himself in a narrow gas-lit corridor. He walked quickly down it and discovered that it turned sharply to the right. As he turned with it, he heard the now familiar swish-thud of the door again and registered the thought that the big man who had pursued him had entered in the same unceremonious way that he had. The thought had scarcely materialized when he felt his right hand seized enthusiastically by a little perky man with a round cherubic face, brightly gleaming gold-rimmed glasses, a pink, bald head and a pair of little twirling legs that almost danced with ecstasy as he shook Anthony's hand.

"My dear Mr. Bretherton," he exclaimed delightedly as he hand-pumped. "I *am* relieved! I've been dreadfully worried about you. I was so afraid you'd lost your train from Wintringham. I know what travelling is these days. None better! Still—never mind, Mr. Bretherton—you're all right—you're just in time. And any miss is as good as a mile."

Anthony was at a complete loss to reply, and before he could enter an effective disclaimer the little perky man was in the saddle and off again.

"What do you think of the bill, Mr. Bretherton? Given you a good show, don't you think? Trust Angel to do the job properly. Can't say we haven't."

Anthony's eyes followed the jerk of the little man's hand, and he saw a red poster in big black type posted on the wall behind him. It read as follows.

ANGEL YOUTH ALLIANCE

At the Assembly Hall on Wednesday evening, November 22, at 7.30 sharp, will be held a "BRAINS TRUST OF SPORT". The Trust will be on sport generally, and the visiting members specially invited to be present are Commander C. M. G. Cadbury (Wessex and England), S. E. R. Tyler, Esq. (Streetshire and England), A. C. Bretherton, Esq. (Oxford University, Corinthians and England), and Miss Ruby Foster-Douglas (Ladies' Open Golf Champion, 1935). Admission by ticket, 1/- and 6d. Come in your hundreds and bring your friends. Question-master: Major F. Q. P. Pointdexter, D.S.O.

The little man permitted Anthony to read to the end and then went on talking. "You've got just about a couple of minutes, Mr. Bretherton, before the rag goes up. And before that I expect you'll want to rinse away the travel stains. That'll be all right. We can hold it for five minutes or so. Just away down there you'll find the 'Gents'. There's a towel and some soap there."

He pointed vaguely down the corridor, and Anthony obeyed him almost mechanically. While he stayed in this Assembly Hall, as he had now found that it was called, he was, at any rate, safe. But what about this fellow Bretherton for whom he had been mistaken? He might very well put in an appearance at any moment.

As he left the washing apartment he almost collided with a telegraph-boy, who thrust a buff-coloured envelope into his hand. Anthony had a brain-wave. He slit the flap of the envelope and extracted the flimsy telegram. His eyes knew for an absolute certainty what they were about to read.

Sorry—too ill to appear. Bretherton.

This to Anthony was the deciding factor. After heavy rain, the wicket had rolled out surprisingly well. He'd take his courage in both hands and play the ball that had been bowled down to him.

Now that he had seen the telegram, there was nothing to fear from Bretherton. But at that moment, just as he had disposed of the Bretherton problem, an icy fear gripped him. What about Commander Cadbury? He'd be bound to know Bretherton—they were both old Oxonians. And both Corinthians. Anthony wasn't sure that they weren't both old Reptonians into the bargain. He tried to think. No—on second thoughts, Bretherton was a Carthusian. Then Anthony remembered something else. Cadbury must be at least forty years Bretherton's senior. If they hadn't been contemporaries, or near-contemporaries—it was just on the cards that Cadbury mightn't know the younger man too well and that Anthony *might* manage to get by!

The little man caught him by the arm again as he was musing thus and pulled him towards the stage. "Here we are. All ready. The others are waiting for you. I told them to hold the rag a few minutes for you. I'll take you along and introduce you to them before the show starts. Come along, Mr. Bretherton."

Anthony felt himself pushed on to a platform. It represented a small stage. There was a table with a cloth and a carafe of water and glasses. Round the table had been placed six chairs. The little man propelled Anthony towards them. Five of the chairs were already occupied.

"I'll introduce you," said the little man again. Anthony was conscious of several pairs of eyes turned up towards him and of the little man talking again.

"This is Mr. Bretherton. You've all heard of him. He's a wee bit late—but of course, it's not his fault—it was through his wretched train. You know what travelling is these days. This is Miss Foster-Douglas . . . Commander Cadbury . . . and Mr.—er— Tyler. And this is our Question-Master . . . Colonel Schofield . . . he's very kindly deputizing at short notice for Major Pointdexter, who's gone down very suddenly with a nasty attack of laryngitis. Too bad, wasn't it?"

The little man beamed. . . . "Now you all know one another and up she goes . . . we really are a little late, you know, as it is. Are you all ready?"

Anthony saw Colonel Schofield regarding him with a glance of fierce indignation and almost malevolent distrust. It was evident that words were failing him. Anthony felt that circumstances called for one action and one action only. Getting on the blind side of the remaining members of the "Brains Trust", he took his seat and favoured the gallant Colonel with a prodigious wink.

IV

Anthony sank back into his chair before the curtain went up and heard Colonel Schofield clearing his throat for action with what seemed like a minimum of goodwill and a maximum of personal annoyance.

At that precise moment the curtain began to ascend, to the inevitable accompaniment of a spirited burst of clapping from the audience. Anthony knew that he had a certain task to perform before the actual "Brains Trust" got into full swing, and he knew, too, that he must set about it at once. He half-turned in his seat while his eyes searched the audience in the hall. He saw the hall was a good-sized place—much larger than he had anticipated—and that there were at least a couple of hundred people present.

Most of the audience—naturally—had taken possession of the front rows. He was not long, however, in finding what he sought. Seated on the right-hand side of the hall, looking into it from the stage, and about four rows from the front, was a row of six men. Anthony had no difficulty whatever in picking them out because the lights in the hall had not yet been turned out. He was able to recognize two of them—the one who had come and stared in his face on the pavement outside the "Spider's Web"—and whom he had seen again even more recently—and the tall, powerful, heavy-shouldered fellow who had almost run neck and neck with him when he had darted for sanctuary down the side-turning. As his eyes caught them one by one and identified them, Anthony could see the six pairs of enemy eyes turned on him both relentlessly and malevolently. Still—he knew where he was—and, better still—he knew where his assailants were. At the moment, the end of the evening—whatever it was destined to bring forth—could take care of itself . . . and in addition—thank the Lord—there was always Colonel Schofield.

By now the clapping had gradually subsided and the gallant Colonel himself was on his feet . . . addressing the audience. This is what Anthony heard him say.

"My dear . . . er . . . friends! You all know why we're here tonight. Otherwise, I suppose, you wouldn't be here. To listen to four . . . er . . . eminent people . . . er . . . Commander Cadman . . . er . . . Mr. . . . er . . . Slater . . . Mr. Bathurst . . . and . . . er . . . Miss Douglas-Stuart . . . she never owes . . . Ha-ha! I am only acting as your Question-Master in the . . . er . . . regrettable . . . but unavoidable absence of my dear old colleague and comrade Major Pointdexter. Er—'Thruster' Pointdexter we always called him. Now there are one or two things which . . . er . . . I must make a point of telling you before the actual show gets going. Now! That is to say at once."

The Colonel cleared his throat again and for no reason at all glared ferociously at the assembled company. One would have been justified in assuming from his expression that the audience at which he looked was composed of a clan of his natural enemies against whom he and many generations of his forbears had sworn eternal vengeance. But Colonel Schofield settled himself firmly on his legs and continued to speak.

"The first half of our programme this evening will be confined to written questions which are in my possession and which I shall . . . er . . . place before the various members of our 'Brains Trust' for them to answer. At 8.15, however, there will be an interval of a quarter of an hour for . . . er . . . refreshments. Both . . . er . . . liquid and solid. Ha-ha-ha! After that, the 'Brains Trust' will answer questions sent up to them from members of the audience. Provided, that is, of course, that those questions are suitable . . . which will be . . . er . . . a matter for my . . . er . . . personal decision. That is all, I think. Thank you, ladies and gentlemen."

Colonel Schofield looked round benevolently and resumed his seat to another terrific burst of applause. He leant forward, emptied a small tray and pulled various slips of paper towards him. Anthony watched the six men who were watching him and then, for the first time, as the Colonel was examining the first slip of paper, Anthony began to take stock of his three fellow "Brains Trust" members. Cadbury, of course, he knew well. Both by sight and by reputation. Must be in his seventies, thought Anthony. Marvellous bloke, too. Certain lines to do with the early days of Cadbury's career ran through his brain. "Colleague of the great Kumar Shri. Full-back for the famous Yi-Yi. Record long-jump. And literary bump. Yes—that's C. M. G. Cadbury."

Anthony jerked himself back from a contemplation of Cadbury's rather imperiously proud features to the first question which Colonel Schofield had selected and was chuckling over to them.

"Our first question," he was saying, "comes from Small Heath, Birmingham. Here it is. From a Mr. Howard Spencer. 'Has there ever been a finer Soccer side than the Aston Villa side of 1897?'"

Colonel Schofield coughed, shed his temporary benevolence and looked round the table aggressively and snapped, "Cadbury!"

The Commander leant back in his chair rather lazily and wiped his monocle. "Well," he said, "as it happens I remember that particular Villa side remarkably well. I rather fancy that the 1897 team won both the League Championship and the F.A. Cup. Yes—I'm right—they did. An achievement which has never been pulled off since. Several teams have almost equalled the feat but not one has been successful. Yes—a grand side. A great side. Skippered—I *think*—by Jack Devey. Very few sides could be compared with them. Preston North End in their early days, perhaps—Proud Preston, one of the Sunderland sides a little later, 'the team of all the Talents', and perhaps one of the more recent Arsenal sides. When Alex James was doing his stuff." The Commander swung one leg over the other. "In answer to the question—I should say 'No'. There's never been, in my opinion, a better side than the Villa side of '97."

"H'm!" said Colonel Schofield. "Tyler!"

The famous Streetshire cricketer shook his head. "I'm afraid I can add little to what Commander Cadbury has said. For one thing, he knows so much more about the question than I do. The side that's being discussed was well before my time. Still—I'd say this. I've heard a rare lot of talk about it and I've always been led to believe by people whose judgment I respect that the 1897 Villa side was *'par excellence'*."

"Thank you, Tyler. That's two people in agreement. Er . . . Bath . . . Bretherton."

Anthony looked at Colonel Schofield, as he amended the name, with a perfectly straight face. He wondered if the Question-Master had "fluffed" his name of malice aforethought or whether the slip had been purely accidental and eminently Schofield.

"Well," he said, "I won't quarrel with the opinions of Commander Cadbury and my colleague Tyler. That Villa side beat Everton in the Cup Final by three goals to two, and in the opinion of many of the best judges, no finer exhibition of football has ever been given in a Final tie. And that goes for both winners *and* losers. Commander Cadbury has tried to remember the Villa skipper. I'll go one better and have a shot at remembering the entire forward line. I think it went, from right to left—Athersmith, Devey, Campbell, Wheldon and Steve Smith. And I fancy, too, that every man in the line was an International."

"Thank you," said the Colonel. "There seems to be . . . then . . . almost unanimous opinion on the matter. That this particular team has never been surpassed. Which is, of course, what the questioner wanted to know. So that he . . . er . . . should be satisfied. Now that . . . er . . . brings me to Question Number Two. This comes from . . . er . . . Welford-on-Avon . . . in Warwickshire . . . and this time it's on another game . . . er . . . Torn Lennis . . . I mean . . . er . . . Lawn Tennis. A Miss Audrey Bubblecup sends it to us. 'Who is the finest Singles Lawn Tennis player of all time?' Er . . . Miss Foster-Douglas?"

Anthony looked at the lady addressed and recognized her immediately from the photographs he had seen of her from time to time in the sporting Press. He knew that she had won the Ladies' Open Golf Championship on two occasions and that not less than six of her brothers had played for Marlshire at cricket and two of them for England. She had a strong, intelligent face and a quick decisive manner of speaking.

"Well—to my mind—that question's easily answered. Although perhaps many people would disagree with me. I should say without the slightest hesitation—Tilden! 'Big Bill Tilden'. For stroke play and absolute domination of a game by . . . er . . . skill . . . technique and his own dominant personality—Tilden every time."

She sat back in her chair and moved her head as though in confirmation of the opinion that she had just voiced.

"Er—thank you, Miss Frobisher . . . you're certainly very decided in your opinion. Er . . . Cadbury?"

The Commander lazed back in his chair as he had done on the previous occasion. "I'm not really very much of a judge. Tennis was never my game. I know, of course, that Tilden was a very great player, but so indeed were the brothers Doherty (Big Do and little Do), Norman Brookes, Anthony Wilding, Donald Budge, Ellsworth Vines, Perry, and a host of others. But please understand—I'm definitely not challenging Miss Foster-Douglas's opinion." The Commander folded his arms and repeated the performance of polishing his monocle.

"Thank you, Commander Cadbury. Er . . . you . . . Tyler?"

"Well—as it happens, I *can* say something about this. And I'm going to differ from the opinion that's already been given. I'm going to take a different line. What about Lenglen? The incomparable Suzanne? As I heard it, the question didn't limit it to players of my sex."

He looked round the table at which he was sitting and then out to the members of the audience. "Did any one of us here ever see a greater player than Suzanne Lenglen? Because if any one of you say you did—I know jolly well that *I* never did! Talk about a whirlwind—a human tempest—Suzanne was all that and then some more. No—I'm bound to say that I disagree with my eminent colleagues. I don't think that she'll ever be equalled, and I'd put Suzanne as the pick of the basket every time."

Tyler concluded with a flushed face and breathing hard. There was no doubting the sincerity of his opinion.

"Er—thank you, Tyler . . . er . . . Barrington?"

Anthony guessed that Colonel Schofield was referring to him and jumped into the breach at once. "I agree with the first two speakers. I'd put Bill Tilden first without the vestige of a doubt. And when Tyler champions the cause of Mademoiselle Lenglen against him, I'm tempted to reply in this fashion. There's an old sporting saying that 'a good big 'un will always beat a good little 'un', and I regard the dictum as eminently sound. Similarly, I would say a good man must always get the better of a good woman. It must be so. Stronger physically and more resourceful. So it's Tilden for me every time."

Schofield thanked him, and in this wise the evening proceeded until the time came for the interval. Question had followed question in quick succession, and among the sports touched on were cricket, both codes of football, lacrosse, coursing, curling and cross-country running. When the interval eventually did come, Anthony knew that he must have a few moments' private conversation with Colonel Schofield. He had something he badly wanted to do, and there was also much to explain.

As the half-time curtain descended to another burst of clapping, he saw his six antagonists move from their row of chairs as one man. He knew, with something like a chill at his heart, what their objective was. To see that he himself didn't leave the building! It was an unpleasant thought. To realize with unerring certainty that he was a hunted man and that the holes of escape were going to be effectively stopped up. That he was the quarry of six determined, resolute men who would have no scruples whatever with regard to the achievement of their personal ends.

When he ran into the Colonel he pulled him to one side as courteously as he could in the circumstances. The Colonel was a little huffy at the encounter.

"Strictly speaking," he said curtly, "I feel that I should denounce you. I never did—and never shall—like deception in any shape or form! Tell the truth, sir, and shame the Devil has always been a favourite belief of mine. Drummed into me by my father at the end of his belt."

"My dear sir," said Anthony, "have no fears—and likewise harbour no qualms. I am an entirely innocent party. I was forced into this. To save my life. Or at any rate—almost that. But I'll explain everything to you later. In the meantime, listen to what I have to say. Get on the 'phone from here to Miss Schofield before the second half of the programme starts and tell her to explore the premises opposite to your place at once. I mean the house where Langley took the cat. Tell her there'll be no danger whatever. Tell her to—"

"Look here, Brotherstone," said the Colonel, "you talk to her yourself. You'll do it better than I shall. You know what you want—I don't. I'll speak to Jefferson here and ask him to take you to the telephone."

"Thank you, sir! Perhaps that would be the better way. It's very sporting of you."

Colonel Schofield beckoned to the little man who had first pulled Anthony into the arena. "Jefferson. Just a moment, please."

The smiling little man came up to them. "Take Mr. Branston to your telephone—will you, Jefferson, please? At once, if you don't mind. He's anxious to use it. Something urgent that he must attend to—otherwise he wouldn't have bothered you." He turned to Anthony. "There you are, old fellow, you run along with Jefferson here and he'll see you right."

Anthony thanked both the Colonel and Jefferson and followed the latter down the corridor into what seemed to be a private room.

"Our Management Committee meets in here," whispered a smiling Jefferson, in an excess of confidence, "the third Tuesday in the month. The Mayor of Angel usually takes the chair. There's the telephone—on that desk over there, and if you want to look up a number there's a directory alongside of it. You won't be long, will you?" he concluded somewhat anxiously.

Anthony shook his head. "I should be through in a couple of minutes, unless I'm *very* unlucky over the call—which I shouldn't be at this time of night."

"Good," said the little man—"it doesn't do to make the interval too long, you know, at these affairs. I know that only too well from experience. If you do, some of the people are inclined to lose interest. I'll wait for you by the stairs at the foot of the stage."

Jefferson slipped out and left Anthony to the telephone and his own devices. Anthony found the Schofield number in the telephone directory and, as he had anticipated, got Priscilla at once. She seemed completely surprised when he told her who he was.

"Listen," he went on, "listen very carefully. I want you to go over to the house opposite—you know the one I mean only too well—and give it as much exploration in a short time as you possibly can. Don't worry—I don't anticipate you'll run into any kind of danger as I'm pretty certain that it's empty and will remain empty for the next hour or so. And by the term 'empty', I mean empty of enemies. At the same time, you *might*—on the other hand—find a friend. Anyhow, keep cool—use all your wits and keep your eyes open—and if the situation should turn against you in any way, I'm relying on your intelligence and native shrewdness to get you out of the jam. Sorry I can't say any more now or answer any questions you may feel anxious to ask. Go right ahead, Miss Schofield, and at the very latest I'll call for your report tomorrow."

Anthony hung up. He looked at his watch and made his way back to the little flight of stairs at the foot of the stage on the O.P. side. Jefferson was there awaiting him, and as Anthony arrived there Colonel Schofield and the other members of the "Brains Trust" joined them. Anthony apologized to them for what he described as his unfortunate absence.

"I'm sorry to appear so unsociable, but there was a telephone call I simply *had* to make and the interval was the only time for doing it. Please forgive me."

Commander Cadbury expressed complete forgiveness with a most comprehensive wave of the hand. "Granted, my dear Bretherton. I'm sure we understand perfectly." Tyler and Miss Foster-Douglas gave similar expressions of understanding.

"Come along then," said the Colonel, even more fussily than usual, "and let's get ahead with this second-half business. If we don't, the audience'll be getting restive."

The visiting company took their various seats at the table and the curtain rose again for the second half of the evening's entertainment. Colonel Schofield addressed the people in the hall. Anthony, anxious again now that he had returned to the job, looked to see if his six antagonists were still there, and had no difficulty in seeing and identifying them immediately.

"They're sticking it to the end," he said to himself, and then schooled himself to listen to Colonel Schofield.

"During the second half of the programme," said that gentleman, "the 'Brains Trust' will be prepared to answer any questions sent up from the audience. First question, please. We'll take them in some sort of order. Row by row—commencing with the first row in front."

The Colonel spoke so clearly and fluently that Anthony realized he had been drinking. A rather pretty girl in a well-cut tweed costume, and who sat in the second row, sponsored the first question for the second half of the evening. And directly Anthony heard it he thought what an excellent question it was.

"To what influence or reason do the Members of the 'Brains Trust' attribute the pronounced supremacy which Cambridge have shown over Oxford in rowing during recent years?"

For some reason which eluded him, Anthony saw the Question-Master glance rather critically at the attractive girl who put the question and bark sharply, "Cadbury."

The Commander waded into the attack with obvious eagerness and alacrity. "As an old Oxonian—that hits home. I'll admit that at once. All of us from the Isis are extremely concerned at the modern monotony of what some of the Press have described as the Putney to Mortlake 'Procession'. There *must* be a sound reason for this overwhelming supremacy that Cambridge has established since the war of 1914-18. Especially when it's remembered—and I trust I'll be forgiven for interpolating this—that in my time at the 'Varsity the boot was rather on the other foot. Almost as much so, in fact. Various reasons have been put forward for Cambridge's success—some, to my mind, frankly fantastic. My own explanation is this. And it's got nothing to do with Steve Fairbairn and the 'Jaggers' style. The tendency over the last thirty years, shall we say, has been for Cambridge to become much bigger than Oxford. For instance—it has many more undergraduates than Oxford. Without any pretensions to being exact, I should say that the present proportion must be something like three to one. Which fact, I submit, must make a tremendous difference over a period of time. It's pretty formidable, you know. My answer, therefore, to the questioner must be 'overwhelming preponderance of numbers'. I can advance nothing else."

Commander Cadbury polished his monocle once again and resumed his original attitude of indifferent ease.

"Thank you, Commander. Er . . . very instructive. Tyler?" Tyler thrust his hands deep into his pockets. "Candidly—I'm sunk. Not being a 'Varsity man, I've never given the subject the ghost of a thought. On the whole I should say there's nothing in it. Just a cycle! Nothing more than that. You're bound to get 'em. They turn up now and then in almost all departments of life. Look at Eton and Harrow at cricket if you want an example of what I mean. Harrow couldn't win the Lord's match for nearly thirty years. Simply couldn't. No matter what they did or what coaches they engaged they just couldn't pull it off for—as I said—about thirty years. It was as near that as makes no odds. From the point of view of the law of average, it was just absurd. So, in reply to our lady questioner—"

They were the last words which Tyler was destined to utter that evening in his capacity as a member of the "Brains Trust". For at that moment there was the noise of a loud report from what seemed to be very near at hand and the entire room was plunged into black darkness. Anthony, armed with his special knowledge and fully alive to the sinister possibilities of the situation, heard the cultured voice of Commander Cadbury cursing softly to himself and then without any pause he heard the same voice say—

"By Jove—that was a bullet unless I'm gravely mistaken. I heard the thing whistle as it went past. Can't understand such a thing! Shouldn't have expected a rough-house here by a long chalk. Shall have to revise my opinion of ancient Angel."

There came a cry of "Candles," and Anthony saw Jefferson and two other men stumble on to the stage carrying a number of lighted candles. As to what he should do himself he was undecided. If the damage to the lighting system (which in itself was not excessively modern) was irreparable, Anthony realized that there wouldn't be any more "Brains Trust" activity that evening and that the whole show would have to close down. He endeavoured to pierce the curtain of darkness with his eyes to see whether the men who had evil designs upon him were still in the same place. But he was unable to see anything clearly, and there was a general noise and confusion in the hall which added to his difficulty.

Cadbury was talking to Tyler and Jefferson and pointing to the backdrop of the trees in Richmond Park. "There you are," he said, "as I told you. That's a bullet-hole right enough. Somebody's making Aunt Sallies of us—but I'm damned if I know why. Surely we haven't been as lousy as all that?"

There was a general laugh at the Commander's sally. Jefferson turned anxiously to Colonel Schofield. His face was white and working with apprehension.

"I think, sir," he said nervously, "that you'd better make an announcement. The people out in the hall are getting a bit out of hand. But please make no reference to the shot that was fired."

"What about the lights?" demanded Colonel Schofield.

Jefferson shook his head at the question. "I'm afraid we shan't be able to get them repaired in anything like time to finish this evening. We must pack it up, sir—I'm sorry and all that, but we've no option, I'm afraid."

"H'm," grunted Schofield; "great pity, I must say. Great pity! Just as we were going well. Still—I'll take your word for it and I'll do as you say."

Holding a lighted candle in his right hand, Colonel Schofield, an acolyte of bad news, advanced to the edge of the stage. Anthony placed himself well behind the table in case the men in front had the temerity to try to get him by rushing tactics. The Colonel was terse and to the point and for once seemed to know what he wanted to say.

"Ladies and gentlemen," he announced, "I regret to inform you that there's been an accident which has unhappily involved our lighting system. Unfortunately, as the necessary repairs cannot be executed in time, it means the end of our entertainment for this evening. We're sorry—extremely sorry—but it just can't be helped. And what can't be cured must be endured. So will you please accept our sincere apologies for the mishap, leave your seats and make your respective ways home as good-temperedly as possible? Good night, everybody."

Through the gloom of the room Anthony could see the shadowy forms of the audience as they filed their way from the auditorium. The shuffling offset the hoarse coughing, and general noises continued for some little time. From his position behind the table Anthony craned his head forward in an effort to see if his pursuers were making their exit with all the others. At any rate, whatever they were doing or intended to do, they had made no attempt to assault him as he had anticipated they might have done. He knew, then, what their next move would undoubtedly be. They would watch the two exits. Both the ordinary exit by which the members of the audience were now going out and the side-street door of salvation by which he had entered earlier in the evening would be covered from now onwards. This meant that there was yet another problem for him to solve. Before he would be able to get back to his hotel that night he would be forced to run the gauntlet again.

As Colonel Schofield returned with his candles from his pilgrimage to the footlights, Anthony came from behind the table and joined him. The Colonel frowned at him severely.

"Something damned funny about this evening," he grunted, "all the way through. And you're included in that. Blest if I know what to make of any of it."

Anthony bore this in patience before drawing him to one side. "At the risk of being dubbed a confounded nuisance I want another word in your ear," he said quietly, "before you start your homeward journey."

V

"Don't tell me," said the Colonel, "that you want to telephone to Priscilla again."

"No, sir," replied Anthony, "nothing like that this time. Something much more sensational—almost highly dramatic—and also, sir, would you be good enough and patient enough to postpone all the questions that you're itching to ask me until later? Firstly, I want you to let me come with you in your car when you drive home. Yes?"

"Certainly, my dear Bathurst. Why not? As a matter of fact I was going to invite you to. I can't see anything particularly sensational in that."

"Perhaps not, sir—but you wait a little while till you've heard the next verse. This is where the catch comes. Where's Jefferson?"

"There is he—by the door. I'll get him up here for you."

Colonel Schofield beckoned to Jefferson. The pink-faced, fussy little man came bustling up. "Bathurst wants you," said the Colonel.

Jefferson stared uncertainly. The Colonel corrected himself. "I mean Brotherstone. I've been getting this fellow's name mixed up all the evening. I don't know what it is exactly that he wants. He'll tell you himself."

Anthony said, "Look here, Jefferson. I want you to do me a favour. There's something going on here tonight which we can't understand. You heard yourself that a shot was fired from the hall out there and has made a mess of your back-drop. In other words—dirty work at the cross-roads. Now does there happen to be a caretaker attached to these premises?"

"Oh, yes, Mr. Bretherton. A very decent fellow, too. An old soldier. Ex-Coldstream Guardsman. Lives in the upstairs apartments. But what's your point, may I ask?"

"Do you happen to know if this excellent old soldier has a wife?"

"He has. Very much so. Always refers to her as his C.O. Big, upstanding woman. Keeps him well in order. It's a bit of a joke in these parts. But why this interest, may I ask, in our caretaker's domestic matters?"

"I want this good lady to lend me a skirt, a coat, a pair of stockings and a hat. They shall be returned to her without fail early tomorrow. In addition to a handsome *pourboire*. I'll give you my word on that. Now—can you arrange all that for me, Jefferson?"

Jefferson looked a trifle dubious.

"Look here," said Anthony, "I'm not asking you to do anything simply as a contribution to the gaiety of nations. I assure you that's not the case. It's really a serious matter, as Colonel Schofield will tell you if you ask him. That bullet wasn't fired across the hall out of sheer animal spirits. Now—Jeffeson—will you help me, old chap?"

The mention of Colonel Schofield's name appeared to work wonders. "All right," replied Jefferson. "I'll join in. No doubt you've an excellent reason for what you're asking me, so I won't pester you with questions. I'll pop upstairs and see what I can manage for you. Is there anything particular about the clothes you're requiring—as regards, say, colour or style?"

Anthony smiled. "Beggars mustn't be choosers. Jefferson, old man, you pop upstairs, see Mrs. Caretaker, and scrounge the best stuff you can—remembering my size as well as you are able. O.K.?"

"Right-o," returned Jefferson, "leave it to me, then, Mr. Bretherton."

Jefferson skipped away down the corridor and Anthony heard his feet ascending a flight of stairs which couldn't be very far away from where he was standing. Anthony, after waiting a little while, went back to the Colonel.

"Hope I shan't keep you hanging about here very long, sir. I've got Jefferson on the job. Ten minutes, say, at the outside."

The Colonel snorted but said nothing. Anthony was unable to gauge what his precise reaction was. They waited there together for the return of Jefferson. When he did return—and the interval was not overlong considering what he had had to do—the little man carried a bundle of clothes and a broad smile on his face.

"Good job Evans and his wife know me well. If they hadn't, I don't know what my reception would have been like. Even so, I was compelled to use all my powers of persuasion and a liberal use of Colonel Schofield's name. But here you are, Mr. Bretherton, how does this clobber suit you? Mrs. Evans would like it all back by eleven o'clock tomorrow morning, and I promised faithfully that she should have it."

He held out the clothes he had brought down with him for Anthony's inspection. There were a dark-coloured skirt, a dark blue coat (long), a pair of dark-coloured stockings and a black hat of the "halo" type. Anthony looked at them for the space of a few seconds and then gathered them up into his arms and walked to the door.

"Back again in five minutes, sir; and to you, Jefferson, my very best thanks for your services."

Jefferson stared at him wonderingly as he shut the door behind him. "Bit of a one, Colonel, our Mr. Bretherton—isn't he?"

This time Colonel Schofield grunted in reply. It appeared that he was far from being pleased. Jefferson still hung around.

"I'd like to have a glance at him when he comes back. So's I can tell my missus. Should be well worth looking at, I imagine."

Colonel Schofield made an impatient gesture and glanced at his watch. "About time he *was* back, Jefferson. Afraid I'm fussy with regard to time-keeping. Hate being kept waiting. I remember when I was in India—"

But what the Colonel's India reminiscence was cannot be recorded here, because Anthony returned to the room before he could complete his sentence. Clad in the borrowed plumes of Madam Evans, the upstanding wife of the ex-Coldstreamer, Anthony presented to Jefferson's eyes a somewhat alarming figure. His hat was perched at a rakish angle and the coat and skirt were tight almost to rending-point. He grinned at his two companions.

"In case you feel over-critical, gentlemen," he stated pleasantly, "don't forget that it will be devilishly dark when we make our exits from here, and that therefore my sartorial deficiencies, plain though they may be to you in the pitiless light of this room, will have much more chance to escape unnoticed. I'm at your service, Colonel Schofield. *En Avant!*"

He turned, shook hands with the staring, open-eyed Jefferson, and walked out of the room in the company of the Colonel, with a distinctly shortened stride. Jefferson continued to stare after them for some time. Then, shaking his head dubiously, he packed up and returned home to his missus. What an evening—to be sure!

VI

"Where's your car, sir?" asked Anthony, as they approached the main door—"far away from the entrance?"

The Colonel shook his head. "It's parked almost opposite—about twenty-five yards farther down."

"Is there a light, do you know, over the porch of the door of the hall?"

"Yes. To the best of my memory—there is. But it's a damnably poor one and not much better than nothing—so it's not worth worrying about. Get well behind me—that's your best chance. And I'll do the talking. Here we are."

The Colonel pushed the door of the hall open and peered into the street. As he did so, Anthony knew that his fears had been thoroughly justified. He saw at once three shadowy figures lurking in the background and not more than half a dozen yards from the entrance to the hall. Anthony took a few mincing steps in the Colonel's wake, took his arm with an almost coquettish gesture and together they made their way towards the opposite side of the road, where the Colonel's car had been parked. The Colonel—and most unexpectedly at that—rose to the exigencies of the situation and played up gallantly. He placed a protective arm round Anthony's waist as they picked their way across the roadway.

"It's all right," muttered Schofield, "we're through. They haven't rumbled you and none of them has moved forward to take a closer look at us. When we get to it, I'll hand you into the car with full ceremonials."

Schofield removed his arm from Anthony's waist and walked a couple of paces ahead of him in order that he might open the door of the car and usher Anthony into it. His formula completed with due dignity, the Colonel hoisted himself into the driving-seat, pulled on his gauntlets, pressed the self-starter and the car moved forward. As they passed the knot of watching men, Anthony raised a hand, did some marvellous work with an imaginary mirror and negligently patted back what might have been a tress of refractory hair, but which wasn't. A couple of hundred yards ahead, Anthony leant forward, came out of character, and spoke quietly to the Colonel.

"Many thanks, sir, indeed, for your very kindly help and also for your timely assistance. Without them I should have been hard put to it. I'm afraid the time is due—overdue in fact—for certain explanations on my part. I'll tell you what happened in the early part of the evening and how I came to be a member of the 'Angel Youth Alliance Brains Trust'."

Anthony recounted to Colonel Schofield how he had been cornered while out walking, how he had circumvented his antagonists, and how Jefferson had welcomed him as Bretherton in a moment of mistaken identity. He then explained in addition the receipt of Bretherton's telegram.

"Well," said the Colonel when he had heard the story, "I guessed that you must have an excellent reason for doing what you were doing, and I was prepared to fall in as long as the proceedings didn't get too outrageous. Your winking at me gave me the tip."

"Very good of you, sir. And I appreciated your attitude intensely. But you will realize the type of people I was up against when you remember how they closured this evening's performance. You noticed that they had no compunction about doing what they did do."

"I don't get that, Bathurst," said the Colonel. "I don't cotton on to the real point behind that."

Anthony considered what Colonel Schofield had said. "I've been thinking of it too, sir. I rather fancy the idea was to prevent the show going the full evening. For some reason or other, they wanted to get away from the hall before the evening had run to full time. Why, exactly—I'm not quite certain. Although I have an idea. I think it was this. They wanted to force me into the open as early as they could. Time will show whether it's sound or otherwise. At any rate, I've important news for you. You can guess what about."

"Langley?" queried Colonel Schofield.

"Langley," answered Anthony. "Miss Schofield's hunch about him was entirely correct. He undoubtedly attempted to communicate with her from the 'Spider's Web' tea-shop when he was confined there as a prisoner."

Colonel Schofield frowned. "*Was* confined? Do you mean that he's not there any longer?"

"I'm afraid that's so, sir."

Schofield looked apprehensive as he peered through the windscreen. "What does that mean—do you think?"

Anthony pulled at his top lip. "I'm not altogether positive about it—but I fancy he's been removed to another place."

"To another prison?"

"I'm afraid so."

"Where—any idea? Or are you at a dead end as regards that? You know what I've always feared."

"No," replied Anthony. "I hold strong hopes thereon. In fact, I'm confidently anticipating that in that direction Miss Schofield may again come to our assistance."

The Colonel changed gear dexterously and took a corner with unaccustomed ease. He half-turned towards Anthony and remarked—"And on what, pray, is that piece of supreme optimism based?" Anthony shook his head. "I suggest, sir, that before I answer that question we interview Miss Schofield herself and hear what she has to tell us."

Colonel Schofield looked up. "Well—we haven't got to wait too long for that. We shall be home in a couple of minutes." Anthony looked ahead and saw that the Colonel's statement was true.

VII

After Anthony had made appropriate changes in his costume by the removal of certain externals, Colonel Schofield ran the car into the garage, carefully covered the radiator, and he and Anthony made for the house. Priscilla ran eagerly out to meet her father as he entered.

"Oh, Daddy!" she commenced impetuously, and then she saw Anthony standing behind the Colonel. "I'm sorry, Mr. Bathurst, I didn't notice you there. I thought Daddy was alone. But I'm so glad you have come. Because I've terrific news for you."

"Well, let's come in and sit down," said her father; "we may as well be as comfortable as we can make ourselves. No point in standing out here."

They followed the Colonel into the lounge. "First of all, Priscilla," he said as he slumped heavily into his chair, "ring for drinks. Bathurst and I will have a spot of Scotch—is that all right with you, my boy?—and you, my dear, can please yourself. Have what you like."

Priscilla did as she had been instructed. The maid, Taylor, brought the drinks in and the Colonel did himself extraordinarily well.

"That's better," he declared—"very much better. Put me right. Damned dry place—that Angel Assembly Hall! Think I shall have to be more discriminating in my engagements—especially the evening jobs—and give these arid desert places a scientific miss." He turned to Priscilla with a twinkle in his cold blue eye. "Bathurst and I haven't exactly had a benefit this evening—but tell us your news first, Priscilla. You say it's by way of being terrific."

Priscilla, who had been obviously awaiting her chance to tell her story, was into her stride immediately.

"Well—I simply must tell you, I've been frightfully worried while I've been waiting, but when you 'phoned, Mr. Bathurst, although I was a bit scared at the time—I did as you suggested and went over to that house at once."

"What house?" snapped Colonel Schofield.

"The house opposite—where all the trouble seems to have started."

"Why were you to go there? Bathurst shouldn't have suggested such an escapade. Pure madness! Had I known of it I should never have countenanced it."

"There was little danger," said Anthony quietly, "otherwise I wouldn't have mentioned the idea to Miss Schofield. I felt certain that the house would be empty when Miss Schofield got there." He looked at Priscilla. "I was right over that, was I not? Yes?"

Priscilla nodded. "Yes. You were right. Let me tell you all about it. I went over there within a few minutes of your ringing me. I wrapped myself up well and put on my tennis shoes and took my best electric torch with me—one I could absolutely rely on. It wasn't too dark, considering, because a good deal of light was coming from Mrs. Christopherson's house a few yards down the road on the other side. Well—I skirted the house of my objective—slipped through the front gates without dallying at all and worked round to the side. It was all very quiet and the house itself quite dark. Not a glimmer of light was showing."

Priscilla paused for breath. She had been speaking very rapidly. "I'll frankly admit," she continued, "that I was as nervous as a kitten. Ever so windy. So much so that I felt absolutely ashamed of myself. Of course I knew what Mr. Bathurst had told me about the place being empty, and I had enough confidence in him—and in his judgment—to believe in it. But, all the same, I'd have given almost anything for somebody else to have been in my shoes or at least to have accompanied me as I crept round that sinister house looking for a way in.

"Well—I eventually found myself at the back entrance. There didn't seem any dog about, so I plucked up my courage a bit and felt it was time to start something."

"Good for you, Miss Schofield," interjected Anthony.

Priscilla smiled at the compliment and went on.

"Then, as I was looking at that back door, I had a brain-wave. At least I like to think it was that. I went round to the front again and rang the bell. To see, of course, if there *were* anybody in the place. You know—just making sure. You see—I was doubtful about any of the servants being there. I felt that it was just possible. I rang twice and also knocked—there's a heavy wrought-iron knocker there as well as the bell—and still there was no reply. Behold me, then, feeling much better, distinctly more confident in every way and *almost* brave.

"I made up my mind quickly, walked round to the back again, grasped the handle of the back door, turned it immediately and found myself inside a sort of outhouse or scullery. Not an inviting sort of place by any means or by any standard. There wasn't a sign or sound of anybody being about, so I made a tour of the rooms on the ground floor." Priscilla turned in her chair and made a quick, impulsive movement in Anthony's direction. "Mr. Bathurst, tell me, please," she said, "what did you anticipate that I should find—when you rang me and told me what you wanted me to do? You said that the house would be 'empty of enemies'—I've been trying to remember since and I think that they were your exact words—but you said also that I might run across a 'friend'. Now that I've done the job, I'm feeling uncertain as to what you really meant. Please tell me."

Anthony seemed a little troubled as he answered her. "I meant exactly what I said. Nothing more and nothing less. My words had no hidden meaning."

"Who was the friend, then, you thought I might meet?"

"Langley—of course. I take it now, from the way you're telling the story, that he's not there?"

Priscilla shook her head, but not in dissent at what Anthony had just said. Much more as an expression of anxiety.

"Mr. Langley is not there. But I'll tell you what I *did* find when I went into one of the rooms a little later."

Anthony regarded her expectantly. "What, exactly—Miss Schofield?" he asked quietly.

"In one of the rooms on the ground floor I discovered a curious arrangement of furniture. No—I scarcely mean that. That's not very well put. I'll try to tell you what I mean. I found a mattress on the floor, a table and a chair. No other furniture. The floor was only partly covered by linoleum. It all seemed so out of place, so incongruous, in a house of that type and size. You know what I mean. It was bare—squalid—sordid, oh—I know the adjective I want—'poverty-stricken'. But that isn't all. What else do you think I saw there? On the floor—in front of the fireplace?"

Anthony gestured his inability to make any adequate suggestion, but looked anxious nevertheless. Colonel Schofield blew his nose after the manner of a gentleman who was not prepared to take sides on any account. Priscilla, having received no reply from either of her listeners to the question she had propounded, proceeded with her story.

"I'm a wee bit disappointed that my question didn't get answered. I quite expected that Mr. Bathurst would answer it—and answer it correctly. Still—he didn't, and I suppose it doesn't matter. Perhaps, in a way, I'm glad that he didn't. But on the floor in front of the fireplace was a little pool of blood. One of my shoes actually touched the edge of it. I was utterly horrified. And besides being horrified, I was terribly worried. I still am—come to that," she concluded simply.

"Why?" cut in her father curtly. "I don't see why you should be so worried. Some blood on the floor? What of it? Might belong to anybody. Somebody's nose may have bled. There might be a dozen commonplace reasons to account for it. That's how I see it."

Anthony nodded. "That's perfectly true. But how *do* you take it, Miss Schofield?"

"You must know how I take it. In the only reasonable way possible. You sent me there in the hope of finding Mr. Langley. I had that in my mind when I entered. I didn't find him. For the reason that he wasn't there to be found. All I did find was blood that he had shed. Isn't that the only sensible explanation I can find to cover the matter?"

There was no mistaking the anxiety in her tone. For some seconds Anthony made no reply to her. Priscilla noted his hesitation and followed up her previous query with another.

"Don't you find yourself in agreement with me, Mr. Bathurst?"

To her surprise, Anthony answered her supplementary question without a hint even of hesitation. "Frankly, Miss Schofield, you compel me to admit that I do agree with you. And I blame myself for sending you to that house too late. But—and I must be fair to myself—I took the first chance that came my way. I had no previous opportunity, you see, of sending you, when I felt that the coast would be clear. All the same, I'm tremendously sorry about Langley."

"What do you think has happened to him, Mr. Bathurst?" Anthony shook his head. "I am not sure. I can't be sure."

"Candidly—do you think that the worst has happened? As Daddy has always said it would."

"On balance, Miss Schofield—no. It's possible, of course—and no good purpose whatever would be served by our blinding ourselves to many obvious facts—but on the whole, I still incline to the opinion that, for the second time, Langley has been removed, for obvious reasons, to another place of confinement. They moved him in the first place to the house from the 'Spider's Web', and now they've moved him again from the house somewhere else. In other words, the original technique has been repeated."

Priscilla nodded at Anthony's explanation. "Yes. It's possible. I can see that. I suppose you have no idea where?"

Anthony shook his head. "Nothing like a certainty. Just the nucleus of a theory—no more than that at the moment. It may develop, though, very quickly, and when that comes along—I'll test it. We shall have to wait and see."

Colonel Schofield helped himself to a cigar and at the same time offered the box to Anthony.

"No, thank you, Colonel," said Anthony, but he noticed that they were Coronas.

"What do you think of doing now, Bathurst?" asked Colonel Schofield.

"How do you mean, sir?"

"Well," the Colonel looked anxiously in the direction of his daughter, "what I meant was this. Do you anticipate any further attack this evening—as far as you yourself are concerned?"

Anthony looked grave. "Candidly, I don't, sir. But I feel, with you, that I must regard it as a possibility, if not a probability. I agree that I can't altogether ignore it. Which brings me to something else, sir. Do you think you could manage to put me up for the night? If you could strain a point in my favour, perhaps Miss Schofield could manage to drive me back to my hotel early tomorrow morning."

Colonel Schofield was graciousness itself in his reception of the suggestion.

"My dear fellow—certainly—by all means. Only too delighted. And—what's more—I'll fix you up with a pair of pyjamas. Ha-ha—you'll look like the cat's whiskers. They'll be a bit on the ample side round the tummy but I've no doubt you'll be able to put up with that—in the circumstances."

"That will be all right, sir, and many thanks for the kindness."

Priscilla had listened to this last snatch of conversation with both interest and anxiety.

"Daddy," she said, "I don't think that I understand. What do you mean—any further attack? Has there been—"

Anthony was quick to reassure her. "We had a little spot of bother this evening. Miss Schofield. Nothing serious and nothing to worry about. It was entirely my fault in the first place for venturing out unprotected. And I think that the incident may yet have its bright side. I'm hoping indeed that I may be able to turn it to good account. But I'll give that idea more consideration in the morning."

CHAPTER V

ANTHONY woke reasonably early, divested himself of his host's nightwear, made the bathroom betimes and entered the breakfast-room freshly tubbed and newly razored before nine o'clock. Priscilla, always an early riser, was already down, and at her invitation he helped himself to kedgeree and to a portion of an astonishingly good game pie. The Colonel himself bustled into the breakfast-room a few minutes later.

"'Morning, Bathurst, and not a bad one either. 'Morning, my dear. Well—how did you sleep, my boy—everything all right?"

Anthony replied in the affirmative, and the Colonel fell on his morning meal with an almost exaggerated gusto. He very soon, however, came at Anthony again.

"Well—and did the nocturnal hours bring you anything in the shape of inspiration? Or were you too dog-tired to think? If you were anything like me—you were."

"No, sir. I was able to do something before I fell off to sleep that I'd been wanting to do ever since I left the Assembly Hall earlier in the evening. I was able to provide myself with a gallery of mind-pictures of the six men who I'm absolutely certain were anxious to put me out of mess last night. I've made pen-pictures of them since and jotted them down in my diary for future reference."

Priscilla, who had been restless for some moments, at last gave vent to her curiosity. "How were you able to do that, Mr. Bathurst? I feel so much in the dark about the whole thing. There's so much that I don't know."

Anthony essayed explanation. Priscilla listened to him attentively. Her face grew graver and graver as Anthony marshalled his facts with regard to the incidents of the previous evening.

"I didn't imagine," she said when he had finished, "when I asked for your help, that I should be embroiling you in such a tempestuous business."

"Perhaps not, Miss Schofield—but there are already two features about our case which never escape me. I can't allow them to. I mustn't—even if I wanted to. There's a dead man and a second man in danger. And two, Miss Schofield, may, so soon and so simply, become three. A very short numerical step indeed."

Priscilla made no reply to this statement. Colonel Schofield pushed away his coffee-cup, lit a cigarette and assumed the mantle of discussion.

"These men, Bathurst. These six men. You say that you've been able to furnish yourself with descriptions of them. I should be more than interested to hear them. I might be in a position to help you. After all—two heads are better than one on a job of this kind."

"Certainly, Colonel. I shall be only too pleased to oblige. The leader—and I'm judging that opinion on the few glimpses I got of them as they were seated in the Assembly Hall—is a man on the short side. About five feet six. With white hair and horn-rimmed glasses. Not a lot of hair. A 'parchment' sort of face—the skin appears to be tightly drawn across it. Gives a sort of mask-like appearance. Summing him up—I get these two main points. (1) Not a healthy face by any means. (2) His name is Gunter and in my opinion he has a harsh guttural voice."

Priscilla nodded at the description Anthony had given. "I can remember him—from what Mr. Langley told me. He's the man the others call the 'Professor'. The house opposite is in his name."

"Number Two," said Anthony, "is a big, powerful fellow. Heavy featured and heavy shouldered. His shoulders are usually hunched. Front row Rugger forward type. Head well down in the scrum. A fourteen-stone man, and one, too, who looks as hard as nails. Altogether the sort of customer I shouldn't care to speak to out of my turn. It strikes me from the glimpses I've had of him that he packs a tidy-sized wallop in each fist. Hands like carpet bags."

Again Priscilla showed signs of assent. "Mr. Langley mentioned him, too. That's the one called Layman. I feel certain of that. He formed much the same opinion of the man as you have. But please go on."

"Number Three," continued Anthony, "is a thin-faced man of middle height. Has sharp, ferrety features. If you like—an ecclesiastical face that has taken the wrong turning. Thin nose and excessively thin lips. Face is inclined to 'work' a little even when he's passive. Nervous disorder of some kind in all probability. A tic of sorts."

"Yes," said Priscilla—"I can recall him. His name's Webber. He waylaid Mr. Langley in his hotel on the first evening he arrived there."

"Post-Ahasuerus?" asked Anthony smilingly.

Priscilla nodded to show that she understood. "Yes, post-Ahasuerus. Not much, though. The same evening."

"I see. Now let me pass on to Number Four. Like Number Three—a man of medium height. But a squatter figure—a much stockier type altogether. To my eye, looks to have foreign blood in his veins. Dark brooding eyes—almost muddy in colour. Strong square shoulders. I know this chap better than I know the others. For the simple Reason that I've met him more than once and his features have become impressed on my mind. If I draw a bow at just a little venture, I'd say that this is the man connected with the 'Spider's Web'."

Colonel Schofield raised his eyebrows. "Then that man would be Newman. Langley inquired after him of me. Langley had the idea that he was the proprietor of another business—baker's and post-office close to the Racecourse."

"I agree," said Anthony, "that's exactly as I see things. He met me—deliberately, I've no doubt—when I emerged from my little sightseeing tour round the 'Spider's Web' after business hours. I fancy that he was waiting for me. But he wasn't absolutely sure from where I'd turned up. And because of that encounter and of what he reported that I might have discovered, he organized the 'rounding-up' activity which I neutralized by popping into the Assembly Hall and becoming an undistinguished member of the 'Brains Trust'. Yes—friend Newman and I are quite able to recognize each other when we come face to face. I must remember that on the next occasion. Which brings us," he concluded, "to Number Five of our fragrant bunch."

"Good job," muttered the Colonel, "that we're approaching the end of the tally. Villainy in the mass has seldom interested me. Still—what about friend Quintus?"

"He," returned Anthony, "is a strange, unusual figure. He's tall. With a big, sprawling, awkward body. Well over six feet, I should say, for a certainty. In many ways he appears to me to be the best of 'em. That is to say the least desperately vicious. There's a certain cheeriness about his face—a quality very definitely absent from all the others. His eyes are large—protuberant—and he has an unusual mannerism which I noted both when he entered the Assembly Hall before the show started and when you and I, sir, walked out at the close of the proceedings. He's constantly lifting his right hand and pushing his bowler hat to the back of his head, where it perches rather than rests. He does this every few minutes—I don't suppose he knows when he's doing it—it's most noticeable."

"Don't know the fellow at all. Can't place him." Thus the Colonel received Anthony's description. Priscilla could give no help either.

"Now for Number Six," went on Anthony—"the whipper-in, as we'll call him. Black hair, snaky-looking eyes and an extremely sallow complexion to accompany them. A man, I should say, who would cheerfully botanize on his mother's grave. I certainly wouldn't put it past him."

The Colonel grunted.

"Outside Newman—I can't definitely place any of 'em. Bar perhaps the fellow Gunter, whom I may have seen. Might do, of course, if I saw 'em in the flesh. Proper bunch of thugs—I don't doubt. I told Langley as much the first time he told me about them."

Colonel Schofield rose from the breakfast-table. "Well, Bathurst," he announced, "don't think for a minute that I'm hurrying you. Please yourself entirely, of course. Welcome guest. But you know that as well as I do. What I meant to say was this. When you want to get back to Angel, just let Priscilla know and she'll take you in the car. D'ye hear, Priscilla?"

"I heard, Daddy. And Mr. Bathurst has only to say the word and I'm ready."

"Many thanks, sir," said Anthony. "That's very sporting of you. But as it happens, I've been thinking things over this morning since I got up, and I've an idea that, first of all, I'll go in the opposite direction. That is to say, if Miss Schofield doesn't mind."

The Colonel stared. "How d'ye mean, my boy? You told me last night on the way here that you wanted to get back to Angel. That's right, isn't it?"

"That's quite right, sir. Except that in the interim I've usurped a privilege of the gentler sex and changed my mind."

"Which way do you want to go, then?"

Anthony put his table-napkin on the breakfast table. "I've a mind, sir, to have a look at the neighbouring village of Eden."

"What on earth for?"

The Colonel was emphatic, and continued after launching the question, "There's absolutely nothing there. Beyond the village street. That consists of about thirteen shops—and four pubs. You won't find very much there to occupy your time, I assure you."

"It's rather a misleading name," said Priscilla, a trifle roguishly, "and certainly flattering."

"I should say so," chuckled the Colonel; "nothing like a Paradise. You'll have a job to find any garden there."

Anthony's eyes twinkled as he replied. "I may not be looking for a garden, sir. But I might be on the look-out for the serpent."

CHAPTER VI

I

THE morning was at November's best when Priscilla Schofield started the car. The air was cool and clear, the mist was being dispersed by a sun gradually increasing in power, and Anthony felt fighting fit as he settled down in the seat next to his charming driver.

"Take me, please, Miss Schofield," he said, as the car gathered pace, "to about half a mile from Eden. Then drop me. I can walk the remaining distance."

"I'll take you all the way, if you like. It won't make the slightest difference to me, you know."

"No," said Anthony; "drop me about half a mile outside the village. That will be better for me from every point of view. I'm wondering, though . . ."

Anthony paused.

Priscilla cut in. "What about, Mr. Bathurst?"

"Well, I'm afraid I'm trespassing on your kindness. Do you think you could cruise around for a while and then pick me up at the place where you drop me—in, say, about another hour's time? Would that be troubling you too much, Miss Schofield?"

"Not a bit," replied Priscilla brightly. "I can do that both with pleasure and with ease. I take it"—she glanced at him sideways—"that you have a definite object in view in visiting Eden?"

Anthony grinned. "I thought I'd made that clear. I have! I told you. Serpent-hunting."

She nodded as she steadied the wheel, "Yes, I think I get it. Or some of it. The dead man, Trimmer, was an Eden man."

"He was. Full marks, Miss Schofield."

She gestured towards a mile-stone, deep in a roadside ditch, past which the car had flashed. "Eden—one mile. Tell me when you come to a likely spot for you to get out."

Anthony nodded. He waited a moment or so before he gave Priscilla the signal. The car came to a trim square patch of grass with what looked like an old-time English maypole rising high from its centre. "Here you are, Miss Schofield," he said, "this looks like a snappy place. Put me down here, will you?"

Priscilla brought the car to a standstill. Anthony looked up the road. There wasn't a soul in sight. He could see the smoke from a few chimney-pots spiralling to the sky about half a mile ahead.

"That's the main street of Eden in the near distance," contributed Priscilla. "Now what time shall I pick you up again? Have you decided?"

Anthony looked at his wrist-watch. "It's twenty past ten now, Miss Schofield. I'll be back here ready for you at half past eleven. Suit you?"

"O.K." said Priscilla. "Half past eleven."

She waved a hand, started the car off again and left Anthony standing on the patch of grass by the old maypole. He was gratified that his descent from the car had been unnoticed—as he was well aware how easily the merest whisper of gossip in a country village can assume the proportions of a side-splitting yell. Anthony buttoned his overcoat, turned up the collar, adjusted his Uppingham scarf and strode forward in the direction of Eden. A quarter of an hour's brisk walking brought him to the principal street of his objective. So far as he could see as he entered it, the village boasted no other.

Anthony walked down it—keeping his eyes well open. For he was following up an idea that had come to him on the previous day. A long shot—perhaps—but there are occasions when the long shot passes the post first. What Anthony was looking for was the village post-office. For a spell, he was unsuccessful. He walked down the north side of the street without success. But half-way up the south side, as he turned and came back, he found the village post-office. It was of the extremely rustic type and one had to walk the length of a cottage front garden to enter it. A telephone kiosk was placed but a few yards from the palings round the garden. Shielding himself as best he could behind this kiosk, Anthony had a good look at the front of the post-office. He was able to see the name of the proprietor.

It was "Frank Mann". The incidence of the name pleased him. For one thing, as he saw it, the Teutonic significance was still persisting.

Trade was obviously sparse and scanty. While Anthony watched, no villager of Eden entered to do business. But just as he was on the point of taking up another position, a telegraph-boy rode up on a bicycle and went in. Anthony walked away, up the street, turning over one or two matters in his mind. As he came to a halt, where the line of shops ceased, he heard the ring of the telegraph-boy's bicycle bell on the return journey. Anthony stood and debated with himself as to whether he should enter the post-office of Mr. Frank Mann. If Mann were one of the six men with whom he was now becoming very directly concerned—and Anthony had a strong belief that such was the case—Mann would know him when he went in. Anthony, standing on the corner of the street, decided that to enter the post-office at this stage of the encounter would be a tactical error. What he would do would be to get a little nearer to Mann's establishment, and, trusting to a small measure of disguise, make an attempt to pick up a little information.

Anthony thereupon pulled the brim of his hat down, muffled, his scarf well round the lower part of his face and put on a pair of horn-rimmed glasses which he made it his practice invariably to carry with him. He determined then to approach the post-office of Eden, if possible, from the rear. Crossing a stretch of waste ground, he moved off in the appropriate direction. His judgment proved correct. As he had anticipated, there was nothing in the shape of a building at the back of the row of shops. They all—including the post-office itself—backed on to an untilled field. There was little difficulty in identifying the backs of the different shops as they came into view. Several spaces occurred between them, and more than once Anthony was able to catch a glimpse of the main street. He was thus easily able to recognize the back of the post-office when he came to it. The back garden of which it boasted was as true to type as the front garden had been. It was long and straggling and it was apparent from the merest glance that flowers and vegetables had been recently grown there, with little regard to situation or order.

Anthony took further stock of the territorial position. He could see that the post-office possessed several rooms at the back. But he could see no way of getting to it, unless he used the way of the back garden. And this operation, he considered, would be as dangerous, while the light still held, as entering the post-office proper. He reluctantly, therefore, made his way back along the field through which he had come. As he came to the main street again, he pulled himself up with a jerk. For, crossing the street but a few yards in front of him, was the powerful "Rugger-forward" fellow who had so closely chased him on the evening before. Keeping discreetly in the rear of him, Anthony made the main street again in order to watch where the big chap was going. He hadn't long to wait for the information, for, about ten yards away, he saw the man turn into the garden that led to the post-office.

"Good enough," said Anthony to himself, for he had now established the fourth rendezvous in the chain of connexion. The house opposite to the Schofields', the "Old Spider's Web" and the two post-offices—one by the Racecourse at Angel and now this one at Eden.

He resolved to walk back in the direction of the old maypole and wait there for the car and Priscilla Schofield. By the time he got there, he calculated, he shouldn't have too long to wait.

II

Anthony stayed with the Schofields for the remainder of the day. During that time he put a proposal to the Colonel which that worthy accepted with alacrity.

"Nothing I should like better, my dear Bathurst—it'll suit me down to the ground. And Priscilla shall drive us to the appointed place. She'd positively hate to be left at home here. What do you say, my girl?"

Priscilla, who had heard the proposals of Anthony, assented with an even greater degree of enthusiasm than had emanated from her distinguished parent.

"Count on me, Daddy. I should have instantly rebelled had you suggested any other course of action. What time do we start?"

"I suggest," replied Anthony, "a little before midnight. Two conditions are essential for us. We want darkness and also the certainty that we shall meet nobody or be in any way disturbed."

"That's all right," said the Colonel in support, "and the idea has an added virtue. It means that you'll be here all the time until we make a start, and therefore will be running no risks. Which is excellent from all points of view."

*

At five minutes to twelve Priscilla got the car away at an appropriately decorous rate of miles per hour. The white road which she had been instructed to take went uphill between high and well-trimmed hedgerows. The night was cold—but visibility was good for the time of year.

After a time, the road became narrow. Priscilla was approaching Eden by a circuitous route—one rarely used by cars. At one point, she had such little room by the hedgerows that the Colonel's face lost some degree of floridity and he began to make strange noises in his throat. The car twisted on and uphill again until it came out on a straight, broad road leading to the village of Cherub. Priscilla accelerated here and the speedometer needle touched fifty. Anthony leant back in his seat with his chin touching his chest. He was running over in his mind the necessary articles he had brought with him—revolver, electric torch, jemmy and brace-and-bit. The car came to the four cross-roads which betokened the limit of the village of Cherub.

"Not far now," said the Colonel; "should do it under a quarter of an hour."

Priscilla nodded her agreement with this statement and abruptly swung the car to the right.

III

They were now running down a lane. It was narrow and winding. But whereas before they had climbed, they were now descending. A turning showed at the end of the lane.

"Turn here, Priscilla," barked Colonel Schofield.

The car swept along a well-made road this time, but only for a short distance. Colonel Schofield issued a further direction.

"First right, Priscilla."

To Anthony's eye, this injunction appeared to border on the impossible. The turning seemed rutted as a cart-track. But closer association with it revealed it to be better than its looks. It twisted and turned for about a quarter of a mile and then it came to its senses, as it were, and settled down as a perfectly well-behaved and respectable highway. Anthony sat up and looked at his wrist-watch.

"Twelve-thirty-five," he remarked; "we've been travelling forty minutes."

Schofield grunted. "Another five minutes should see us there," he contributed.

Priscilla drove the next four hundred yards in silence. Then Anthony saw the maypole rising from its bed of grass. But this time it was to the south, and he saw that they would hit the main Eden road by the corner where he had stood and seen the man whom he took to be Layman. The maypole looked eerie and ghostly by night, like the finger of a giant poised menacingly over an innocently sleeping community.

"Stop at the corner," said Anthony, as the car slid smoothly past the outlying buildings of a farm, "and you and I, Colonel Schofield, will get out. Then Miss Schofield can turn round and be ready and waiting for our get-away when the time comes. What do you think?"

The Colonel nodded. "I agree, Bathurst. I can't think of anything better. I was about to make a similar suggestion myself."

He pointed to an ancient three-fingered signpost, which announced the details of three roads—to Angel—to Angel-in-the-Wood, and to Seraph's Vale. Priscilla halted the car. Anthony and the Colonel alighted. Schofield tarried to have a few final words with his daughter.

"You wait here, Priscilla, until we come back. Be ready to move off at once. Don't get windy if we seem to be away a long time, and don't worry in any way. No harm will come to us. Bathurst and I are quite able to take care of ourselves, believe me." Colonel Schofield chuckled—almost, it might be, in anticipation.

Priscilla nodded and rested her hands on the steering-wheel.

"O.K., Daddy. I understand perfectly. Rely on me."

The Colonel and Anthony made straight for the back way across the fields which Anthony had taken that same afternoon.

"There's a ditch to your right, sir," Anthony warned the Colonel. "I shouldn't get too far over that way, if I were you."

"I won't," replied Schofield. "I have no love for foul water at the dottom of a bitch—er . . . you know what I mean, my boy."

They went on in silence. Somewhere away in a tree, in another field probably, an owl hooted. Suddenly Anthony halted. To his left, his eye could see the rough, wooden gate of the back garden of Eden post-office.

"Behind me, sir," he whispered. "Just here!"

Colonel Schofield turned and Anthony came to the wooden gate.

IV

The Colonel followed him, close on his heels. They tried the gate, but it held. It had been fastened by some means which at the moment neither of them was able to see. Anthony tried the hinges, but they had been secured.

He whispered to the Colonel. "I'll jump it," he said, "and then perhaps I can let you in better from the other side."

Going back a few paces, Anthony ran and jumped the gate. He landed nicely on a patch of grass in the garden. Going back to the gate, he discovered that a row of nails was the obstacle. He quickly prised out three of them and was then enabled to open the gate enough to yield Colonel Schofield entrance. Together they walked up the wet grass towards the house. Neither spoke. About halfway up the garden they came to a stretch of derelict latticework. But the struts were broken and it was a comparatively simple matter to find a way through. The grass stopped now and they came to rambling, uncared-for patches of flowers and vegetation. Anthony could see a tree not far from the house, and with a silent gesture pointed out its proximity to Colonel Schofield.

They came to the back door. Anthony flashed his torch on to it. "Doesn't look very formidable," he whispered to his companion. "I'll have that open in no time."

Anthony was as good as his word, and they found themselves standing in a low-arched doorway. Anthony let his torch pick up the surroundings. The room in which they found themselves was of some size and the furniture looked surprisingly good. Anthony found a switch and clicked it on. But the lamp was of poor quality and yielded but a dim, dull light.

"Living-room," muttered Schofield; "better than I should have anticipated."

Anthony quoted Kit Marlowe. "'Infinite riches in a little room.'"

He walked to the inner door and then beckoned to Colonel Schofield. They crept into the passage which evidently led to the shop premises. The Colonel went first and Anthony closed the door noiselessly behind them.

"Come with me," whispered Anthony.

They progressed to a flight of stairs and cautiously began to climb it. It brought them to a landing which ran the entire length of the side of the house—from the front to the back. There was no light at all in this passage. They halted at the summit of the stairs and, as they stopped, a church clock in the distance struck a musical "one". Anthony produced his electric torch again and flashed it along the length of the passage. There was carpet laid on the flooring and there were three doors, all to their left-hand side. Anthony breathed a sigh of relief when he spotted the carpet, for Schofield was a heavy man—heavy-laden and heavy-breathed. He put his fingers to his lips and Schofield and he stood there in the darkness, listening. Not a sound was to be heard.

Anthony crept across the carpeted floor and went to listen outside each of the three doors. Schofield saw him shake his head twice. The first of these gestures seemed to indicate certainty—the second doubt and even perhaps something like disappointment. But at the third door, that is to say the door nearest the rear of the premises, Anthony stayed for some few seconds. And then he turned towards Schofield and beckoned him as he had beckoned him before. Schofield joined him outside the door and Anthony noted with a strong degree of satisfaction that the Colonel was able to move almost noiselessly across the heavy carpet. And then slowly, and with excessive care, Anthony turned the handle of the door.

V

Schofield, standing a few paces to the side, watched Anthony's face. But it was impassive. It gave no hint of what it saw or of what it expected to see. The aperture grew wider. Schofield continued to watch. He felt excitement mastering him. The door by now was almost wide open. Schofield still searched for a clue as to what Anthony was feeling. Was it surprise, amazement or satisfaction?

Satisfaction that he had travelled the right road and found the true solution at the end of it?

Then, suddenly, Schofield heard the click of Anthony's torch again and equally suddenly Anthony half-turned and plucked Schofield into the bedroom behind him. That was the moment when Schofield knew it was a bedroom. He could see the bed and a figure more "on it" than "in it". He crept on tiptoe to where Anthony was standing. The figure on the bed looked shapeless and inert. It gave no suggestion that it was recumbent in healthy sleep. In the room, too, were a plain, cheap, white wood table and a kitchen chair. Once again Anthony gestured to the Colonel to remain silent. Schofield nodded. The injunction was easiness in itself as far as obedience to it went. He would have been hard put to it to have uttered a syllable. Anthony went quickly up to the bed. His torch showed Schofield certain details which he hadn't grasped before. A strap was round the ankles of the prostrate man and his wrists, also, were tied together. Schofield formed the opinion that the man was in a sort of feverish and disordered doze. The beating of the heart was unsteady and at regular intervals a tremor shook and shuddered through his limbs. He lay quiet and still for the most part, when these symptoms were not in evidence, but very quickly a moment came when he writhed in pain.

Schofield held his breath. What did Bathurst intend to do next? He watched Anthony with a curious feeling of fascination. He saw him bend over the prostrate figure on the bed, place his left hand over the mouth, and use the right hand which held the electric torch to shake the man gently by the left shoulder. The man moaned a little and then Schofield saw his eyes open.

"Who's there!" he said wearily. "It's not breakfast-time yet, is it? I don't seem to have been asleep more than a few minutes."

Anthony bent down to him and whispered something. The Colonel, from where he was standing, was just able to hear it.' "We're friends, Langley. Friends! You know Colonel Schofield. But please don't make the slightest noise or it will ruin all our plans. Quiet, man! Understand?"

The Colonel could see now that the man on the bed was Langley. The Langley whom he had known. Langley, too, recognized him, for he nodded twice—once to Bathurst and once to him. Anthony bent down again and with quick, firm and decisive strokes cut the bonds that had held Langley's hands and feet. Schofield went up to the bed to help. Anthony unstrapped Langley's wrists and ankles. Langley waved the former in the air to relieve himself of pain and flexed his legs likewise. Anthony held up his finger to enjoin the strictest of silences. He whispered again to Langley.

"Is there anything you want to take away with you?"

Langley shook his head. "All I have here is what I stand up in." He smiled ruefully at his rescuers. "Or what I lie down in. That would be nearer the mark."

Anthony went to a ewer and wetted his handkerchief. He bathed Langley's forehead with it. Langley raised himself to a sitting posture and shivered at the sharp touch of the cold water.

"You're not feeling too good?" said Anthony quietly.

Langley nodded. "It goes that way sometimes. But where do we move from here?"

"Can you walk?" asked Anthony.

"Yes. I think so. Although I haven't walked far for some little time." He grinned at the Colonel. "Not since Doctor Fell won the Angel Autumn Handicap—or whatever the blessed race was." He passed his hands over his forehead. "I can't remember."

Anthony gave instructions. "Langley, take off your shoes and give 'em to me—you come along in your socked feet. I'll sling the shoes round my neck. You're too hefty to be lugged on my back—and the Colonel's out of training. Don't make even half a sound, and follow the Colonel. You'll be in between us. I'll come last."

Anthony motioned to the Colonel to lead the way out of the room. Langley, who had understood what was expected of him, staggered behind the Colonel. Anthony brought up the rear. He went across to the bed again, pinned a piece of paper to the pillow and closed the bedroom door soundlessly behind him, and once again the journey was made along the carpeted landing. This was accomplished without mishap and the three men descended the flight of stairs. Not a board creaked, and within a period of a few moments Colonel Schofield, Anthony and Langley stood once more (as far as the first-named two were concerned) in the garden. Anthony gave Langley his shoes. The latter put them on.

"You go first now, Bathurst," said the Colonel; "there's that piece of broken latticework to circumvent. Langley and I will come up behind you."

Anthony spoke to Langley. "Feeling all right?"

Langley grinned again. "I wouldn't say that, exactly. But not too bad—considering."

"O.K. Keep next to me then. Not too far behind. Colonel Schofield can bring up the rear. Now, listen. We've got a fairish distance to travel. And as you can see, it's pretty dark. Fit?"

"How far really have we to go?"

"The length of the garden. And then about another three hundred yards. Can you make it?"

"I think so. Anyhow—I'll have a shot at it. Lead on, Horatius." Anthony wasted no more time and went straight ahead. Langley stuck it very well and they were soon through the gate of the garden again. Anthony noticed that Langley had again begun to stagger a little. He stopped in his tracks and waited for Langley to come up with him. Langley put his hand to his head.

"I'm frightfully sorry," he said, "but I'm nearly all in. I've had a pretty thin time lately."

Anthony put an arm round him and supported him. "I'll give you a hand. Keep going for a little longer and you'll be all right."

Langley nodded, and the trio got going again. The way was arduous, and with Langley in the state that he was, they made but slow progress. But helped by Anthony's strength and the Colonel's encouragement, Langley stuck to his task doggedly and eventually they came to the end of the journey.

"Good man," declared Anthony, "that's the bundle. Round the corner, you'll see two sights for sore eyes."

"Two?" queried Langley weakly. "Did I hear you say two?"

"You did," replied Anthony, "and what's more—I meant it. First of all you'll see a real motor-car on real wheels—wheels that go round—and, secondly, you'll see a charming girl in the driving-seat. You may even know her."

"Did you say—a charming girl?"

"'Sright," replied Anthony. "By name of Schofield. Priscilla Schofield."

Langley half-stopped and turned towards him. "That, my dear sir, is the best news that you have so far given me. And I mean that."

He swayed ominously. Anthony and the Colonel between them held him up. They turned the corner.

"There you are," said Anthony, as Priscilla waved to them. "There's the promised land, the car and the lady! And she's spotted us. Only a dozen yards to go. Come on, Langley—last lap!"

Langley nodded and put every ounce of his strength into the final effort. They reached the car, and as Priscilla leant over and opened the door, he toppled forward in a dead faint. Anthony and the Colonel between them hoisted him in and he slumped on to the back seat. Priscilla looked anxiously at the recumbent figure.

"Shall I—" she started to say. Anthony nodded as though he had divined the question she had intended to ask.

"Drive home, Miss Schofield, please, as fast as you can make it. And don't worry about Langley—he'll be O.K. in a little while."

Priscilla trod on the juice. The clock in the distance struck two.

CHAPTER VII

I

THE morning that came after was flooded with November sunshine the colour of pale amber. The white-rimmed foliage that still survived in the garden of Colonel Schofield looked like so many shining jewels. Langley walked in the garden for a little way between Anthony and Priscilla. Sleep and a bellyful of good food had worked wonders with him. The tired, dazed look which his eyes had held was now vanished, and they were keen and eager with excitement and interest. But Anthony's eyes twinkled as he rallied Langley with questions.

"What I want to know, my dear chap, is why you've been in hiding for so long? When we've all been so hot and bothered about you?"

Langley shook his head. "What I can't understand is how you found me. How in the name of all that's wonderful did you connect with that place at Eden? I give it up—but I hand it to you all the same."

Anthony returned one of Langley's own grins. "You led the trail to the 'Old Spider's Web'—and my congratters on how you did it. I followed it up, but found that the bird had flown. Then I reasoned that your next port of call would be Gunter's house, where you first arrived with Ahasuerus. But Miss Schofield took an opportunity and as a result convinced me that you had left there—and my next step up the ladder of deduction was the post-office that breathed o'er Eden. *Voilà!*"

Langley flushed a brick red. "Mr. Bathurst—" he started.

"Cut out the 'Mister'," said Anthony.

"Well, Bathurst, then—there's just one thing I must say to you, it won't take me long, and that's thank you."

"Oh, skip it. You'd have done the same for me. But tell us all you know, why you're here, how they got you in the first place, who killed Trimmer, and why there's all this 'ere smoke coming from that there fire."

"Hear, hear," said Priscilla, "and please remember that I'm just as curious to know as Mr. Bathurst is."

Langley smiled at this evidence of her enthusiasm. "Seems to me," he replied, "that there's just as much that I don't know about you as you're in the dark about me. So what about—"

Anthony cut in. "That can wait. I happen to have won the toss, it's 'a sticky dog' and you've been put in first. So get on with the job. Neither Miss Schofield nor I can wait in patience any longer."

"O.K. That suits me." But the forced gaiety had gone from Langley's voice and general manner.

"We must keep on the move," said Anthony; "it's lovely, but it's cold."

"Go through the end gate," said Priscilla, "and we can walk towards Cherub Magna. It's a delightful walk at any time."

"Good. Now, Langley."

"My job is to get a real jumping-off place or starting-point."

"Start," said Anthony, "from where you left Angus Mount." Langley stared at him. "How do you know about that? The commission was entrusted to me with the utmost secrecy. I thought that I was the only man who—"

Anthony waved a deprecating hand. "My dear Langley, when you did your vanishing trick and I was pressed into service by—er—interested people, I had to get down to the beginnings. My efforts led me to Angus Mount. What could be simpler?"

Langley nodded but he gave them the impression that he was far from being satisfied and that there was still much to be explained to him.

"Start," went on Anthony, "by telling me the particular headache Angus Mount Ltd. were suffering from. That much I absolutely couldn't extract from them."

"Mount," explained Langley, "were extremely concerned with a number of people in the district of Angel who were singularly successful in backing winners. There were four of them. Their names were Gunter, Webber, Layman and Miller. Their addresses were all care of their bankers—the London and Midland Counties. Mount weren't at all satisfied with the bona fides of their transactions. In other words, they smelt an exceedingly large-sized rat. For this reason—the four backers concerned always found these highly lucrative horses when the meeting was at Angel. Elsewhere they weren't anything like so successful. Just ordinary give-and-take betting. Lose a little—win a little! Mount commissioned me to smell round, see what I could get on them and report back. I drove down to Angel just before the last Autumn flat meeting—and then, by a curious coincidence, Miss Schofield took a hand. Unwittingly, of course—but all the same a definitely, well-developed hand. She gave me a kitten to take home—and like a nitwit I took it to the wrong house. Yes—I took His Majesty Ahasuerus in a welter of innocence straight into my own particular lion's den. Into the house of Gunter. Pretty shattering, wasn't it?"

Priscilla looked at Langley round-eyed. "To think that I should have done that! I shall never forgive myself—never."

"Go on," said Anthony, "I'm just beginning to get interested. What happened after that?"

"Well," continued Langley, "their consciences made them suspect me from the outset. I played the silly-twerp card for all I was worth—but I knew, of course, when I heard one or two names bandied about, that Miss Schofield had delivered me straight to my objective. The evening finished up with a rough-house. Ahasuerus let me down rather. He decamped in a very ungentlemanly manner to keep a date somewhere. Naturally, this was a bit of no good to me, because I was forced to produce him as evidence, and I had to do a bit of bashing to get out of the place whole. The gentleman named Layman took one of my best drop-kicks on his wrist and in the confusion that followed I made it. But they followed up with another merchant—one Webber.

"He came along to the 'Bear and Ragged Staff' and did a spot of threatening. I began to realize that I was in a tough spot, and, to use your recent phrase, that there was plenty of fire at the back of Angus Mount's smoke. So I decided to put in a spell of scouting. And I did what was probably a foolish thing. I broke into Gunter's. It was a comparatively simple matter to do so, and I hid in the cloak-room. In the hall. I was able to overhear quite a lot, but just as things were becoming interesting, somebody came along and tried the door and I had to scram. Pronto. Through the window at the back. When I got out on to the road I found that the so-and-sos had pinched my car.

"The next day my car turned up at the 'Bear and Ragged Staff' with a 'stiff' in it. It transpired afterwards that he came from the Eden district and that his name was Trimmer. The fact that he had thumbed a lift out of me the day before made the incident even more interesting. No doubt he had been put on to me by Gunter and Co."

Langley stopped and Anthony cut in. "You said just now that when you were in hiding at Gunter's you heard quite a lot. May I ask what it was you did hear?"

"Oh yes. It was both relevant and appropriate. Criticism was levelled against one of the party for having 'roped in' somebody into the joint plans who wasn't proving entirely satisfactory. A gentleman by the name of Trimmer may have filled this bill—that's my suggestion. In fact I've considered the question from that aspect for some little time now."

Anthony frowned. "Did you hear the name of Trimmer actually mentioned in the conversation?"

Langley shook his head. "Oh no. One of the gang—I fancy it was Mann—was the object of the censure. Evidently he had spilled some of the beans, at least, to a man who, I suggest, was this fellow Trimmer. As a result, Trimmer paid the penalty. Dead men tell no tales, they say, so they 'outed' him and dumped him in my car."

"I see. And within limits I accept it and regard it as feasible. Now go on, please, and let us have the rest of your story."

Langley smiled at Anthony's persistence. "O.K. But I don't know that there's a great deal more for me to tell you. The day after those baa-lambs won my car off me, I went to the Angel Race-meeting. In the circumstances of my own special commission, I regarded it as a significant place for me to visit. While there—Miss Schofield can confirm this—the Police came for me. Re the bloke who'd been dumped in my car. I told the sergeant who interviewed me the truth, the whole truth and nothing but the truth. That interview, by the way, may be regarded as my last public appearance—prior, of course, to the early hours of this morning."

Anthony nodded in acquiescence. "I had an idea that was the case. Let us have the details, Langley, please."

Langley grinned amiably. "Again, I'm afraid there's very little for me to tell you. As I've already said, I was contacted by the Police authorities while I was actually on the Racecourse. Which certainly didn't belong to my idea of spending an enjoyable afternoon. After I had gone over to the station with the blokes that came for me and told them all I knew—which wasn't much—I was told I could clear out. Naturally, I took them at their word, and was peacefully strolling back to the 'Bear and Ragged Staff'. All I can remember with any degree of accuracy is hearing a car behind me pull up. I half-turned, took a hefty welt on the back of the head—I can feel the bump now, by the way—and the next coherent thing I remember is coming to in that rather secluded apartment adjoining the tea-room at the 'Old Spider's Web'."

Priscilla interrupted with a pertinent question. "How did you know that was where you were?"

"Well—I had the advantage of previous knowledge. I had already associated the man Newman with the place, and when I was interviewed by him soon after taking up residence there I felt pretty certain as to the identity of my surroundings."

"Friend Newman," said Anthony, "has also crossed *my* path. And there's one important matter to which I would call your attention. He keeps a post-office in Angel."

"He does," replied Langley. "I found that out during the short time I was on the job here."

"And don't forget," supplemented Anthony, "that the name of the guest-house from which we removed you of recent date was 'Eden post-office'. I commend the coincidence to your notice."

Langley nodded. "I know. But in the meantime, don't forget, I've stayed at Gunter's."

"Did they threaten you at all?"

"Not—er—exactly. Newman, at the 'Spider's Web', and Gunter, *chez-lui*, indicated that I was to be kept a prisoner 'until'—I don't know what 'until' meant exactly—but I'm pretty certain that they're planning something like a big coup within the next few days."

Anthony pulled at his top lip consideringly. "Do you think," he asked Langley, "that after that coup had materialized, your life would have been in danger?"

"I've had the idea in my mind, I must confess. Pretty grim and all that—I know. That's why, when I was removed from Gunter's to Eden, I put up a bit of a scrap. But the odds were heavily against me and I took a prang on the snout for my pains. You should have seen the blood that poured out of me when that happened."

"Priscilla has," said Anthony; "you've been her own true Sir Galahad ever since."

Both Langley and the lady coloured at Anthony's teasing. "I don't follow, though," said Langley; "however did Miss Schofield manage to get inside that house?"

"I sent her," replied Anthony nonchalantly. "I was successful in tracing your movements, you see, by guess and by God—or, if you like, by luck and just a little of the science of deduction."

"I think," said Langley quietly, "that, before we progress any farther, you had better tell me your side of the story."

II

"I made my entry into the cast," said Anthony, "through the good offices of Miss Schofield here. I ought to mention that she has endured a good deal of self-castigation on your account. For she cherishes an idea that it's entirely due to her that you landed yourself in this mess. You and I, Langley, know differently, but I doubt whether we shall ever be able to convince her that we're right and she's wrong."

Priscilla made a laughing disclaimer, but Anthony continued.

"When I took the case—the case of the vanished Langley—I naturally came down here. And one of the first things I did was to strike lucky." Langley seemed about to demur, but Anthony waved away the anticipated gesture. "No—I was appallingly lucky. Angus Mount had engaged another firm to look for you and their emissary simply couldn't bear me out of his sight for more than five minutes at a stretch." Anthony's eyes twinkled. "Well—I fancy he told me much more than I told him, with the result that after a word or two with the Yard I made contact with a gentleman named Monkhouse—representing your friends Angus Mount Ltd. Monkhouse wasn't exactly loquacious, but I learned enough to send me back to Angel with certain definite ideas. Shortly after my return, you and Miss Schofield gave me further impetus towards a fuller understanding of the pattern. As I told you just now, we received your ingenious message from the 'Spider's Web'. You hid that, I presume, in the establishment's laundry?"

Langley nodded. "Yes. The old magazine had been left behind in the inner apartment, and my difficulty, after using it, was how to convey it to Miss Schofield. All I could do was to poke it in a heap of towels and tablecloths thrown in a corner and waiting to be picked up at the weekly laundry call. I thought that there was just a hundred-to-one chance it *might* get into her hands if anybody at the laundry spotted it."

"Good man," responded Anthony. "Well, it came to this. I took a clandestine view of the 'Spider's Web' one evening after the establishment had closed for the day, and felt positive that you had lately been accommodated there, but for certain reasons had been required to change your apartments. The only place I could think of in this connexion was Gunter's place. In fact, I did a spot of 'phoning to that gentleman in an attempt to give him severe wind-up. As a result of this little effort of mine—at least this is my opinion—you were transferred to Eden. In the meantime, however, friend Newman had managed to get a line on me, and he and his henchmen attempted to take concentrated and aggressive action."

Priscilla looked up somewhat anxiously. Langley sought details of the statement. Anthony explained laughingly.

"Oh—it's all right. Thanks to the able and timely assistance afforded me by a number of people—chief among whom was Colonel Schofield—I managed to evade their clutches and find at least temporary sanctuary. Which brings us almost to the present moment. Our problem now—and it seems to me, Langley, that it has become our joint problem—is to discover the genesis and motif behind the whole business and to lay these interesting gentlemen by the heels. You see that, having put my hand to my own particular plough and produced the vanished you, I'm prepared to lend you a hand on yours as well." Anthony dropped an eyelid in Priscilla's orbit of vision.

"Thanks very much, Bathurst," said Langley, "but before we discuss our plans for the *coup de grâce*, how did you cotton on to that post-office at Eden? I haven't quite got the hang of that."

"I was interested in Eden—because the dead man, Trimmer, came from there. I got Miss Schofield to drive me over. While I was there, I had the inestimable good fortune to see one of the gang go into that post-office. I happened to be particularly interested in this chap because on the evening previously he had come perilously near to putting me out of mess."

Langley frowned as though in an effort of remembrance. "What was he like—this chap? Can you describe him?"

"Easily. In that gallery he stands out, rather. He's a well-built, heavy-shouldered, hefty chap. To myself, I always class him as one of the 'Rugger-forward' type."

Langley nodded. "O.K. I've connected. That's the fellow named Layman I mentioned. I had the pleasure at our initial meeting of landing him a juicy kick on his wrist. I can still hear him howling when I got him on the bone."

Anthony nodded. "I remember you mentioning it."

Langley went on. "There's another thing I can tell you about him. At times, he wears a naval uniform—of sorts. The day after I took Ahasuerus home I spotted him in it. Don't know whether the point's worth anything or not."

Anthony seemed to be thinking it over. "What do you think," persisted Langley—"can we link it up anywhere?"

"Don't know," answered Anthony; "we may be able to—later on, perhaps. Very often in this game, either a chance remark or a fortuitous happening will connect two things that you've certainly failed to connect previously, try how you would."

"I agree," said Langley; "that has occurred to me more than once, even in my limited experience."

"What do you two people intend to do?" asked Priscilla, "because I think it's time we turned for home. Are you returning to the 'Bear and Ragged Staff' or are you going to become Daddy's guests and stay on here?"

Anthony looked at her with a question in his eyes.

"It's quite all right," she said; "I've discussed the point with him, and he's frightfully keen for you to stay on."

"That's extremely kind of you, Miss Schofield—but I was debating in my mind whether staying on here might mean danger and unpleasantness for you. For instance, what will they do when they look for Langley in his bedroom and find their bird has flown? You see—I left a message of comfort behind—straight from New Scotland Yard."

Neither Langley nor Priscilla replied. Anthony waited. Eventually Langley spoke. "The day after tomorrow," he said slowly, "is the opening of the National Hunt season at Angel. It's a two-day meeting. There are at least two important events down for decision on the card. And I rather fancy"—Langley spoke very slowly—"from one or two things that I heard drop when I was their uninvited guest, that Gunter and company are all set for a big coup."

"Good," returned Anthony; "then we've about forty-eight hours to get the better of them."

PART THREE
CURTAIN

CHAPTER I

I

THEY returned to the house, and after an early lunch Anthony announced that he intended to hold a council of war. Colonel Schofield took the chair.

Anthony said, "Look here, sir; as I see things, Langley must 'stay put' here for the next two or three days. The main point behind that is consideration for his personal safety."

Langley protested, but the effort was unavailing. The others agreed with Anthony's contention and the suggestion was accepted.

"Now, sir," Anthony went on, addressing the Colonel in particular, "can you rig me up in a suit of overalls? Such as you might use for washing down your car or any similar job."

"I think there's an old suit of that kind in the garage. The chauffeur used to wear it—on occasions. Priscilla could put her hands on it for you."

"Thank you, sir. Then I think I'll ask Miss Schofield to be good enough to drive me almost into Angel in about half an hour's time and get her to pick me up again somewhere about five o'clock this evening. Just about the time it gets really dark."

"What do you do in the meantime, Bathurst?" asked Langley.

"Scout round," answered Anthony, with a smile; "as a matter of fact, there are one or two matters I want to check up on."

"Let me come with you," said Langley.

"You can't. You know that perfectly well. There was a decision taken on that just now. You 'eard!"

"I know all about that—but I don't see—"

Anthony cut him short without ceremony. "It's far safer for you not to show your face in Angel—for a day or so at least. So don't argue with me, my lad."

Langley subsided again, but it was obvious to see that the concession went much against the grain. Anthony turned to Priscilla.

"What do you say, Miss Schofield? Can you find me that old suit of overalls and be ready with the car by half past one?"

"I think I can," replied Priscilla; "at any rate, I'll have a shot at it. Will you want the overalls to wear before we set out for Angel?"

"I shall, Miss Schofield," responded Anthony grimly; "you'll have to look the other way when the car starts. Because I shan't be quite the thing—you know. Anyhow, let me know when you put your hand on the overalls."

Priscilla dashed off on her errand. Langley shook his head in supreme dissatisfaction.

"Lucky chap," he muttered.

"Perhaps," said Anthony, "but you never know. There may have been one or two occasions in the very distant past when I haven't noticed that condition very particularly. Maybe you'll be right this time, though."

He lit the cigarette which Langley tossed over to him, and before he could dispose of the match Priscilla was back with an old suit of overalls.

"What about these, Mr. Bathurst? Will they do?"

Anthony gave the clothes a quick glance. "Admirably, Miss Schofield. I'll be with you in less than a quarter of an hour."

The Colonel issued orders in support of Anthony's design. "Get the car ready, Priscilla. Don't keep Bathurst waiting."

Priscilla raised her hands in mock resignation and winked gracelessly at Langley as she made her exit. When she came back, Anthony was already coming downstairs. Priscilla stared at him open-mouthed.

"Good afternoon, Miss Schofield," said Anthony; "can I do you now, Miss?"

II

"Put me down, Miss Schofield," said Anthony, "just before we come to the old theatre. I've noticed that it's usually pretty lonely round there. Which is precisely the condition I desire for my alighting."

He rubbed the back of his hand down his cheek and achieved additional decoration. Priscilla grinned at him.

"Hope I don't dream tonight."

"Hope I haven't overdone it," inquired Anthony anxiously. "No-o," said Priscilla consideringly, "don't think so. You see—I know you as you really are and there comes the inevitable comparison. No—I think you'll pass muster. But try to look just a wee bit more 'hangdog'. You know, as though you're about to go on strike for another halfpenny an hour."

Anthony made the effort. "How's this, Miss Schofield?"

Priscilla gave him an appraising glance. "Much better," she announced; "you'll pass now for the real article."

She steered the car into the main Angel road and later turned and said to him, "The theatre—the old Macready Theatre—I presume that's the one you mean—is about half a mile ahead. So be ready to jump out quickly, Mr. Bathurst, when I stop the car."

"Say the word, Miss Schofield," said Anthony, "and I'm O.K. And I think that we'll repeat the programme we used at Eden. Pick me up here, please, at five o'clock this evening. Yes?"

Priscilla nodded. "I'll be here. Rely on me."

"Thank you, Miss Schofield; here we are, and I'm fit. Cheero, then, till this evening."

Anthony opened the door of the car and slipped out. The old theatre looked as forlorn and as deserted as he had ever seen it, but he walked quickly past it and heard Priscilla's car moving off rapidly in the reverse direction. Anthony walked on. As he progressed, he did his best to get into the skin of the part he was about to play.

He soon left the Macready Theatre behind and came to the newly-built modern cinema. He observed that it was described as a "Super" Cinema. He formed the opinion that he would like to encounter a cinema that didn't advertise this description. This particular building modestly blazoned the title of "Majestic". Anthony came to the busier parts of Angel and without hesitation made for the Racecourse. After all, Newman had a post-office near there, and Anthony was feeling a lively curiosity therein.

He was gratified to notice that nobody he passed betrayed anything more than an ordinary interest in him, so that he concluded with satisfaction that Priscilla's assessment of his appearance had been eminently sound and that he was "passing muster" all right. He encircled the square, passed the Shelley Memorial and the Coronation Gardens and came out by the new theatre, near the banks of the river. The modern theatre, he noted, was called the Thespian. As he crossed the fine expanse of grass that led to the bridge that he must cross he knew that his luck was in. For, walking along one of the gravelled paths that intersected the grass carpet at various space-intervals was a strongly-built man clad in a dark blue uniform and wearing a gold-braided peaked cap. Anthony recognized the man at once. It was the man whom he knew as Layman.

III

As Layman came more closely to him, Anthony knew that this encounter might well supply the acid test as far as his appearance was concerned. He slouched along, therefore, remembering the hangdog expression which Priscilla had recommended, and to his relief Layman evinced no interest in him whatever.

Layman came out of his path on to the grass where Anthony was walking and took the lead by a couple of paces. "Good," thought Anthony, "this will suit me very well—it may turn out to be just what the doctor ordered." He allowed Layman, therefore, to get well ahead of him, but he kept the uniformed man well in sight and followed him assiduously. When Layman jumped on a 'bus bound for Lubbock, he got on behind him, and when Layman got off, Anthony followed suit.

As he had half expected, Layman made for the river. Anthony slommocked after him, and when he came to the actual waterside he saw Layman make a straight line for the ferry-boat that was standing in to the little jetty. Anthony knew that the ferry was used to cross between Angel and this much larger town of Lubbock. Some of a group of men standing by touched their caps to Layman as he went aboard—and Anthony began to think things. Acting on impulse, he followed Layman on to the ferry-boat. Layman made for the bridge and Anthony realized with increased interest that he must be the skipper of the craft.

"Once aboard the lugger," thought Anthony, and then he heard the first bells coming from the bridge. Anthony looked at his watch. The time was appropriate. Layman's turn of duty, evidently, started at 2 p.m.

The boat was not unduly crowded. The after-lunch traffic, it seemed, was not yet at full pressure. Anthony lounged on the deck and appropriately rubbed his nostrils with his forefinger. There was a coolish breeze blowing and most of the passengers huddled in groups abaft the funnel. More bells were heard from the bridge, and after a good deal of shouting, clanking and deft ropework at the fenders by a blue-jerseyed lad, the *Edna Smith* got under weigh. She moved slowly and easily away from the jetty-side and was soon making good and rhythmic progress towards mid-stream. As they crossed, Anthony could see the green sweep and white rails of the Angel Racecourse as he had never seen it before. The grandstand, perched precariously on one side, looked, with its tiers of seats, like a chocolate-box in the distance. The landing-stage on the side of the river, towards which they were travelling, seemed to be placed right in front of the course, but, in Anthony's judgment, as he essayed to assess the correct distance it would probably be about a quarter of a mile away.

As they came nearer to the course Anthony could see the enclosures, the paddocks, the Tote and the number-board quite clearly from his position on the deck of the *Edna Smith*. Layman, from his coign of vantage on the bridge, must have a splendid view of the course and all its activities.

They were running towards the landing-stage now, and Anthony knew that the journey across the river was almost accomplished. More bell-ringing came from the bridge to the engine-room below and the *Edna Smith* began to reverse and turn her bulk, with her screws thrashing the river-water almost triumphantly. Layman took her in well and deftly and, as the craft backed and turned towards the landing-stage, Anthony heard her siren hoot three times discordantly. A gangway was thrown across and, with others he stepped ashore. He considered it sound policy to go ashore rather than to stay in the ship and go back on the next return journey. As he weighed things up, he thought that there was the possibility that

Layman *might* spot him and have his suspicions aroused—which was the last thing that Anthony desired to happen.

So Anthony, killing time for, say, about half an hour, took a stroll along the outskirts of the Racecourse and noted with interest the preparations for the morrow. The hurdles were up at their intervals along what was obviously the two-mile course and there were also the great thorn fences for the longer distance "chasing" events. Anthony planned to return to the ferry-boat at three o'clock and make the journey back to Lubbock. He had no wish to make it later, for the seeds of an idea had begun to germinate in his fertile brain.

IV

It was at two minutes past the hour that Anthony spotted the *Edna Smith* coming back again to the landing-stage adjacent to the Angel Racecourse. As she came nearer, Anthony could easily pick out the bulky form of Layman on the bridge. He watched the adroit and skilful manoeuvring for position to bring her in, as he had seen it before as a passenger, and then he heard the siren commence to hoot, followed by the venomous thrashing of the screws. On this occasion, *Edna* permitted herself a nap hand of strident hoots, and Anthony walked forward to go on board again. The blue-jerseyed assistant did his customary job with the fenders and the gangway, and with a motley group of others Anthony was aboard the *Edna Smith* again.

He slouched across the deck with his hands thrust deep in his pockets and his greasy cap pulled well over his forehead. From a well-screened seat on the deck, he was able to keep Layman well in view almost all the time of the crossing. Although a big man, the movements of the skipper of the *Edna Smith* were alert and quick and everything he did appeared to be actuated by determination and a fixity of purpose. And the seeds of the idea which had begun to germinate in Anthony's brain took root and grew, and when he boarded the 'bus at Lubbock, a few minutes later, in order to return to Angel, he was resolved to telephone to Chief Inspector MacMorran at the first opportunity.

CHAPTER II

ANTHONY alighted from the Lubbock 'bus by the Hathaway Bridge at the southern end of Angel and walked straight into a telephone booth. He was successful in picking up MacMorran within a few moments.

The message that he delivered to the Scotland Yard man was curt and crisp.

"I want you, Andrew, to come down here at once. In the morning—or perhaps in the afternoon, to be precise—I fancy that I shall be able to show you something. You can catch the five-twenty-two this evening out of Paddington. Come straight to the 'Bear and Ragged Staff' and you'll find I've fixed everything for you. Supper—a steak and chips with a tankard of really good beer. How does that sound, you old ruffian?"

MacMorran listened quietly and it is possible that the terms of Anthony's concluding sentence offered both inducement and blandishment that were strong enough to turn the scale.

"Just a minute," he replied cautiously; "just a minute, Mr. Bathurst, before you rush me off my feet. Let me look at my desk-diary to see how I'm placed for tomorrow. It's quite likely that I can't make it."

Anthony heard the rustle of Andrew MacMorran's papers. He waited patiently for MacMorran's decision. When it came, it was as Anthony had expected. MacMorran had never let him take the can back yet, and Anthony knew that while things were in his power he never would.

"I've had a look at my engagements over the next two or three days—and I find they aren't too bad. So once again I'll listen to the voice of the charmer and come along. What was the time of that train you mentioned?"

Anthony told him and continued with something else. "One other thing, Andrew. Bring another man with you. Hemingway, if you can manage it."

"H'm," grumbled MacMorran, "you're running things a bit fine, you know. You aren't giving him much time. What do you want him for?"

"It's like this, Andrew. I haven't been able to work things out yet with any real clarity or semblance of plan. I haven't had time. And—what makes matters worse—as things are with me, I shan't have time! Hence this urgent call to you for help. As I see things, there'll be a certain move made tomorrow and it will be our job to throw the spanner in the works. If I have you *and* Hemingway here with me, I can dispose of my forces should I deem it necessary."

"All right. As usual, you'll blarney me into giving you your own way. I'll bring Hemingway along with me."

"Good man, Andrew! And if I shouldn't be at the station to meet you tonight—there's a good reason for the doubt—take Hemingway along to the 'Bear and Ragged Staff' with you and you'll find everything O.K. Thanks very much, old man."

Anthony replaced the receiver and slipped quietly out of the box. He looked at his wrist-watch. There would be ample time for him to have tea in an appropriate establishment before he need keep his rendezvous with Priscilla Schofield.

In a side-street he found the very place he wanted and in keeping with the clothes he wore. It was of the old-fashioned coffee-house type. Anthony entered, gave his order, and within an exceedingly short space of time found himself served with a hot mug of tea, a plate of bread-and-butter and a couple of Yarmouth bloaters. He fell to with a will.

II

Priscilla met him and drove him back to her father's house without incident.

"Made any progress?" she inquired simply.

"I *think*," he replied slowly, "that I've been lucky enough to acquire certain very definite ideas as to whys and wherefores. The cogent point seems to me to be this. Our mutual friend, Layman, is skipper of the good ship *Edna Smith*, which plies her ferry-boat trade across the river between Angel and Lubbock. I treated myself to two journeys in her."

Priscilla raised her eyebrows. "What is, then, the big idea? I don't get it. Ferry-boats and crime to me don't exactly team up."

"Before I answer that question categorically, Miss Schofield, we'll sit in conference this evening and talk things over. You and I and your father and Langley. Langley's advice, I am sure, will be invaluable to us."

"O.K.," returned Priscilla, "I can wait for it. That's the worst of you detective experts. You're a cagey lot. Still—as I said just now—I'll possess my soul in patience."

They made good time home. Anthony divested himself of his mechanic's garb and after dinner he called the three others into conference.

"As you know," he said, after the Colonel had filled the glasses, "I went into Angel this afternoon with certain ideas. The ball rolled well for me and I walked almost slap into our mutual acquaintance, Layman. This was too good a chance to be lost. So I kept on his track and he led me to a ferry-boat that runs between Angel and Lubbock. The name of the boat is the *Edna Smith*. He happens to skipper the boat, and skippers it remarkably well, too, I should say, from my observations of this afternoon. One of its two destinations is the landing-stage quite close to the Racecourse."

"Quite right," put in the Colonel; "I've noticed it put in there many a time. Seen it when I've been on the course itself."

"Good," said Anthony; "well, now you have the general lay-out of the river territory as I want you to envisage it. The *Edna Smith* setting out for Angel from Lubbock on the other side of the river, with Layman, the skipper, on the bridge."

Anthony turned to Langley. "Got the idea, Langley?"

"Why—yes," replied Langley, "of course."

"Good man," went on Anthony—"because that's where you come in."

"I? How do you mean?"

"Because I want your expert advice."

"Expert turns to expert," murmured Priscilla; "now comes the tug-of-war."

"What advice?" queried Langley.

"Re the Sport of Kings, Langley. Matters equine. Have you any details of tomorrow's card?"

Langley stared. Anthony went on.

"Is there an important race tomorrow with a reasonably small entry? In the region, say, of about half a dozen horses going to the post?"

Langley scanned the racing column of the Colonel's newspaper. "Yes," he replied at length, "the big race of the day. The Grand Midland Steeplechase. Run over three miles. It happens also to be the most valuable event on the card. Worth £750 to the winner."

"Good," said Anthony again, rubbing his hands; "then if my theory's going to hold any water—that's the race that our friends hope to make a substantial profit out of."

"But how's it worked?" asked Langley. "I presume that it's phoney—that there's something fishy about it somewhere."

"I believe this," said Anthony quietly, "that Layman will convey the name of the winner to his compatriots *after* the race has been run." Langley regarded him incredulously. "But how in Hades can he do that? And even if he did—how the blazes could they get a bet on? They wouldn't have time. No—I'm sorry—but I don't see it. I'm afraid that you're barking up the wrong tree, Bathurst."

Anthony smiled at Langley's certainty. "There's an old saying, Langley, that there are more ways of killing a dog than by choking it with a sausage. I have a definite idea as to how the job's worked. Based very largely on my observations of this afternoon."

"I'd love to hear it," said Colonel Schofield; "this yarn's just about my own personal handwriting."

"Well," said Anthony, "I hadn't intended to give details until I was more certain of my ground. That's a position which I don't think I can give away—yet. But I'll say this. Layman gets the winner from the announcement board directly the winner's number goes into the frame—and he immediately sends it to Newman."

"But *how*?" persisted Langley—"that's the part I don't get."

"Wait until tomorrow, Langley, and see what happens. I've got Chief Inspector MacMorran coming down tonight with one of the best men attached to Scotland Yard. They're going to the 'Bear and Ragged Staff'. I shall confer with them there early tomorrow morning."

III

Anthony met MacMorran and Hemingway a few minutes after breakfast on the following morning.

"Andrew," he said, after he had shaken hands with each of the professionals, "there's a hell of a lot to do—and precious little time to do it in. But first of all I want you to see the local Police—there's a Sergeant Lawton in charge of the case—and arrange to have the telephones attached to two installations listened-in to between one o'clock and half past four this afternoon. It'll take a bit of wangling, perhaps, because the 'Yard' isn't in on this case officially, but I'll bank on your powers of persuasion. The two services are both post-offices. One's kept by a man named Newman—it's just by the Racecourse— and the other's kept by a certain Mr. Mann—High Street, Eden. If you see to that, Hemingway can come with me to the offices of the Lubbock and Angel Ferryboat Services Company. I shall be all the better for a touch of professional backing. Now, is that all dear?"

MacMorran grinned. "Don't rush me. Let me get it all straight. You want me to see the Police re this telephone stunt. I must do that, naturally. I'll jot down those addresses. And then you want Hemingway to go with you to the ferry people—have I got it correct?"

"That's all O.K., Andrew. And if we get busy at once, I'll meet you here again"—Anthony looked at his watch—"at half past eleven. Hemingway and I will come into the cocktail-bar as near to that time as we can make it. Is that a bet?"

"All right, Mr. Bathurst. And when we meet, you can give me the dope. At the moment, you know, I'm taking most things for granted."

Anthony grinned at him and then waved "Come on," to Hemingway.

IV

Hemingway followed Anthony into the offices of the Lubbock and Angel Ferryboat Company.

"Your pigeon," Anthony whispered, as they were on the point of being shown into the secretary's office. "I want them to do something for me. So it's Scotland Yard for ever—see what I mean?"

"Leave it to me, Mr. Bathurst," answered Hemingway. "I'll fix that all right for you."

Anthony judged it discreet in the circumstances to let Hemingway enter the room first.

"What can I do for you, gentlemen?" inquired the secretary. He was a thin, pale-faced, insipid-looking fellow, but he seemed anxious to help all he could and was in no way awkward. Hemingway produced the necessary documentary evidence as to his own official status and then waved the details of the inquiry over to Anthony. Anthony stated his case. He stated it thus.

"Our inquiry, Mr. . . . . er . . ."

"My name's Webberley," said the secretary with a somewhat anaemic smile.

"Thank you—Mr. Webberley. Our inquiry concerns an employee of yours—a gentleman by the name of Layman."

Webberley raised his eyebrows. "That's so . . . We have a Layman in our service. One of our most—er—competent and—er—efficient captains. He's been in charge of our boat *Edna Smith* for some years now. Three or four, I should say . . . without troubling to consult the Company's records. And how can I help you with regard to Captain Layman?"

"Would you be good enough to tell us, Mr. Webberley, whether your Captain Layman was on duty on the *Edna Smith* on these afternoons? Give me just one moment for reference and I'll let you have the dates that we're concerned about."

Anthony examined his diary with regard to certain dates that he had obtained from Langley. He called them out to the secretary. "The dates are as follows, Mr. Webberley. November the 11th and 12th of this year. September 23rd and 24th. June 10th and 11th, and February 18th and 19th. All of them falling in this year of grace."

Webberley frowned. But it was more apologetic than anything else. "That will take me some little time, I'm afraid. I shall have to . . . er . . . investigate the staff record book. I'll have it brought in here at once." He pulled the telephone towards him and lifted the receiver. "Is that you, Dean—bring in the staff record book, will you? At once, please."

Webberley sat back in his chair and meticulously adjusted the hang of his trouser on his crossed leg. "I trust, gentlemen, that you harbour no . . . er . . . unpleasant suspicions as to . . . er . . . Captain Layman's conduct or personal integrity? I should . . . er . . . deplore—"

Anthony replied to him. "Nothing, Mr. Webberley, that would directly implicate the good name of your Company. I can assure you of that."

"I am relieved to hear that. Ah—here we are."

He took a book from the hands of a mouse-like man who had crept to the secretary's side. Webberley turned the pages. "Let me see. We start, I think, in . . . er . . . chronological order . . . with February 18th. That was the earliest date you mentioned. Here we are. Yes. And the 19th. Yes. June. Ten-eleven. H'm—h'm. Er . . . September . . . and er . . . November. I think you wanted to know re the eleventh and the twelfth. November . . . let me see. Ah! H'm."

Webberley held the open book on his knees. He nodded affirmatively. "Yes, gentlemen. Captain Layman was on the afternoon duty on all of those dates you specified. I am able to confirm that for you."

"And the duration of the afternoon period of duty would cover what hours, Mr. Webberley?"

The secretary pursed his lips at the question. "Well—it would vary a little according to the time of the year. Not a lot—but a little. And the river's tidal, you know. But if you said between noon . . . at the outside . . . and, say, seven o'clock in the evening . . . again at the outside . . . you would be on quite safe ground."

Anthony turned to Hemingway. "You might make a note of those days and times, will you?"

Hemingway nodded and made the necessary entries in his diary. Anthony waited for him to give the O. K. This soon came and Anthony rose on the point of departure.

"Thank you, Mr. Webberley. You have given me the information that I wanted. As I said—many thanks. I don't think we need detain you any longer."

Webberley smiled and bowed Anthony and Hemingway out of his office. Anthony grinned at the professional and patted him on the shoulder.

"We will now, my dear Hemingway, return to meet your respected colleague Chief Detective-Inspector Andrew MacMorran. I find the idea of that cocktail-bar distinctly attractive."

V

MacMorran was already there when they arrived. Anthony stood drinks before he referred to the main business of the meeting.

"Well, Andrew?" he said eventually, "how did you get on? Did you pull it off?"

The Chief Inspector tossed his head in mock indignation. "You sent me off on a nice errand, didn't you? Talk about treading on the Chief Constable's corns! Still—I did my best and explained in the first place I was in on the London end of the case and needed their very keenest co-operation. You know—the Angus Mount angle. This enabled me to soften your Sergeant Lawton down, and after taking instructions from at least three big noises at County Headquarters and by putting a trunk call through to the old man, he agreed to do what I wanted. Notes will be taken of all 'phone conversations on the two lines you mentioned which will take place between 1 and 4.30 this afternoon. Does that suit you?"

"Admirably, Andrew. Now spill what we picked up this morning, Hemingway, at the offices of the Ferryboat Company."

Hemingway complied. "Make a note of that, Andrew," said Anthony, "because before we're through with this case that information will have acquired a very definite value. Ah! there we are. By the way, Andrew—two people I asked to come along to meet you. They're coming towards us now." Anthony beckoned. "Chief Inspector MacMorran, Superintendent Hemingway—Miss Schofield, Colonel Schofield."

Priscilla smiled and the Colonel unbent in a jerky nod. "If you two gentlemen would do me the honour of lunching with me at my house—I'd be delighted. We're lunching early today—twelve o'clock sharp." He winked at Anthony.

"I'll accept on their behalf," said Anthony.

"There's room in the car," went on the Colonel, "so we'll have another drink and then . . . ahem . . . get cracking." The Colonel stiffened as he used the colloquialism and then looked round guiltily to see if anybody by chance had heard him.

"By the way," asked Anthony—"where's Langley?"

"At the house," replied Colonel Schofield with a throaty chuckle. "At the house with specific instructions to lie low and say nuffin, like . . . er . . . the white . . . rabbit in *Alice in Wonderland*."

Priscilla glanced a little indignantly in her father's direction. But the drinks came, were disposed of with alacrity, and the party generally made for the Colonel's car.

Lunch was ready when they arrived and at half past twelve Anthony began to issue his instructions. "The big race this afternoon," he said, "is timed for two-fifteen. The Grand Midland Steeplechase. A three-mile race. According to my paper this morning, six horses will face the starter. There may be less. But there are unlikely to be more than six because the full entry was only nine."

At that moment he noticed that Langley was regarding him strangely. There was a peculiar look on Langley's face. Anthony asked him a question.

"What's the trouble, Langley? Have I slipped up over anything I've said?"

"Oh no," replied Langley with a shake of the head—"not at all. But what you did say struck me as being rather remarkable. That is to say from my point of view. When you spoke to me about it yesterday, I must have been utterly and completely dense."

"I don't get you," said Anthony; "in what way do you mean?"

"Why—you asked me about a race with what you termed a reasonably small entry. I told you the Grand Midland 'Chase. That's when I was stone blind." Langley leant over the table to give greater emphasis to his words. "When I was commissioned by Angus Mount to come down here, they told me that Gunter and Co. were almost always successful in backing the winner in races with comparatively small fields. You see the coincidence now, don't you?"

Anthony rubbed his hands and a familiar gleam (to MacMorran and Hemingway) came in his grey eyes. "Excellent, Langley, excellent. That makes me feel more certain than ever that I am on the right track." He went on. "Now with regard to this afternoon. Thank God the weather's fine and clear, for one thing. MacMorran, Hemingway and I will accompany Miss Schofield in the car as far as the Macready Theatre. I shall be dressed as yesterday—I intend to be on the safe side as far as possible. After Miss Schofield has dropped us, Andrew and I will get across to Lubbock by the ferry. From there we shall be all set for the return journey to Angel. Miss Schofield will drive the car back here and pick up the Colonel and Langley. The three of them will proceed to Eden and the Colonel will enter the post-office there at, say, twenty minutes past two. That time should do. I don't suppose they'll be 'off' for a minute or so after the scheduled two-fifteen time. As far as you are able, sir, keep a close eye on Mann himself—he's the Postmaster there. Keep him in conversation as much as you can—I rather anticipate that you'll experience some little difficulty in that direction." Anthony grinned as he said this. "And watch him closely to see what happens. The more detailed report you can pass on to MacMorran upon your return, the better we shall all be pleased. Oh—and by the way, Langley, don't show too much of yourself in the car. Now, I think that does for that particular portion of our arrangements." Anthony turned to Hemingway. "That leaves only you, Hemingway. I fancy that we left you, if my memory serve me correctly, outside the Macready Theatre, with the Inspector and me making for Lubbock. I want you, Super, to make your way from the theatre to Post-office Number Two. It's in Racecourse Way and the name of the proprietor is Newman. Get in there about the same time that Colonel Schofield enters the post-office at Eden. And carry out as much as you can an identically similar programme to that which you heard me outline to him. O.K.?"

Hemingway nodded. "Leave that to me, Mr. Bathurst. I haven't let you down in the past and I shan't start on this job."

"Good man! Now we're all set—yes?"

The others nodded. "Right-o then! Miss Schofield! I'll be at your service—suitably clad for the occasion—with Inspector MacMorran within the space of ten minutes."

Anthony dashed from the room. "Knows his vegetables," said Langley as the door closed.

"Mr. Bathurst, do you mean?" said MacMorran.

"That's what I meant," said Langley.

"If he didn't," declared MacMorran, "you wouldn't find Hemingway and me here."

CHAPTER III

I

ANTHONY, MacMorran and Hemingway alighted from the car at the Macready Theatre and waved to Priscilla as she backed, turned and drove back in the direction of her house again.

"Here," said Anthony to Hemingway, "is where you part company with the rest of us. We'd better not all move off together. You know your destination. Cheero, and good luck."

Hemingway crossed the road without saying a word and strode off. Anthony looked at his watch. "He's all right, Andrew. Got bags of time. In our case we want the Lubbock 'bus. I know the way. I've travelled this road before."

Anthony and the Inspector took the same route as Anthony had used when he encountered Layman, picked up the Lubbock 'bus in good time and boarded the *Edna Smith* at five minutes to two precisely. MacMorran cast a shrewd glance and smiled appreciatively in Anthony's direction.

"You certainly look the part. If I ever want my car given the once-over, I'll send for you."

"Thanks, Andrew. But I'm afraid my terms'll be too steep for you." As he spoke, he nudged MacMorran in the ribs with his elbow. "Don't look up for a second. But Layman has just gone on to the bridge. And, in my opinion, he looks a trifle worried."

MacMorran played cautiously, looked up at the sky and also across the river before he essayed a glance in Layman's direction. Although the early morning had been clear, with visibility excellent, the day had not lived up to its prior promise. There was no rain, but it was distinctly dull now and Anthony felt uncomfortably certain in his bones that the rain would come before nightfall. The river was dark and swirling and the clouds were growing more sombre as the day had worn on and by now had established their mastery over the morning sun.

"I agree with you, Mr. Bathurst," said MacMorran, after a few seconds' interval, "friend Layman has something very definitely on his mind."

Anthony looked at his watch again. "It's gone two o'clock. According to my reckoning, he'll be late getting away this afternoon. The crossing normally takes about ten minutes. He'll hang about a bit, you'll see."

"You mean that he's deliberately delaying starting off?"

"That's my idea, Andrew. In a nutshell. Come and sit leeward. You get a good view of my lord from that seat over there. By Jove— oh, that's really excellent! Just what the vet ordered."

"What are you muttering about, Mr. Bathurst?"

Anthony prodded the Inspector with his elbow. "Cock your eye in the skipper's direction," he said; "notice anything? Different from the same view of a few moments ago—eh?"

MacMorran re-directed his gaze casually and then answered in low tones. "Yes. I've spotted it. You mean the field-glasses, I take it?"

"Good for you, Andrew. That's what I meant. It's seven minutes past the hour now. He'll be casting off any minute now—if I'm any judge."

Anthony's prognostication was correct, for, almost simultaneously with his statement; they felt the *Edna Smith* moving away from the waterside.

"Now, Andrew," said Anthony, "keep your eyes glued on Layman all the time that we're crossing over."

As they watched, they could see the skipper's fingers working nervously round the strap of the field-glasses suspended round his neck. Anthony watched the hands of his wrist-watch as they crept towards the quarter. "Our man's taking his time, Andrew," he said quietly, "making a much wider sweep of the river than he did the time I came before. Ah—he's turned a little now—making more for the usual course. I should say we've come about half the distance. It's two-seventeen. I shall expect him to move straight across from now on."

MacMorran watched and saw that Anthony was right. The *Edna Smith* was now proceeding slowly but smoothly towards the Angel Racecourse.

"Watch him, Andrew," said Anthony after a brief interval; "see what he does. It's just on twenty minutes past. According to my reckoning—this is about the time when he'll get very busy."

MacMorran slid off his seat and crouched, half-turning, over the side of the ferry-boat. From this new position he was able to see Layman and the man's general movements very much better. He saw the skipper of the *Edna Smith* raise the field-glasses to his eyes as the boat ran steadily towards the Racecourse on an even keel.

"We're about four hundred yards from the landing-stage," remarked Anthony quietly; "he's timed the whole business remarkably well—unless there was an unusually long delay at the starting-gate. Keep on watching him."

"I am," replied MacMorran from the side of his mouth. "He's not moving. His eyes are fixed intently on some object. Or—what I should say—the field-glasses are."

"If you follow the direction in which he's looking, Andrew, you'll see the white-painted board on the Racecourse. In that frame, within a very short time from now, there will be hoisted the numbers of the three placed horses in the Grand Midland 'Chase that is now being run over a distance of three miles. When Layman lowers his glasses, see what happens—and don't say I didn't do my best to prepare you for it."

"He's still watching," said the Inspector, "keeping quite still."

"Columbus sighting the New World—eh?"

"Looks very much like it. Nothing at all suspicious about him that I can see. Hope you aren't giving me the can to take back."

"Something gave trouble at the starting-gate," remarked Anthony laconically. "That's the explanation of the delay, Andrew. Don't worry. The long-anticipated dénouement will come along all right. Possess that canny soul of yours in patience."

"He's still standing stock-still," went on MacMorran, "just the same—all the time. He doesn't seem to be ready to—No—no—he's dropped the glasses and taken a few steps along the bridge. Things are moving."

"Wait for it, Andrew," said Anthony—"wait for it, my lad."

"What do I wait for?" asked MacMorran. "I'm a man that's always liked to have his—"

Before he could complete his sentence MacMorran heard the answer to the question he had just put to Anthony. The siren of the *Edna Smith* hooted discordantly. As it always did when the ferry-boat stood in towards the landing-stage. One! Two! Three! Four! Five! Five sharp, clearly-defined and clearly-separated blasts came from the *Edna Smith*. Anthony consulted a copy of a newspaper that he took from the pocket of his greasy overalls.

"Five of 'em, Andrew! You heard! And as I see things, if the official card agrees with the list of runners in this paper—and from the entries, I think it does—the Grand Midland Steeplechase has been won by 'White Man's Burden'. Events will prove me right or otherwise."

MacMorran sat back as the *Edna Smith* bumped and rocked against the side of the landing-stage and then he looked at Anthony with curious interest. At the same time he commenced to finger his chin reflectively.

"So that's how it's done—eh? Picked up by the confederates at the post-offices and then some monkeying with the time-stamp—eh? Di-da-di-da-di-da." He looked at Anthony Bathurst. "Have I cottoned on to the idea, Mr. Bathurst?"

Anthony grinned at him. "Andrew, according to my reckoning—you're a hundred per cent right. Take top place in the class—will you?"

The Inspector fell to consideration. "What do we do now?" he inquired. "Get off the boat?"

"I fancy so, Andrew. There's no point, as I see it, in our remaining on and going back to Lubbock. Besides, we should, first of all, pick up the indefatigable Hemingway. I should say that when we meet him he'll be bursting with news. Knowing him as I do, I don't imagine that the encounter will be long delayed."

They walked down the gangway on to dry land. Anthony, as he disembarked, flung a quick upward glance towards the bridge of the *Edna Smith*. But Layman, having superintended the bringing-in of the ferry-boat, had temporarily disappeared. MacMorran spoke over his shoulder to Anthony, walking a few paces behind him.

"What price would they get? Any idea?"

"As it happens, Andrew, on their system of finding the winners after the race has been won, they have to put up with the favourite sometimes. And possibly, too, at very cramped odds. Then, of course, the stake would be their maximum. The maximum, I mean, from the particular layer's angle. Today I should say they've raked in quite a juicy little winner. According to the betting forecast in the morning paper, the S.P. should be in the neighbourhood of fives. That's grateful and comforting, considering how small their field always is."

"Always is?" queried MacMorran—and then corrected himself. "Oh—of course, I remember—you pointed out that they always choose 'em that way."

"Exactly," confirmed Anthony; "people don't care two hoots, they don't notice five—but they *might* be a little perturbed if they heard—say—a sweet seventeen coming from the *Edna Smith*." He took MacMorran's arm.

"Take this turning, Andrew—and we ought to run into our good friend Hemingway before many minutes have passed. Newman's post-office is at the end of this road on the right-hand side."

"I rather think," said the Inspector, "that the case may be difficult to ram home to them."

"Perhaps," said Anthony; "maybe you're right. We shall be able to assess the chances of that more accurately when we compare our respective accounts of the various proceedings. Ours, Hemingway's, Langley's and the Schofields'. We should be able to string the bits and pieces together and make a fairly respectable whole of them. Enough to equip Angus Mount Ltd., anyway."

"Also—what about the murder?" asked MacMorran.

"My prediction," said Anthony, optimistically, "is that one of the bunch will squeak. I'm confident about that. When we get 'em in the bag you'll see a large yellow streak somewhere—or I'll eat my hat."

"We'll see. It often does go that way. And if—" MacMorran broke off suddenly. "There's our man," he said, "crossing the road." Anthony looked up and saw Hemingway crossing over to join them.

II

Hemingway came up. He looked grave and somewhat preoccupied. "Well," said MacMorran, "and what have you got to tell us? What happened?"

"I went into the post-office, as we arranged, just after a quarter past two. A man came out from the shop-parlour to serve me. A shortish, dark-eyed man."

Anthony nodded. "Newman himself."

"I asked for some stamps, two postal orders of odd amounts, and when he'd served me with the orders I put a question to him concerning my purely hypothetical savings-bank account." Hemingway's eyes twinkled. "If my trouble and strife had heard me, she'd have collapsed in the shop there and then. I asked him the most you could draw out of your bank-book 'on demand'. I pretended to be on the daft side, and kept him talking as you wanted me to. Suddenly he asked me to excuse him for a minute or two—he said the telephone in the house was ringing. It wasn't—or at any rate I hadn't heard it. But I could hear him talking on the 'phone just afterwards, so I concluded he must have got through to somebody."

"You couldn't hear what he said, I suppose?" asked Anthony.

"No, sir. Not a word. He was fly enough to shut the door behind him."

"Did you hear a ship's siren going just before he asked to be excused serving you?"

"No. Not that I noticed. I was too keen on keeping the bloke on the chin-wag to pick up any what you might call external sounds or noises. Well—to continue the story—it was a good five minutes before he came back to serve me. This time with the excuse that he had a near relation lying dangerously ill and that he was constantly being 'phoned because of that. After a few minutes' more conversation, I thanked his worship and scrammed out of the shop. There you are, gentlemen—full score—words and music. Has thy servant performed well and truly?"

"I'll leave that to Mr. Bathurst to answer," said the Inspector; "it's his show—not mine."

"Yes, Hemingway," said Anthony, "that's all right. So far—so good—and all according to Cocker. It only remains now for the other contingent to report on much the same lines and then for you, MacMorran, to hear what the conversations between the two post-offices really were. The Schofields should be back home again by now—I suggest we 'phone to the house and ask Miss Schofield to come in with the car and pick us up."

"Good idea," returned MacMorran; "you can do your stuff in that direction as soon as you like. I was becoming afraid I had to walk all the way back."

Anthony found a 'phone-box, and within the hour Priscilla had picked them up outside the Macready Theatre and driven them back to her father's house.

III

As Priscilla handed round the cups of China tea and plates of hot buttered muffins, Anthony turned to the Colonel and Langley.

"I haven't yet asked Miss Schofield. I presume she waited outside in the car with you, Langley, but what happened?"

The Colonel squared his shoulders. One of his big moments was definitely on the way, and dammit, sir, he wasn't going to miss it.

"Priscilla and Langley stopped outside in the car—as you said. And, mindful of your instructions, I warned Langley to keep his head well down."

Langley grimaced gracelessly behind the Colonel's back.

"I walked in," continued the Colonel. "Just like that." He gestured with dramatic emphasis. "Quite—er—coolly and . . . er . . . nonchalantly. And, as far as I could judge, at the exact time you told me to. Although I say it, I make it a golden rule never to fail anybody in a moment of crisis. My old regiment would subscribe to that—I can tell you. And I didn't fail this afternoon. I asked the unwholesome-looking fellow behind the counter how long it would take for a telegram to get from there to Hampton Lovett in Worcestershire. That bowled him, by Jove! Neck and crop, my boy. You could see he was damned annoyed at my turning up like that, just at that moment, but he made some sort of show of answering my question until I heard the telephone ringing in the living-room behind the shop. At least, that's where it seemed to me to be coming from. Well, Mr. Mann, as you call him, came all over dithery when he heard it and it was as much as he could do not to rush off and leave me there stone-cold in the shop. As it was, he muttered a mumbled apology about urgent business or something and disappeared. But he was back very quickly and sent a telegram—or even, perhaps, telegrams. I could hear the instrument at work. When he'd finished doing this, he came back to me with what was nothing more or less than a barefaced lie! He said that he'd instituted inquiries and my wire would take about two hours and a quarter to get to Hampton Lovett. I was speechless—I can tell you—and a damned good mind to call the scoundrel's bluff. But I didn't—I bottled up my indignation and came out. I flatter myself to think that in the circumstances I behaved creditably."

"Colonel," said Anthony, "you've really done a grand job of work and I owe you my sincere congratulations. You've rounded off the case in the manner of a master. The affair went exactly as I had visualized it. Layman sent the number of the winner by 'siren' code. Newman—listening and waiting for it—picked it up. That part's as easy as falling off a log. Money for old rope. Then Newman, without waiting a second—'phones it through to Mann at the Eden post-office and Mann wires it off to as many bookmakers as the enterprising gang have managed to obtain on their list. The telegrams from Eden are, of course, ante-timed." He looked round at the others. "One way of getting rich without working for it."

He noticed the expression on Langley's face. "What's troubling you, Langley?" he asked.

"Just one point that's not terribly clear to me, Mr. Bathurst. Why take the trouble—and lose valuable time into the bargain—because that's what it must mean—of 'phoning to Eden? Why doesn't Newman send the wires from Angel?"

"I'd thought of that point," smiled Anthony, "and I fancy I know the answer. The post-office run by Newman in Racecourse Way is *very* near to the course. Don't you think that this unusual proximity would have aroused suspicions at the other end at once? As it is—they've had a much longer run for their money. Or rather for Angus Mount and Company's." Anthony shrugged his shoulders.

Langley nodded at the explanation. "Yes—I see—and I think you're on sound ground."

MacMorran took another muffin from Priscilla and passed up for another cup of tea. "It remains for me to have access to the recorded conversations. They should clinch the matter. And if you good people will excuse me—or, better still, excuse us—Mr. Bathurst, Hemingway and I will get down to Angel as soon as possible. Lawton expects me some time this evening. I told him I'd be as early as I could make it."

"Certainly, Inspector," replied Colonel Schofield—"and Priscilla once again shall drive you into the town."

Langley made plaintive noises. "Do I go?" he asked.

MacMorran looked at Anthony. "On this occasion," said the latter, "your persistence shall be rewarded."

IV

"Hallo," said Lawton breezily to Langley as they entered the Sergeant's room, "you here again? Seen you before, my lad. What's your trouble this time?"

Langley grinned at the greeting and answered in the same strain. "I'm with the others, Sergeant Lawton. Chief Inspector MacMorran, Superintendent Hemingway, Mr. Anthony Bathurst—complete with self. Come for some highly important information. Which you, and you alone, can give us."

"Oh, of course," commented Lawton with a touch of irony, "and wrap it up for you as well, I suppose?"

Langley turned to MacMorran. "The man's hopeless, Inspector. I'll pass him over to you. See what you can do with him."

A uniformed constable brought chairs. They accepted them. MacMorran made himself comfortable.

"Well, Sergeant," he opened, "what's the best news you've got for me?"

Lawton took papers from his drawer. "I'll read it to you. Then you can judge for yourself. The first, which I'll call 'Message A', was sent from the post-office situated at Racecourse Way, Angel, to the post-office in High Street, Eden. The time—the official time of the recording, that is—is given as two-twenty-eight p.m. B.S.T. Here's the wording of it. *'Is that you, Harold? This is Ted. Number Five's the size you want. Fit you like a glove. Won't know you've got 'em on. Get busy at once.'"* Lawton looked up from his reading. "Did you get that all right?" he inquired.

"Carry on, Alvar Lidell," interrupted Langley, "you're sure doin' fine."

Lawton ignored the ribaldry. "The second—which we'll describe as 'Message B'—travelled exactly the reverse route. It was timed two-fifty-nine p.m. Thirty-one minutes after the other one. It ran as follows: *'Number Five O.K. Ted. Taken your advice and ordered seven pairs.'"* Lawton replaced his papers. "There you are, gentlemen, you've had it."

MacMorran looked at Anthony. "Satisfied?"

"I am," replied Anthony, "but the more important point is, are you?"

"I think so. Knowing what I do know. The whole bag of tricks, I mean. It adds up, doesn't it?"

Anthony nodded. "The evidence is accumulative all right."

"My next step," said the Inspector, "is to get in touch with Angus Mount. By the way—what did the winner actually start at, did you hear?"

"Sevens," replied Anthony laconically: "very tasty."

"You know," went on MacMorran, "I've been thinking things over. Our friends can't win a rare lot this way. All bookmakers protect themselves, you know, against this sort of thing. They limit the stake for wires despatched up to the advertised time of the race to something like a couple of quid. I'm not certain of the amount—but it's something like that. And they also bar telegrams sent in batches from the same post-office. I happen to know that too. I fancy they draw the line at four."

Anthony fell to calculation. Then he turned to Hemingway. "I've been thinking. They say second thoughts are best. Could you be certain that Newman didn't send any wires?"

"No. He could have done so easily in the time he was away."

"If he did—supposing they work half a dozen bookies (you can bet your boots Mount isn't the only one) and operate from two post-offices—each man in the gang has £4 on at seven to one six times. Net profit, £168 per man." He jerked a question at Langley. "How many meetings a year at Angel?"

"Over the sticks *and* on the flat do you mean?"

"Yes. Covering the full calendar year."

"Seven, as a rule."

"There you are then—over £1,000 a year per head of villain."
Langley shook his head. "The price wouldn't always be sevens."

"It might conceivably be more—on the flat. But averaging it at
fours, it's not so dusty. Better than the proverbial slap in the belly,
etc. *And* free of Income Tax! No mean consideration that, these days."

MacMorran rose. "Well—thank you, Sergeant Lawton, for the
information and also for what you've done. The next step, as I see
it, is with me."

V

MacMorran, Anthony and Langley went to town on the following morning and called at the offices of Angus Mount Ltd. After a
little preliminary negotiation, they were interviewed by the debo-
nair Monkhouse.

"Why," said the latter genially, as they were shown into his
room, "look who's here! Langley of all people, and my very good
friend Bathurst!"

The Inspector grunted and introduced himself. In a few brief
sentences he stated his case. Monkhouse listened with interest, punc-
tuating MacMorran's recital of the facts with many affirmative nods.

"Yes," he said, when the Inspector had finished, "we were 'Aunt
Sallied' again. They knocked us up another catcher. I'll send for the
wires. Some firms protect themselves against the 'batch telegram'—
but we don't—and there are a good many more like us."

He spoke into the telephone and a clerk brought in a bundle of
telegrams. Monkhouse picked out the Eden and Angel despatches.
"Timed out at two-fourteen p.m. Well, it seems to me there's a clear
case for prosecution."

"You'll put the matter in the hands of the authorities, then?"
asked MacMorran.

"Certainly," replied Monkhouse, "and as far as Angus Mount
are concerned—you can go the whole hog! Also, gentlemen, my
congratulations, on behalf of the firm, on a very neat piece of work."

MacMorran pointed to Anthony. "There's your man for the bouquets—if you must chuck 'em."

Monkhouse's eyes twinkled as he shook hands with Anthony. "Do you know," he said, "I guessed as much."

"You mustn't believe all the Inspector says," laughed Anthony.

VI

Twenty-four hours later, the six arrests were made, and Gunter, Layman, Webber, Newman, Miller and Mann were lodged in jail. A week afterwards, Mann, the Postmaster at Eden, turned King's Evidence as Anthony had predicted and confessed to his share in the conspiracy. He also described how Trimmer had been approached by him to assist in the working of the plot at the Eden end of the scheme, because he himself worked the post-office alone, how Trimmer had demanded a larger cut than was first offered to him and how Gunter had killed him when he had turned nasty and threatened to squeak.

"How many of the bunch will hang?" asked Langley of the Inspector.

"Does it matter?" answered MacMorran, "but probably only the leader, Gunter, known to his intimates as 'the Professor'. The others may be charged as accessories. But it depends on how the trial goes. The evidence will settle most of the queries."

Anthony chuckled to himself. "What's tickling you?" asked MacMorran.

"I was laughing at myself," replied Anthony. "And how I saw in the names of those wretched people the rudiments of a gigantic Nazi plot. A stupendous conspiracy! In future, Andrew, when I'm inclined to get up-stage, just remind me of it. And of how my dreams of a world-shattering conspiracy turned out to be nothing more than a mere sordid swindle."

"I will," said MacMorran, "until you get tired of hearing me talk about it."

Richard Langley stood with his foot on the running-board of the Schofields' car. Priscilla sat with her hand on the driving-wheel.

"You know, Priscilla," he was saying, "there's only one possible way for this business to end. I've seen that for a long time."

Priscilla remained demure. "Oh—and how is that?"

"You must marry me. Any other conclusion is absolutely unthinkable. What do you say yourself?"

"I might consider it. But goodness knows how Daddy will react to the idea."

"That's easy," said Langley loftily. "We'll tell him that you've simply *got* to get married. When he hears that he'll—"

"I beg your pardon, Mr. Langley!"

"Why—oh—I see what you mean!" Langley's face broke into a broad grin. He opened the door of the car, got in, seated himself deliberately, put his arm round her and kissed her.

"I've dreamed of that," he said, "for a very long time."

As he spoke a blue bundle of fur streaked across the road. "Look," said Langley delightedly. "The old gentleman himself. Ahasuerus in person."

He kissed Priscilla again. "In my will," he said, "and should I predecease him, I shall leave a sum of money to provide Ahasuerus with a daily bowl of cream."

"Whatever for?" asked Priscilla, with mischief in her eyes.

"Your guess, Miss Schofield," said Langley, as he kissed her for the third time, "is as good as mine."

THE END

KINDRED SPIRITS . . .

Why not join the

DEAN STREET PRESS
FACEBOOK GROUP

for lively bookish chat
and more

Scan the QR code below

Or follow this link
**www.facebook.com/groups/
deanstreetpress**